BLACK ORCHID BLUES

by PERSIA WALKER

AKASHIC
BOOKS

This is a work of fiction. All names, characters, places, and incidents are the product of the author's imagination. Any resemblance to real events or persons, living or dead, is entirely coincidental.

Published by Akashic Books
©2011 Persia Walker

ISBN-13: 978-1-936070-90-9
Library of Congress Control Number: 2010939106

First printing

Akashic Books
PO Box 1456
New York, NY 10009
info@akashicbooks.com
www.akashicbooks.com

BLACK ORCHID BLUES

CHAPTER 1

Queenie Lovetree. What a name! What a performer! When she opened her mouth to sing, you closed yours to listen. You couldn't help yourself. You knew you were going to end up with tears in your eyes. Whether they were tears of joy or tears of laughter, it didn't matter. You just knew you were in for one hell of a ride.

Folks used to talk about her gravely voice, her bawdy banter, and how she could make up new, sexy lyrics on the spot. Queenie captured you. She got inside your mind, claimed her spot, and refused to give it up. Once you heard her sing a song, you'd always remember her performance. No matter who was singing it, Queenie's voice would come to mind.

Sure, she was moody and volatile. And yes, whatever she was feeling, she made sure you were feeling too. But that was good. That's what could've made her great—*could've* being the operative word.

I first met Queenie at a movie premiere at the Renaissance Ballroom, over on West 138th Street. The movie I'd soon forget—it was some ill-conceived melodrama—but Queenie I would always remember.

It was a cold day in early February, with patches of dirty ice on the ground and leaden skies overhead. It was late afternoon, an odd time for a premiere, so the event drew few fans and, except for Queenie, mostly B-level talent.

It was a party of gray pigeons and Queenie stood out like a peacock. For a moment, I wondered why she was even there. She was vivid. She was vibrant. And when she found out that I was Lanie Price, *the* Lanie Price, the society columnist, she went from frosty to friendly and started pestering me to see her perform.

"I'm at the Cinnamon Club. You must've heard of me."

Well, I had, actually. Queenie's name was on a lot of lips and I'd heard some interesting things about her. I could see for myself that she was bold and bodacious. I decided on the spot that I liked her, but I couldn't resist having a little fun with her, so I shrugged and agreed that, yeah, I'd heard of . . . the Cinnamon Club.

Queenie caught the shift in emphasis and was none too pleased. She raised her chin like miffed royalty, pointed one coral-tipped fingernail at my nose, and, in her most regal voice, said, "You will appear."

I smiled and said I'd think about it.

The fact was I had a full schedule. A lot of parties were going on those days, and it was my job to cover the best of them. However, I finally did find time to stop and see Queenie a couple of weeks later. I called in advance and Queenie said she'd make sure I had a good table, which she did. It was excellent, in fact, right up front.

To the cynic, the Cinnamon Club was little more than a speakeasy dressed up as a supper club, but it was one of Harlem's most popular night-spots. It was on West 133rd Street, between Seventh and Lenox Avenues, what the white folks called "Jungle Alley." That stretch was packed with clubs and given to violence. Only a few weeks earlier, two cops had gotten into a drunken brawl right outside the Cinnamon Club. One black, one white—they'd pulled out their pistols and shot each other.

That was the neighborhood.

As for the club itself, it was small but plush. The lighting was dim, the chairs cushioned, and the tables round and tiny and set for two. All in all, the Cinnamon Club seemed luxurious as well as intimate.

It was packed every night and most of the comers were high hats, folks from downtown who came uptown to shake it out. They liked the place because it was classy, smoky, and dark. For once, they could misbehave in the shadows and let someone else posture in the light. That someone else was Queenie. The place had only one spotlight and it always shone on her.

Rumor had it that she was out of Chicago. But back at that movie premiere, she'd mentioned St. Louis. All anybody really knew was that she'd appeared out of nowhere. That was late last summer. It was midwinter now and she had developed a following.

You had to give it to her: Queenie Lovetree commanded that stage the moment she stepped foot on it. Every soul in the place turned toward her and stayed that way, flat-out mesmerized and a bit intimidated too. Only a fool would risk Queenie's ire by talking when she had the mic.

A six-piece orchestra, one that included jazz violinist Max Bearden and cornetist Joe Mascarpone, backed her up. Her musicians were good—you had to be to play with Queenie—but not too good. She shared center stage with no one.

At six-foot-three, Queenie Lovetree was the tallest badass chanteuse most folks had ever seen. She had a toughness about her, a ferocity that kept fools in check. And yes, she was beautiful. She billed herself as the "Black Orchid." The name fit. She was powerful, mythic, and rare.

Men were going crazy over her. They showered her with jewels and furs and offered to buy her cars or take her on cruises. In all the madness, many seemed to forget or stubbornly chose to ignore a most salient fact, the one secret that her beauty, no matter how artful, failed to hide: that Queenie Lovetree wasn't a woman at all, but a man in drag.

When Queenie appeared on stage, sheathed in one of his tight, glittering gowns, he presented a near-perfect illusion of femininity. He could swish better than Mae West. His smile was dirtier, his curves firmer, and his repartee deadlier than a switchblade. From head to toe, he was a vision of feminine pulchritude that gave many a man an itch he ached to scratch.

That night, Queenie wore a dress with a slit that went high on his right thigh. Folks said he packed a pistol between his legs, the .22-caliber kind. If so, you couldn't see it. You couldn't see a thing. Queenie kept his weapons tucked away tight.

Gun or no gun, he smoked. When he took that mic, the folks hushed up and Queenie launched into some of the most down and dirty blues I'd ever heard. He preached all right, signifying for everything he was worth, and that crowd of mostly rich white folk, they ate it up.

During the set, Lucien Fawkes, the club's owner, stopped by my table. He was a short, wiry Parisian, with hound-dog eyes, thin lips, and deep creases that lined his cheeks.

"Always good to see you, Lanie. You enjoying the show?"

"I'm enjoying it just fine."

"I'll tell the boys: anything you want, you get."

After Queenie finished his set, the offers and invitations to join tables poured in. He took exuberant pleasure in accepting them, going from table to table. But that night, they weren't his priority. He air-kissed a few cheeks, exchanged a few greetings, and then slunk over to join me.

"The suckers love me," he said. "What about you?"

"I'm not a sucker."

"Well, I know that, Slim. That's why you're having drinks on the house and they're not."

He sat down and turned to the serious business of wooing a reporter.

"So, what do you think? Am I fantastic or am I fantastic?"

"I'd say you've got a good thing going."

"You make it sound like I'm running a scam."

I hadn't meant it that way, but given his fake hair, fake eyelashes, and fake bosom, I could see why he thought I had. "I'm just saying you're perfect for this place and it's perfect for you. Everybody's happy."

"It's okay," he said. "For now."

"You have plans for bigger and better things?"

"What if I do? There's nothing wrong with that."

"Not a thing. I've always admired ambitious, hard-working people."

"Honey, I ain't nothing if not that." He leaned in toward me. "People say you're the one to know. That you are the one to get close to if somebody's interested in breaking out, climbing up. Because of that column of yours. What's it called?"

"'Lanie's World.'"

"That's right. 'Lanie's World.'" He savored the words. "And you write for the *Harlem Chronicle*?"

Acknowledgments

I'd like to thank my agent Lukas Ortiz and Johnny Temple at Akashic for believing in this book. My thanks also go to Jerry Eisner, Catherine Maiorisi, Jane Aptaker, Sara J. Henry, and Elizabeth Zelvin for their patient rereads of the manuscript. Last, but not least, a word of gratitude to Shelton Walden for his constant encouragement.

"Mm-hmm."

"You think you can write a nice piece on me?"

"Well," I hesitated. "There *is* some small amount of interest in you, but—"

"Small? People are crazy about me. The letters I get, the questions. They want to know all about me. Where I come from, what I like, what I don't, what I eat before going to bed."

I shrugged. "But they've heard so many different stories that—"

"I promise to tell you the whole truth and nothing but."

"Well, thanks."

I'd been in the journalism game for more than ten years. I'd worked as a crime reporter, interviewing victims and thugs, cops and dirty judges. Then I'd moved to society reporting, where I wrote about cotillions and teas, parties and premieres. It seemed like a different crowd, but the one constant was the mendacity. People lied. Sometimes for no apparent reason, they obfuscated, omitted, or outright obliterated the truth. And often the first sign of an intention to lie was an unsolicited promise to tell the truth, "the whole truth and nothing but."

In some areas, of course, I was sure Queenie would be factual, but in others . . . it didn't matter. I'd decided to interview him. I was sure to get a good column out of him. I just wasn't sure this was the place to do it.

People kept stopping by. They shook his hand and praised him and begged him to join them. Men sent drinks. They sent flowers and suggestive notes. But they were out of luck that night. After every set, he'd rejoin me, tell me a little bit here, a little bit there.

"I like action," he said, "lots of action, diamond studs and rhinestone heels. I love caviar and chocolate, sequins and velvet. Most times, I'm a lady. But I can smoke like an engine and cuss like a sailor. The men love me cause I treat them all the same. I call them all Bill. By the way, you got a ciggy?"

I shook my head. "Never took to 'em."

He turned and tapped a man sitting at the next table. "Butt me, baby."

"Sure," the guy said, grinning. He produced a cigarette and lit it.

Queenie flashed a dazzling smile, said in a husky voice, "Thanks, Bill," then turned his back before the fellow could make a play.

"Bill" shot me a rueful look. All I could do was give him a sympathetic smile.

During one of the longer set breaks, Queenie invited me back to his dressing room, "so we can talk without them fools interrupting." He described how at age fourteen he'd fallen in love with a sailor who smuggled him to Ankara.

"He was the greatest love of my life, but that bastard sold me."

"Sold you?"

"Yeah. To a guy in a bar." He saw my expression and added, "But seriously, I'm not lying. And that guy turned around and sold me again—to a sultan for his harem."

Believable or not, Queenie's tales were certainly fascinating.

He described corrupting wealth and murderous intrigues. Sultan's wives were poisoning each other and one another's children in a never-ending struggle for power.

"For a while there, it was touch and go. I didn't eat or drink nothing without my taster."

"How terrible," I said, with appropriate horror and sympathy.

At the next break, he talked about his further adventures in Europe. When he was nineteen, he said, the sultan sent him off to an elite finishing school near Lake Geneva, in Switzerland.

"Honey, I couldn't take that place. I made tracks the minute they weren't looking. Went to Paris. Got me a nice hookup. Performed at the Moulin Rouge. Would've stayed there too, but a rich uncle came and found me."

"A rich uncle?"

"Mm-hmm," he said, with a perfectly straight face. "He's dead now. But that's okay, cause now I've got lots of rich uncles." He gave a wicked wink. "A girl can't have too many, you know."

I just had to shake my head. At my expression, Queenie threw his head back and laughed. His shoulders rocked with deep, raunchy amusement. He laughed so hard, tears rolled down his cheeks.

"Oh shit," he said, trying to regain control of himself, "I'm ruining my makeup."

I've seen and heard enough to be fairly immune to what shocks most people. So it wasn't Queenie's stories that got me. It was the obvious pride and conviction with which he told them. People talk about being larger than life, but it usually doesn't mean a thing. When applied to Queenie, it did. And his tales were as tall as tales can get. Sure, they were hokum. That was obvious, but it was okay. It was more than okay because it would make rip-roaringly good copy.

Back in the clubroom, watching him onstage, I mused about his real history. No doubt it was like hundreds of others. He'd been a touring vaude-villian, or had grown up singing gospel in some church down South, then either ran away from home or was kicked out. He was a young boy with a pretty face, the kind that would attract certain types of men. Boys like that, out on their own, they lose their innocence fast. Queenie was no exception.

No doubt he'd spent years on the circuit, in smaller clubs, dark and dirty. Underworld characters had smoothed his path and a wealthy man or two had taught him to love the finer things in life—men who lived double lives, with women during the day and men at night. Now Queenie was here in New York, the big time. It was his chance, and he was going to run with it, milk it for all it was worth. I certainly couldn't blame him.

Queenie liked to flash a big diamond ring. When he sang, the ring caught the light. It was a lovely yellow diamond, set in yellow gold, surrounded by small white diamonds. I had a good eye for jewelry, but at that distance I couldn't say whether it was fake. If it was real, then it was worth ten times a poor man's salary. If it wasn't, then it was a darn good imitation—and even imitations like that cost a pretty penny.

"That got a history?" I asked when he rejoined me.

He glanced at the ring, smiled. "Honey, everything about me has a history."

"Care to tell me this one?"

He fluttered his large hand and held up the ring for a long, loving look. Then he smiled. His golden eyes were feline. His husky voice just about purred. "Not this time, sugar. But I will, if you do a good piece on me. If you do it right, then I'll give you exclusive access to Queenie Lovetree. You'll be my one and only and I won't share my shit with anyone but y—"

Gunfire exploded behind us. I jumped and Queenie's eyes widened. Heads swiveled and the music shredded to a discordant halt. Then someone gasped, another screamed, and people nearby started diving under tables.

At first, I wondered why.

But as people scrambled to get out of the way, I could see the club's bouncer, a man named Charlie Spooner, and the coatcheck girl, Sissy Ralston, emerging unsteadily from the area of the entrance. They wound their way past the tables, coming toward us, hands held high. Directly behind them, a man emerged from the shadows. He wore a Stetson, a big black one, pulled down low to cover his eyes, and a long, black trench coat with a turned-up collar.

It was a very sexy look, but the true eye-catcher was the tommy gun he held on his hip, his black-gloved hands firmly grasping the two pistol grips. It looked real, it looked deadly, and he had the business end of it pressed against Spooner's spine.

The bouncer was a good guy, a decorated veteran of the 19th Infantry. He was married, with a kid on the way. He'd been on the job six months, had taken it, he told me, because he could find nothing else. Now his olive-toned skin had turned ashen gray; his usually jovial face was tight with fear. He had survived bombs and missiles and landmines overseas. Had he gone through all that simply to die in a stupid nightclub robbery at home?

I knew the Ralston girl too. That child couldn't have been more than sixteen. She was just a kid trying to earn money for her family. Her father had died the year before and her mother was a drinker. Sissy was the sole support for her seven-year-old brother and six-year-old sister.

There they were, the bouncer and the coatcheck girl, so terrified they could barely put one foot in front of the other.

Death march. I flashed on stories my late husband had told me about the war, stories of soldiers and civilians marched to their execution, of whole villages lined up against a wall and shot. A chill went through me. I tried to think, tried to restrain the fear and think.

A million questions raced through my mind.

Was this the result of some bootleggers' war? Or was it supposed to be a robbery? If so, would he take the money and run? Or was he the type to kill us all just for the hell of it?

He was covered. That meant he wanted to make sure no one could identify him. Did that mean that if no one did anything stupid, just gave up the jewels and wallets and fancy timepieces, he'd let us all live to tell the story?

I glanced across the crowded room, at the white faces peering out of the smoky gloom, and didn't see a hero among them, thank God.

The gunman shoved Spooner and Ralston to the small open space just before the stage and had them stand side-by-side.

"Everybody, wake up!" he yelled. "Take your seats and show your hands."

But we were all too scared to move.

"I will count to three and then start shooting—for real. One . . . two . . ."

My heartbeat was pounding a hot ninety miles a minute, but my hands and feet felt cold. From the corner of my eye, I glimpsed Queenie slipping his right hand under the table. The gunman saw it too. He swung around and leveled his weapon on us.

"Bring it out," he said. "Nice and slow."

Queenie gave him an insolent look and mouthed the word *No.*

I was stunned. I'd talked to Queenie long enough to know he thought he could handle anyone and anything, but what the hell was he thinking? Okay, so he had pride. He didn't want people to see that he was scared. But this was not the time to act all biggety and try to impress people. He could get us killed.

"Queenie," I hissed, "do as he says."

"No."

The gunman's lips twitched, but he said nothing. He looked Queenie in the eyes, made a slight adjustment in his aim, and squeezed the trigger.

Copper-jacketed pistol rounds erupted from the muzzle in a sheet of flame; a shower of shiny brass cases rained down from the breech. The bullets found Spooner and ripped a trench in his chest. Blood splattered everywhere. The Ralston kid crumpled in a dead faint. People shrieked. Some ducked down again, but others raced for the door. They were screaming, tearing at each other.

"Shut up and get back here!" the gunman swung around and yelled. "Shut up or I'll mow you down!"

The bouncer pawed at his ravaged chest. He plastered his big hands over his gaping wounds, as if he could hold in the blood. Then he looked up at me, in mute sadness. He stumbled forward a step and his heart gave out. He sagged to his knees and fell, facedown.

The gunman stared at the dead man before pointing an accusing finger at Queenie. "You!" he said. "You made me do that!"

Queenie had gone gray under his elaborate makeup, ashen and speechless. He finally understood. This was not one of his tall tales, where he could play the star. This was real.

"Back to your seats everybody!" the gunman yelled. "Get back in your seats and show your hands. Do it, or I'll start shooting. And I won't stop till the job's done."

This time, folks moved. They scrambled to get back in place.

The killer turned to Queenie and me. "Come over here, the both of you, where I can see you."

We stood up and edged around the table, keeping our distance from him.

The gunman was taller than me, but not by much, which made him short for a man. The coat seemed to have padded shoulders, but I had the feeling that he would've appeared broad even without them, that he was built like a quarterback, muscular and stocky.

For the most part, he'd successfully concealed his face, but some of it showed above the mask. His eyes had a distinctive almond shape and they were light-colored: blue or gray, I couldn't be sure. And the band of skin showing over the bridge of his nose, it was light too. In other words, this was a white guy. Last, but not least, I detected an accent. European, northern European, perhaps. So, not just any white guy, but a *European* white guy. He'd sure traveled a long way to cause trouble.

"Now, you," he told Queenie, "take the heater out or she's next." He pointed the gun at me.

I half-turned to Queenie to see what he'd do. *Please, don't do anything stupid.*

Queenie slipped his hand through the slit of his dress. And lingered there. He was going to try something dumb, like shoot from down there. I could see it in his eyes.

Don't do it. Don't do it.

Queenie looked at me and I looked at him. If he pulled a stunt like that and I managed to survive, then I was going to kill him myself. That's what I was thinking and that's what I put in my eyes.

I guess he got the message.

He eased out a small black handgun and aimed it downward. My lungs expanded and I inhaled big gobs of sweet relief.

"Put it on the floor and kick it over here," the gunman said.

Queenie did as told. He kept his eyes on the submachine gun the whole time. I still didn't trust Queenie not to try something and I guess Mr. Tommy Gun didn't either, so I understood why he was keeping his weapon trained, but I wondered why it was trained on me.

"Get over here." The gunman indicated the space right in front of him.

Queenie glanced at me. His eyes held doubt, fear, and resentment.

"Do what he says," I whispered. "Please. Just do it."

"Come on," the gunman growled.

Queenie's gaze returned to the gunman. Stone-faced, he held up his gown, then stepped delicately and ladylike over Spooner's body. He stood before the gunman, chest heaving, eyes narrowed, and said with tremulous bravado, "Well?"

The gunman slapped him. He was a full head shorter than Queenie, but wide and solid. Queenie swayed under the blow but didn't stumble. He seemed more stunned than anything. His hand went to his lip and came back bloodied. His jaw dropped in alarm.

"My face! You piece of shit! You hurt my face!"

The gunman slapped him again. This time Queenie went down. He tripped backward over Spooner and landed on the floor in a pool of blood. He scrambled away from the body with a horrified cry, and got to his feet. His hands and dress were smeared red. From the expression on his face, all resistance had finally been knocked out of him.

The gunman gave me a nod. "You! Come here."

Queenie and I exchanged another glance. Then I took a step forward. The gunman produced handcuffs from his pocket and tossed them at me. I caught them instinctively.

"Cuff up the songbird," he said. "You," he told Queenie, "hands behind your back."

If there was one thing I'd always told myself I would never do, it was to be an accomplice to a crime. I had read, and written, so many stories in which victims had cooperated with their killers. They had done so in the minute hope of surviving, but all they had really done was make it easier for their killer to get them alone, isolate them and do what he felt needed doing.

I'd always said I would resist. I wouldn't make it easy. Oh no. Not me.

But now here I was and things appeared differently. They weren't so cut and dry. Someone else's life was at stake, not just mine.

I could refuse or cooperate. If I refused, then he'd probably shoot me and cuff Queenie himself—or worse, shoot someone else. If I went along and bided my time, there was some hope I'd survive and that everyone else would too.

Everyone, but maybe not Queenie.

"Well," the gunman said, "who should I shoot next?" He glanced down at the Ralston girl, still unconscious on the floor. "How about her?" He turned his gun, took aim.

"No!" I pulled Queenie's hands behind his back and slipped on the handcuffs.

He flinched at the touch of cold metal. "Please, no, Slim. You—"

"It'll be all right," I said, trying hard to sound calm.

I snapped the cuffs shut, and when the gunman ordered me to step back, I did.

He made Queenie stand next to him and checked the cuffs. "Good." Then he grabbed Queenie and started backing out. He slinked to the rear exit, backstage left, and kept the singer in front as a shield.

Queenie panicked. "Oh come on now, people! Y'all ain't gonna let him take me like this, are you? Somebody do something. Please!"

People stayed frozen to their seats. No one was willing to play the hero. Not in the face of that weapon.

Queenie's eyes met mine. "You! Slim, you—!"

The whine of police sirens rang through the air. The cops were probably headed to another emergency, but the killer assumed the worst. He pushed Queenie aside and sprayed the room with gunfire. All hell broke loose. People stampeded toward the door. Wall sconces exploded. The room fell dark. Plaster and dust showered down.

I heard screams. I heard cries. I dove under a table and covered my head. Bullets ripped up the floor two inches from my face. I couldn't believe they didn't touch me.

"Motherfucker! Get your hands off me!" Queenie cried.

I heard the back door bang open. I heard a scuffle and a scream. Then the door slammed shut and all I heard was the heavy thumping of my terrified heart.

CHAPTER 2

Five seconds went by. Five eternal seconds. I counted them down. *One one-hundred. Two one-hundred. Three one-hundred. Four . . .* I was still trembling from head to toe, but my breathing was approaching normal. The police sirens were getting louder and I finally crawled out from under the table.

Despite the shadows, I could detail the destruction. The bullets had torn open bodies as well as furniture. Four people lay sprawled over their tables or slumped in their booths. Blood and shattered glass covered everything. The air was thick with gun smoke.

Now others emerged from their hiding places. Stunned patrons staggered to their feet. The musicians, who had flattened themselves on the floor, slowly straightened up. The sirens drew nearer.

I couldn't risk being found here. If I were spotted, I'd end up at the police station instead of the newsroom, where I needed to be, writing my story.

It was colder than a mother-in-law's kiss outside. I was wearing a thin black cocktail dress with lace at the shoulders and hemline. Sexy as all get-out, but no protection against the cold. I needed my hat and coat, but they were at the check-in. I couldn't risk going back over there.

I felt around for my purse, found it on the seat, and made for the back exit. I pushed open the door and gasped at the sudden rush of frosty air. I stumbled outside, shivering, and took a moment to get my bearings. It was well after midnight and the only light came from the stars above. The city landscape seemed foreign, filled with shadows I could barely identify. Garbage, milk crates.

If Queenie's body had been at my feet, I would've stumbled over it before I saw it.

Pressing myself against the side of the building, I moved swiftly toward the street. Snow and ice blanketed the ground. The wind pierced me to the bone and I shivered from head to toe. I could hear the rumble of curious and confused voices. I could see the flashing beams of a patrol car. I made it to the corner, ducked down, and peeped around the edge.

The first cop car screeched to a halt in front of the buildings. So those sirens *had* been for us. Who called the coppers? Maybe one of the waiters.

A crowd had gathered and the folks who'd been on the inside were starting to stumble out. The bulls pushed their way through and seconds later ran back out. Soon, there would be more cops and then detectives and they would have questions.

My car was parked half a block away. Earlier, I had been annoyed at not finding a space closer to the club. Now I was grateful. I had a better chance of reaching it on foot and driving away unnoticed than of trying to start it up right there.

So I hustled off, teeth chattering, and remained well behind the crowd. My luck held. No one noticed and no one called out my name.

I paused at a pay phone and rang Sam Delaney, my editor. He answered on the first ring. I could imagine his face, his dark eyes, his strong hands, as he gripped the phone.

"Lanie? Where are you? I just heard over the police band. Are you all right?"

"I'm fine, Sam. Fine." I told him the details and dictated the setup for the story.

"You coming in?" he asked.

"I'm on my way."

I hung up, shivered and rubbed my upper arms, then hopped into my car. Sam would phone downstairs and tell the guys to hold the presses. Then he would start writing the story. By the time I got there, he would have all the basic stuff down.

I made myself focus on the story. Set all emotions aside. There was no time for them. No time to feel anything. That would came later, but right then and there, I didn't want to feel anything, anyway. I wanted the comfort of detachment and reason.

Sam was the only one in the newsroom when I arrived. The place was as silent as a tomb. During the day, it was a human beehive. You heard typewriters clacking, phones jangling, and radios blaring. You heard the wire service printers thumping out endless reams of print and the *whomp* of the pneumatic tubes shooting final edits down to the typesetters. In short, it was so loud the noise hit you like a wall when you walked in.

But in the evenings, the newsroom was deserted and the heavy silence had a tangibility of its own. Normally, you would've at least heard the rumble of the printers downstairs. But that night they were paused and waiting for the story of the Black Orchid kidnapping and the Cinnamon Club massacre.

Sam waved me into his office, the man-sized fish tank that sat at the far side of the newsroom. He was as handsome as always, and impeccably dressed. He wore a blue-gray shirt and a finely printed dark blue silk tie under a gray vest. He was at his typewriter, pounding the keys with a viciously accurate two-fingered hunt and peck. I tossed my purse into a chair and started reading over his shoulder.

I double-checked what he'd written, suggesting where to add color and detail. Then we switched seats and it was he who edited over my shoulder, smoothing phrases, rounding out sentences, making the copy strong, the telling swift and neat.

I couldn't have worked this way with everyone. Sam was a wonderful editor, one of the best. He wasn't just your advocate, but the advocate for your story. He helped untangle complicated ideas and pushed you to think of new angles. He saw potential, both in you and your piece. He was patient; he was funny. He was smart and he was kind. He was also the first man I'd dared to care about in the three years since my husband died.

Hamp had collapsed on a Seventh Avenue street corner, not ten blocks from our home. At thirty-seven years of age, he'd died of a heart attack. It came without warning, just one day out of the blue, like a hammer from the heavens, and he was gone.

Hamp's passing had not only broken my heart, but left me terrified to love again. I hadn't realized how much until Sam took over the newsroom. Now I was learning bit by precious bit to stop using grief as a wall against future pain and disappointment.

As Sam leaned over my shoulder, his clean male smell filling my nostrils, I felt a surge of joy, a terrified joy. I could've been one of the unlucky ones. It could've been me who caught a bullet and was on my way to the morgue. It could've been me who was stretched out with a tag on one toe. Instead, I was alive and here in my newsroom with Sam.

"He was jumpy," I said of the killer. "Shot up the place for no reason."

"Sounds like an amateur."

His office phone rang and he snatched up the receiver. From his side of the conversation, I gathered that it was the typesetter wanting to know how much longer we'd be. I glanced at the wall clock. We had another five minutes, tops, to get the story done. The whole paper was on hold. An entire crew was waiting.

But that's not what worried me.

Sam hung up. Over the next four minutes, we checked the copy once more, and I took comfort in his nearness as he read along with me.

"That last paragraph," he said, "it—"

Outside Sam's office, the main newsroom door banged open. I looked up and saw the source of my worry stride in. Detective John Blackie. I knew him from when I covered crime for the *Harlem Age*. Now I worked for the *Chronicle*, but our paths still crossed, because every now and then my writing about highbrow Harlem meant writing about highbrow crime.

"Sam, you might have to finish this without me."

He didn't answer.

Blackie rapped sharply on Sam's office door, but didn't wait for an invite. He stepped inside, saw what we were up to, and said, "I hope you're done with that, Lanie, cause I'm gonna need you to come with me."

"Give me just a minute."

He shook his head. "Sorry, it can't wait. I got a boatload of witnesses who say you were there tonight, at the Cinnamon Club. You saw the whole thing."

"Sure I did, but what about the witnesses? They weren't just looking at me."

"None of them got as close to the shooter as you did."

"What about the Ralston girl? She stood right next to him."

"Are you kidding? The poor kid's scared witless. She can barely remember her own name."

There was no use in arguing. I glanced at Sam.

"It's okay," he said. "I'll finish up here, then I'll join you."

"No need for that," Blackie said. Then he saw the look in Sam's eyes. "All right, but don't expect me to wait till you get there."

I picked up my purse and went to Blackie, my reluctance obvious.

"Where's your coat?" Sam asked.

"You ran out and left it, didn't you?" Blackie said.

Sam took his coat down from the rack and draped it around my shoulders. "Don't worry, I'll take care of your baby here." He nodded at the typewritten pages. "Then I'll come to the station, make sure everything's going all right."

CHAPTER 3

The precinct house was one block east of the newspaper office, a brisk five-minute walk in the freezing cold. The station was usually quiet at that hour—it was around two—but on that night, it was abuzz. Reporters, photographers, the curious, and the worried crowded the front entrance, held back by stressed uniforms.

Blackie kept a firm grip on my upper arm. He pushed and shoved and barked orders, cutting his way through. "Move, people! Move!"

Those forced aside regarded me with interest, bewilderment, and envy. "Hey, why does she get to go in?" one reporter yelled out. I knew most of these fellows and was on good terms with many of them. But professional friendliness can evaporate in the heat of competition. Some of them looked about ready to throttle me.

Then I was through the crowd, up the steps, and into the clubhouse.

Inside was more nervous, agitated, fearful humanity. There were a number of people who'd been at the Cinnamon Club. Their faces were scraped, their clothes dusty and bloodied. They sat on benches, some in shock, some alone, some comforted by others who argued with officers about needing to get their loved ones home. And there were cops, cops everywhere. I'd never seen so many outside the St. Patrick's Day parade.

Blackie guided me through it all. He took me down an ugly corridor to an even uglier back room. He left me there, "just for a minute," and hustled off.

The closing of the door left a sudden quiet. It was a small room with three chairs and a desk. There were no windows, just walls, and they were bare and dirty. A bare bulb hung from the ceiling. The place was a closet, tight and claustrophobic. It made me feel like a crook, as though I'd done something wrong.

I took a deep shuddering breath. I wrung my hands, folded them over one another, and then wrung them again. I fumbled in my bag for a cigarette, but remembered that I hadn't brought any. Sometimes I carried them for social events, when smoking was expected. It was one of those things that sophisticated people were supposed to do: smoke. But I'd never liked cigarettes, never enjoyed their bitter aftertaste, and they'd certainly never calmed me.

The "minute" passed and Blackie wasn't back.

It was chilly inside the room. I was grateful for Sam's coat and hoped he wouldn't catch cold, running down to the station without it. Hugging myself and rubbing my upper arms, I paced back and forth. What a miserable night, and it was far from over.

The door opened and Blackie walked in, followed by a young woman. She was in her mid-twenties, had dark blond hair parted to one side, dark brown eyes, and wire-frame spectacles. She wore a dark blue shift and carried a thin pad and pencil. A stenographer.

Blackie introduced us, then we all sat down. When he offered me a cigarette, I shook my head and said, "Let's get on with it."

So began a grueling hour and a half. Under questioning, I gave a statement, repeated it, and repeated it again.

"A caper like this," Blackie said, "it must've taken two people. One in the club, another with the getaway car. Did you see anybody else?"

I shook my head. "No."

After Blackie was done, another detective came in—I didn't catch his name—and he had questions too. Some Blackie had asked; others were brand new. Most I didn't have answers to.

Eventually, I was taken to another room. There I sat with a police artist and tried my best to supply details I didn't have but they desperately needed.

I saw Lucien Fawkes in the corridor. I'd forgotten about him—he must've been in his back office when it happened. Was he the one who'd called for help?

We gave each other a cursory nod, but didn't speak. The bulls were keeping him busy. I could imagine the kinds of questions they were throwing at him, because they'd thrown them at me too.

How well do you know the Black Orchid? What kind of person is he? Did he ever give any sign of being in trouble? Did he worry that someone was after him?

I could honestly say that I'd only had that one real conversation with the man, and that much of what he'd told me was fluff. But Fawkes wouldn't be able to get off so easily. He was Queenie's boss, had worked with him for months. Surely he'd gotten to know his headliner in that time.

I would've given my eyeteeth to listen in. I doubted they were getting anything useful out of Fawkes, but I wished I could've been a fly on the wall just in case.

CHAPTER 4

It took Sam another couple of hours to put the paper to bed. By the time he arrived at the station, I was ready to go home. We said our goodbyes to Blackie, and Sam walked me to my car. It was back up the block, parked in front of the newspaper offices.

"They got anything?" he asked.

"Don't think so."

"When we get you home, I'm going to run you a nice, hot bath and—"

"Sam." I came to a stop, hesitated.

"Yes?"

"I think I'd rather be alone tonight."

I could feel his surprise, then his frustration. His lips tightened. He took a moment and glanced away. When he spoke, his voice was calm and controlled.

"You've been through hell. I know that and I'm not the kind of man to take advantage of it. I thought you knew that—"

"I do."

"Then why—"

"I just . . ." I sighed. "Need to be alone."

"That's exactly what you don't need."

I didn't answer him.

He gripped me lightly on the shoulders. "All I want to do is hold you, make you feel safe. Please, let me do that for you."

I closed my eyes. A part of me wanted to give in, but another part, a stronger part, refused. "I'm sorry. I can't." I pushed him away, gently but firmly. I wanted to say something to assuage the hurt in his eyes. How could I explain that this had nothing to do with him? I gestured back over my shoulder, toward the police precinct. "When I was in there . . ." I shuddered, unable to go on.

"That's what I mean. Now's not the time to crawl back into your widow's shell. You shouldn't be alone."

I bit my lip, then slowly but deliberately shook my head. "You're wrong."

He took a deep breath, glanced upward, and slowly blew out his cheeks. For a moment he was silent, praying no doubt for patience. Then he summoned that slightly tense but loving smile he so often had to use with me. I reached up to kiss him. It wasn't the kiss I wanted to give him; it certainly wasn't the kiss he deserved. He turned his head at the last minute and I couldn't be sure it wasn't on purpose. So I ended up kissing his cheek. His skin was warm and he smelled good. For a split second, I regretted my stubbornness—but only a split second.

Once we reached the car, he walked around to the driver's side and opened the door for me. I started to take off his coat to hand back to him, but he told me to keep it.

"It's okay," I said. "It's warm in the car."

"Not really."

"I only have a short ride home."

"You'll need it tomorrow, until you can make it back to the club and get your coat."

"What'll you do?"

He shrugged. "I don't need a coat, not when I have you." He put a hand over his heart. "Thoughts of you keep me warm through and through."

I had to smile. I climbed in, behind the wheel.

He shut the door and bent to speak through the window. "Get some rest."

I felt guilty. "Sam, about coming home with me. I—"

He shook his head, a crooked smile lighting his face. "Naw, baby, you don't have to apologize. You don't ever have to apologize to me."

He leaned into the window and gave me a light kiss, one that despite its brevity conveyed wistfulness and regret. Then he stepped back with a bow, making an obvious show of getting out of my way. I bit my lower lip, my heart heavy, my mind confused, and started to pull out. On impulse, I stuck my hand out the window to wave, but I was too late. He'd already turned away.

CHAPTER 5

I drove the four blocks to my town house on West 139th Street and pulled into an empty parking space. For several minutes, I just sat there, hands gripping the steering wheel. I felt physically exhausted and mentally drained. I leaned forward, rested my chin on my knuckles, and closed my eyes.

Bad idea.

It all came back. Images of Charlie Spooner, his chest ripped open; of Queenie's face and the fear in his eyes; I could smell the gun smoke, hear the screams, see the bullets tearing up the floor in front of my face. And always in the background, Queenie's cries. I could see him being dragged through that back door. Hear him, once proud, now begging for someone, anyone, to save him; and I could see myself, hiding under a table, heart pounding.

I sighed, opened my eyes, and rubbed my forehead. I had done nothing to help Queenie; in retrospect, I wasn't sure there was anything I could've done. But that didn't stop me from feeling guilty. No, not just guilty, but dirty, used, and utterly spent.

I'd covered crime for years at the *Harlem Age*, so this wasn't the first time I'd witnessed violent death. It wasn't the first time I'd witnessed a shooting, either. But it was the first time I'd seen a friend, Spooner, shot before my eyes. It was the first time I'd been talking to one of the victims only minutes before the crime. And it was certainly the first time I'd been made an accomplice.

Or was it?

One day, when I was a child, maybe five or six, in Virginia and out with my mother, we were walking past a park. It was the middle of the afternoon. I don't remember where we were going, but my mother was in a hurry to get there. I also remember looking up and seeing two men. They held a woman by the arms, and were dragging her toward the park. She was struggling, weeping, looking around for help. All I recall of her face is her fear. But I can still see her dark velveteen hat, her dark gray coat. She had a black leather purse with a silver handle slung over one arm. I can still hear her, so terrified she couldn't scream. She was babbling, begging for help. She kicked and tried to dig her heels into the ground. But it didn't matter—they were pulling her inexorably into the darkness.

People were walking past, stone-faced, my mother included. How could they? Couldn't they see what was going on? Why weren't they helping? I tugged at my mother's sleeve and pointed. She hushed me. "It's none of our business." Look straight ahead, she told me, but I couldn't. My eyes followed that woman into the bushes.

I never found out what happened to her, but I've always wondered. I've always been haunted by the thought that I could've done something. I've always felt puzzled and somehow dirtied by the fact that my mother refused to do anything.

I hadn't thought of that woman in years, but I thought of her now. I thought of how we'd helped those men do whatever they did to her, simply by doing nothing.

Of course, I was a child back then. I couldn't have done anything. But I wasn't a child anymore. I had to take responsibility for my role in the crime that had just taken place.

I went over it again, but didn't see what I could've done differently. And I couldn't stop thinking about it.

My hands were ice cold and, despite Sam's coat, I was shivering. I needed to get out of the car, go inside, get warm. But I couldn't bring myself to move. Instead, I sat there, staring out the windshield, at the quiet, familiar street.

I lived in a small, highly insular part of Harlem dubbed "Strivers' Row," an appellation that began as a term of mockery but soon became a badge of pride. The enclave's distinctive town houses were home to many of Harlem's most renowned "strivers," including entertainers, lawyers, doctors, and other professionals.

The mention of Strivers' conjured up images of red Roman brick or Georgian yellow town houses. It meant private gateways and courtyards, quiet dignity and distinction, all designed by some of the best architects of the day, including Stanford White.

Strivers' Row consisted of only two blocks—West 139th and West 138th Streets—and it ran only one block east and west, from Seventh to Lenox Avenues, but those two blocks contained some of the most elegant town houses in all of New York City.

Of course, I was partial.

I glanced over at my house, sitting there looking so pretty. Hamp and I had purchased it shortly before his death. Since then, the house had become a source of both pain and comfort. Everywhere I looked, I saw signs of Hamp. To live there meant living with a continual reminder of what I'd had and what I'd lost.

There was one part of the house where memories of him had been softened, if not fully overlaid, and that was the kitchen. Sam had labored long and dusty hours in there to build me a set of cabinets. He'd started over the Christmas holiday and worked on them every weekend, assembling them bit by bit, until they stood lined up against the walls like perfect soldiers. Like Sam, they were solid, dependable, and attractive.

I thought of those cabinets now. How I'd fought to keep Sam out of my heart, out of my home. Then, in December, after the terror of the Todd case, I turned to him. He was everything he appeared to be, and for a few weeks I'd known some semblance of peace.

But only a few weeks.

Soon, the fear, the reluctance to become involved again, resurfaced with a vengeance. I knew I could trust him. At least, I thought I could—there was so much about him I didn't know. He was singularly silent about his past.

But that wasn't it. Lack of knowledge about his past wasn't the reason I'd pushed him away.

What then?

I didn't know. Earlier in the evening, when I'd first gotten out of the club and arrived at the newsroom, I'd been so glad to find him there. There was no place on earth I would rather have been, and I was grateful, so very grateful, that I didn't have to be there alone. Thoughts of him had sustained me even through those grueling police interviews.

When had my feelings begun to change? Had it been while I waited for the portrait artist?

Yes, perhaps then. I'd sat in the regular waiting room, fully exposed to the jostling misery of that frantic crowd. By the time I sat down with the artist, all I could think of was getting out of there, of going home and being alone.

Totally, restfully, blissfully alone.

Sam hadn't understood that. I hadn't understood it myself and couldn't explain it to him.

I frowned.

Then again, maybe he *had* understood. There were many times when he seemed to understand me better than I understood myself. Perhaps this was one of them. He'd understood me and known better. Perhaps he was right and I was wrong.

Exhausted, I again allowed my eyes to close for a second. Memories from the nightclub instantly flared up once more, images of the agony in Charlie's face, the terror in the Ralston girl's eyes, of the man and woman lying slumped in their seats, the acrid stench of gunpowder, of blood and fear. I opened my eyes, gasping and feeling sick.

My gaze traveled up the long empty street. Everyone else on this tranquil block was in bed. No. Lights did burn in one window: diagonally across the street, at the home of the Bernard family. Hmm. Was it the miseries of the evening keeping them up, as with me? I hoped not. I hoped that it was simply a good book.

For a moment, I had the wild wish to go over there, ring their bell, talk to them, enjoy their normalcy. But I couldn't do that. It wasn't just that it was late—well past two in the morning—it was also that, well, I'd been a poor neighbor to the Bernards. I'd known them through my husband, but I'd rarely seen or spoken to them since Hamp's death. My fault, not theirs.

My gaze moved down the street. Other than the Bernards' single light, all the windows along Strivers' were dark. This was a street of couples and families. Behind most of those windows were husbands and wives, cozied up together, finding comfort and strength in each other's company. I could've had that tonight, but would it have been real and lasting, or just something to get me through the loneliness of the night? Did it matter?

I drew a deep breath and let it out slowly.

Sometimes, I didn't understand myself. I really didn't.

With another deep sigh, I turned off the engine and stepped out of the car. I went up the stairs to my front door, unlocked it, and entered, but paused in the vestibule.

I peered at the gleaming stairway leading up to the second floor and beyond. I thought of all those beautiful but empty rooms, more than ten of them. For the first time in a long while, the house seemed achingly empty. I'm not superstitious, but in my heart of hearts, I've always believed that houses are alive, that perhaps they're imprinted by the thoughts of their creator and the succeeding hopes and sorrows of their owners.

For a moment, I felt as though the house itself was speaking to me. I could sense its disappointment. I wasn't the only one to have lost dreams; the house too felt a wrenching void. It was a big place, with generous spaces. It was meant to be filled with noisy, laughing children and grumpy but lovable relatives. Instead, it stood empty.

I knew I had to change, to do something, but how?

It was too much to think about just then.

The house was warm—I could feel the warmth on my skin, but it didn't touch the chill inside me.

I hung up Sam's coat, then went upstairs. I undressed, slipped into a lace cotton gown, and slid under the covers. I lay there shivering for a while, then got up and fetched more blankets. They didn't help.

Fact was, I longed for a man's arms to hold me. That night, especially, after what I'd gone through. Was I going to spend the rest of my life like this? I didn't want to.

As it so often did, my gaze moved to Hamp's photo on the night table. I couldn't see the details of his image in the dark, just the outline of the silver frame glinting from a stray bit of moonlight. It looked cold.

Like the grave.

My beloved husband was in the grave. He was gone. Really, really gone.

I closed my eyes and the sobs erupted, harsh, hot tears. I was alive, yes, but I felt cold inside, as cold as the dead.

CHAPTER 6

Thursday morning, the Chronicle led with the story of the Cinnamon Club massacre. By that afternoon, the citywide dailies had picked it up. By evening, people who'd never before heard of the Black Orchid or the Cinnamon Club were talking as though they'd known about them forever. There was talk about guns and the increase in crime and how Harlem had turned wild "ever since the ofays moved out and the darkies moved in."

Five people were in the hospital. Six had died outright, including Spooner and the maître d', the latter having died at the door in the first burst of gunfire. One of the victims happened to be a Harvard kid. His death turned what would've been forgotten as a local crime into a citywide manhunt. He was the nineteen-year-old scion of a wealthy, conservative Park Avenue family. The parents were aggrieved and ashamed. Plenty of white folk hung out in Harlem, but not in places like *that*. They tried to keep the boy's name out of the papers but by afternoon it had leaked. The only thing left for the family to do was to come out swinging, and they did. They wanted the shooter who'd killed their boy, and they wanted him like yesterday. To get folks going, they announced a nice little reward to the tune of five grand.

Sam and I met in his office to discuss the story. We focused on the two big questions: who and why? I thought the second question would lead to an answer to the first. After some consideration, Sam agreed.

Why had the Black Orchid been taken? Was it an act of revenge by a disgruntled suitor, or was it a move for money? Would a ransom note follow? If so, then who did the kidnapper expect to pony up the cash? Maybe he didn't realize that Queenie had no family. Once he did, what would he do?

"What would you do," Sam asked, "if you had a celebrity hostage who had no relatives? Who'd you turn to?"

"The person who stood to lose the most."

"Queenie's boss, Lucien Fawkes?"

"Yup." I shivered from a sudden chill. I had pushed aside my morbid thoughts of the night before as the aftereffect of the shooting. But I still felt cold inside, like a member of the walking dead. Seeing those people lose their lives the night before . . . it had done something to me. Images of the carnage kept slashing through my mind. I told myself to focus.

"At least twelve hours have passed since the kidnapping," I said. "Chances are that he's been contacted."

"Do you honestly think he'll tell you if he has?"

I shrugged. "Probably not. But he might drop something." I drew my sweater close and folded my arms across my chest.

Sam regarded me over steepled fingertips. His eyes, which missed little, reflected concern. "You all right?"

I gave a little smile. "I'm fine. Why?"

"I don't know . . . you seem . . . You sure you don't want to take today off? After last night—"

"That's the last thing I want, especially after last night."

"Sure?"

I nodded.

His expression said he disagreed, but he knew better than to argue. He continued, "What would be more interesting is if Fawkes definitely *hasn't* been contacted. If he says he hasn't been and you believe him . . ."

Our eyes met.

I nodded again. "Then I'd have to wonder why."

CHAPTER 7

We agreed that I would swing past the Cinnamon Club that evening. Chances were it was closed, not only because of the loss of Queenie, but also out of deference to Charlie Spooner.

But the club was open. It was jumping, in fact. A line of people stretched around the corner and down the block. And a new man stood at the door. His demeanor was somber and he said his name was Charlie. I didn't hide my surprise and he gave a sad smile.

"Mr. Fawkes said to tell everyone that that's my name, as sort of a memorial to the other guy."

I glanced back at that crowd waiting to get in. "Sure, I understand," I said. And I did. Lucien had his eye on the bottom line.

This "Charlie" was different from the original, tall and slim and muscular. I thought I detected a lyrical accent.

"Where are you from?"

"Morocco."

"You worked with Lucien in Paris?"

"*Oui.*"

I extended a hand and introduced myself. "Well, it's good to see you here—though, to tell you the truth, I'm surprised to find the place open."

"We had men working all day to get it ready, to clean up the glass, paint the walls, put in new lights. Monsieur Fawkes, he said it would show greater respect to Charlie to keep the club going than to let it stay closed."

Respect to Charlie? Sure, sure. I bit back the words that came to mind. "Lucien in tonight?"

Charlie nodded and stepped aside.

I stopped by the coat check to pick up my coat. They had a new girl, but she didn't say her name. As a matter of fact, she didn't say anything. Seems to me she looked a little scared. I gave her a tip, even though I believed it rightly belonged to the Ralston girl, and then went into the main clubroom.

They had a new maître d' too. A very officious-looking guy with an attitude. I told him where I was going and started past, but he put up a hand to stop me.

"You're a reporter, right? Well, Mr. Lucien said he don't want to talk to no more reporters."

"He'll want to talk to me."

"That's what they all say."

I admit I have a temper at times. This threatened to be one of them. "You like your job?"

"Well, yeah." He looked surprised at the question.

"If you want to keep it, then you'll either let me by or tell Lucien that I'm here."

That shook him. He asked my name, then told me to wait.

It was strange being there, after what had happened the night before, surreal. Just about every trace of the crime was gone. The floors were dark, so any bloodstains would've been invisible in the dim light, anyway. But blood on the walls would've been evident, as well as any bullet holes and the shattered wall sconces. I would've bet the floors had been thoroughly scrubbed. The walls were certainly clean and smooth. New lights shone in place of the old, and the unmistakable aroma of fresh paint and disinfectant mixed with the acrid smell of cigarette smoke and bootlegged liquor.

The maître d' reappeared. "Lucien will see you."

"Thank you."

Lucien's office was in the rear. A crowd packed the tiny bar, waiting for tables. I shouldered my way through and headed for the archway to the right of the stage. It opened to a row of four doors. The manager's office was the first; the rest were dressing rooms and a toilet.

I gave a quick rap on the manager's office door and went in. Lucien was behind his desk, working on receipts. He peered up at the sound of my entrance. His woebegone eyes were even sadder than usual and he looked ragged. How late had the cops grilled him? He was still at the station house when I'd left. He welcomed me now with a gesture to take a seat.

"Business is good tonight," I said.

He made a sound of disgust. "They are not here to drink or eat. Only to take up seats, see where it happened."

From here, with the door open, Lucien had a bird's-eye view of the nightclub.

"You must've seen it all," I said. "Are you the one who called the cops?"

"*Oui.*" He ran a hand through his hair in frustration. "I need Queenie back out there, pulling in real customers."

"Has he contacted you?"

"Who?"

"The kidnapper."

He gave a cynical smile. "Now, you wouldn't really expect me to tell you if he had, would you?"

"Why not?"

"You print the wrong thing and Queenie dies."

"I wouldn't do that."

"You've done it before."

I winced. He was referring to a column I'd written that past December. It had led to a man's death—not a nice man, but still.

"I've learned my lesson. I can help, if you let me."

His eyes remained wary. A moment passed. "The answer is no. No one has contacted me."

"Doesn't that worry you?"

"Of course. If he doesn't want money, then what does he want?"

"Maybe he contacted someone else?

"*Qui?*"

"I wouldn't know. I was asking you."

"You sound like the cops." It wasn't a compliment. "Queenie has no family. So who else, other than me? I have no answer." He shook his head, his lips turned down. "Maybe something happened. Something . . . to delay the ransom demand."

Or maybe the kidnapper didn't mean to return Queenie at all.

"Could it be a fan?" I wondered out loud.

"You mean some sick man who thinks he's in love with him?"

I nodded.

Lucien thought about it, then shrugged. "I have no idea."

"Has Queenie been getting letters?"

"Of course. All the time."

"Do you have any of them here?"

"Not down here, no. There could be some in his dressing room."

"What about his apartment?"

He shook his head. "I don't know where he lives."

"I thought this gig came with an apartment."

"It does, but Queenie didn't want it."

I frowned. "Excuse me for asking, but does he actually earn enough here to afford someplace else?"

Lucien hesitated. "Let's just say, he has a handsome income."

"Enough to cover housing, costumes, board?"

Another smile that drew up only the corner of his lips. "Don't tell me you've forgotten about Queenie's other source of income?"

The men, the admirers. "Oh, of course." I filed that away, making a mental note to find out where Queenie actually lived, then got to my feet. "So, dressing room it is. I'd like to take a look."

He shook his head. "Impossible."

"Why?"

"Queenie would not like it."

"You don't know that."

"It won't happen," he said, his accent thick. "Queenie would kill me if he found out."

If Queenie survived to come back. "Have the police searched his room?"

"You are not the police."

"That's not what I asked."

"Yes, they have searched there."

"When?"

"About an hour ago, right after the set started."

"Did they find anything?"

He shrugged. "I don't know. They didn't tell me."

"Lucien, I need to get into that room."

"Why?"

"Because. Maybe I can find out something."

"Maybe? That isn't good enough." He rose and came around the desk. "Why don't you let the police handle this? It's their job."

"Since when have you started trusting cops?"

It was a shot in the dark. I didn't know if he'd had trouble with the law, but I'd never met a club owner who hadn't.

"You do know they'll be back," I said. "The longer Queenie's gone, the harder they'll start looking at you. Sooner or later, they're going to see some-thing you don't want them to see. Maybe it won't be what they're looking for, but it'll be something—like that game you've got going on in the back room, or the liquor party down in the cellar."

"I'll take my chances."

"You want to be stubborn, fine. Suit yourself." I shrugged. "But if you were smart, you'd help me do my job, and help yourself while you're at it."

"I do not see the connection."

"It's simple. I'm the main reporter on this story. If I put something in the paper, people will pay attention. If anybody is in the position to give the cops somebody to look at—somebody other than you—it's me."

I studied him; he studied me. After a while, he sighed. "*Bien.*" He reached down, pulled out his main desk drawer, and produced a set of keys. "Follow me."

CHAPTER 8

Lucien unlocked the door to Queenie's dressing room and froze. "*Mon Dieu!*" he whispered. He stood there mouth agape.

The room had been ransacked. A thick rack of costumes stood to one side and a vanity overflowing with makeup was on the other, but the rest was chaos. Each and every container—makeup, hatboxes, shoeboxes, and the like—had been opened, the contents spilled and examined.

"I had no idea the police did this," he said.

"You weren't here?"

"They told me to leave. And later, I didn't check, just locked the door." He put a hand to his forehead and the lines on his face deepened. "I know they have to do what they have to do, but . . ."

"You see anything missing?"

He shook his head. "I don't know. I can't tell."

"Okay, let's look. Maybe we'll find something interesting—threatening letters or something."

The room was small and crowded and the floor was covered in clutter. Lingering traces of Queenie's heavy perfume, sweet and musky, touched everything. It interwove with the smell of greasepaint, dust, stale cigarette smoke, and sweat.

I searched the vanity, the mirror, even behind the mirror, the drawers. I turned out pockets and turned over papers, most of which were playbills. I searched every conceivable hiding place I could think of. I didn't know what I was looking for. I just hoped I'd recognize it when I saw it. But thirty minutes of searching turned up nothing. Nada. Zip.

I did notice one thing, though: nothing in that room seemed to belong to

Queenie himself. Yes, the room was full of the trappings of fame—the now wilted flowers, the empty jewel boxes, the signed photographs—but most of it had originated from fans. Despite all the clutter, the room was utterly devoid of anything personal. Even the costumes were too small for Queenie to have worn.

"You have seen enough?" Lucien asked.

"These dresses, they don't belong to him."

"He brought his own. We should go now."

"And the rest of these things, none of them seem to have anything to do with him."

Lucien bit back his impatience and took a breath. "It became very clear to me early on that he had another life, and that he wanted to keep the two of them apart."

"Really? Maybe we should start at the beginning. Just how did you find him?"

"This is not the best place to talk."

"Oh, I think it's the perfect place." I perched on the edge of the vanity, making it clear that I wasn't going anywhere.

He wasn't happy about it, but he apparently decided that cooperation was the fastest way of getting me out of there.

"All right," he said. "The fact is, I did not find him. He found me. He just walked in one night. It was last August. I had never seen him before. I told him I didn't need a new singer, that I was doing quite well with the one I had. He asked, 'Is *quite well* good enough for you?' I thought he was arrogant, but there was something about him. *Un certain je ne sais quoi.* Let's say I liked his guts. Furthermore, I could not make him leave. He would not go until I agreed to audition him."

He shrugged, made an open-palm gesture. "*Eh bien.* The rest, we know. He was dynamite. I wanted him and I did a bad job of hiding it. We haggled. He demanded a greater cut than I had ever given anyone. *Non,* I said. No way. Then he looked at me and said, 'We will see, sugar. We will see.' Those were his very words, and sure enough, I saw."

"Saw what?"

"The people. The crowds he brought in. It was not just the numbers, but the *kind* of people, real spenders, night after night. I was hooked. I gave in. He was worth it."

I tilted my head and narrowed my eyes. It was time to shake him up a bit. "Are you lovers?"

He blinked "*Quoi?*"

"You heard me."

He straightened up, indignant. "It is none of your business, *mais non*."

I studied him for a moment, then decided to believe him. "Did the police ask you that?"

"They were too well-bred, a tendency you obviously do not share."

"Absolutely not." My gaze drifted back over the costumes. "Queenie replaced Morgana, right?"

"Morgana had nothing to do with this."

"How do you know?"

"I . . . simply do."

I could still hear Morgana out there performing. He was singing an up-beat number with determination. Hoping to get his gig back. Hoping that Queenie would stay gone. Or was it more than hope? Was it certainty? Had he helped make Queenie disappear?

But if Morgana were behind the kidnapping, a ransom note would have been on Lucien's desk by now. Morgana would've made that a major part of his plan, even if that plan didn't include Queenie's return.

"Who do you think did it?" I asked Lucien. "You must have a theory."

He started to say something, then hesitated.

"Lucien?" I said. "Do you know something?"

He shook his head. "I—" He broke off to go to the dressing room door. He cracked it open, peeped out to see if anyone was in the area, and shut it. Then he came back and spoke in a hushed voice. "What I tell you now, I did not tell the police, but it is nothing for you to print."

I regarded him sideways, doubtful but willing to hear him out. "Okaaay."

"He was not taken for the money."

"No?"

"*Non*. Big Frenchy DeMange: you know of him?"

"Of course." DeMange ran the Cotton Club for Owney Madden, a mobster who'd made a fortune in bootleg whiskey and speakeasies. The entertainment at the Cotton Club was all black, light-skinned black to be sure, but black nonetheless, and the patronage was all white. "What about him?"

"He wants my Queenie. He has been trying to talk to him."

It was my turn to be stunned. "How do you know?"

"Queenie told me."

"And you believed him?"

"Of course."

It might've been true. It might've been a lie too. Queenie could have been trying to boost his worth by claiming he had options. I wouldn't have put it past him.

Outside, in the clubroom, Morgana finished with a flourish. The crowd responded with tepid applause.

"Was Queenie interested?" I asked.

Lucien shook his head. "He said he'd never work in a place like that, one that put colored people on display, like in a zoo. His words, not mine. He would not work for people who would not let Negroes come in, sit down, and enjoy themselves. And when he said it, he was angry. That is why I believed him. He was furious and I think he meant it."

Hmm. Social awareness: Queenie had many good qualities, I was sure. But social awareness? The Queenie I'd interviewed had shown no interest in civil rights or a willingness toward self-sacrifice. More like an overweening sense of self-absorption.

Would someone like that really give up a chance to perform at the Cotton Club? Being on stage there told the world that you were top-drawer. It meant performing before some of the richest, most influential people in all of New York City.

And let's not forget the financial aspects of such a gig. Queenie's pay at the Cinnamon Club probably wasn't bad but, despite what Fawkes said, it couldn't have been the best, either. It was certainly a far cry from what he would've been getting at the Cotton Club.

Prestige. Money. I couldn't imagine Queenie turning down either. Nor could I imagine DeMange being so desperate for performers that he'd resort to kidnapping one.

"You really think DeMange is behind this?"

"Maybe not. But it could be someone who wants to get in good with him. And there are others, some who don't just want Queenie, they want this place. But mostly, it's Queenie. One of them told me—only last week he said it—that if Queenie wouldn't work for him, he would make sure he didn't work for anybo—"

The dressing room door opened and Morgana strutted in. He stopped at the sight of the chaos. "What the hell?" His gaze moved between Lucien and me. "Did she do this?" he asked Lucien.

"Of course not," Lucien snapped.

"Well, whoever did, they better not have stolen nothing."

"This is not your place anymore," Lucien said. "There is nothing of yours in here to steal. You're only using the place while . . . until Queenie comes back."

Fuck you, Morgana said with his eyes.

"Have time to talk?" I asked.

"Not really."

"You can talk to her after your next set," Lucien told Morgana.

"Fine," Morgana said. "Until then, you can get the hell out."

"Tell you what," I said. "You're on break now, right?"

Morgana nodded.

"Why don't you rest while I straighten up?" I suggested.

"You mean, act like you're my maid or something?"

"That's right. What d'you say?"

Morgana threw a glance at Lucien, who said nothing. The singer gave me a cold smile. "All right, sister. Start working."

CHAPTER 9

Lucien left us alone. Morgana sat at the vanity, retouching his makeup before the mirror. I tried to make quick order out of the mélange of tossed dresses, hats, playbills, and knickknacks. Morgana kept a wary eye on my reflected image, while patting his face with powder. He was indignant that I would even imply that he had a hand in the kidnapping.

"I didn't have nothing to do with that shit. I can't stand that bitch and yes, I would've been happy to get rid of her, but I saw pretty early on that I wasn't going to have to do nothing."

"What does that mean?"

"It means, I could see that somebody else was gonna do her."

"Which somebody?" I paused in the housekeeping, my arms full of feather boas.

Morgana arched one overplucked eyebrow. "Why should I tell you?"

I put down the boas, came up behind Morgana, and whispered in his ear: "Because if you don't, I might drop a dime that you wanted to see Queenie disappear."

He nearly let go of his powder puff. "You wouldn't."

"Oh, but I would."

It was a weak threat, and I didn't think Morgana would go for it. I was wrong.

"Damn." He sucked his teeth and rolled his eyes. "I knew this maid act of yours was too damn good to be true."

"Come on. Spill."

He blew out a big irritated sigh. "All right, but . . . you won't tell anyone where you got this, will you?"

"Not if my life depended on it."

"Well, sister, mine does. You dig?"

I nodded.

He pressed his lips together, reluctance oozing from every pore. "I seen her with this goon. Don't know his name. Just heard that he knocks heads for a living."

"For who?"

He shrugged. "I don't remember."

"Morgana—"

"I don't know."

"Can you describe him?"

"Not too well."

At my clearly cynical expression, he twisted round to face me. "Look, I've only been here once in the past six months, only once since that bitch had me thrown out, and that's when I saw him." He held up a large index finger. "That one time. All I remember is that he's a big guy, built short and wide, like a bulldog. Had real broad shoulders."

I tensed. "White? Black?"

"White. Had light-colored eyes too. Can't say what color exactly, but they were light all right."

I kept my voice even. "When was this?"

"'Bout a month ago. He slammed Queenie up against a wall and it wasn't pretty. I just happened to be walking by. I thought he was going to break her neck, right then and there."

"What did you do?"

"What do you think? I kept on walking."

CHAPTER 10

Things would change a few years later, but back then, if you were gay and into the scene, you had a lot of Harlem nightspots to choose from. The crowd that danced at one place partied later at another. There was 267, for example, over on West 136th Street, and Edmond's Cellar on West 132nd and Fifth Avenue. There was the Yeahman and the Garden of Joy. There was Lulu Bell's on Lenox near 127th and buffet flats like Hazel Valentine's Daisy Chain on 140th.

The Daisy Chain was also known as the 101 Ranch. It had a chorus of men who would come out and dance, dressed in the best of women's finery. It was at the 101 that they came up with the Shim Sham Shimmy. That dance just took off. At one point, everybody was doing it.

People knew about these places mostly by word of mouth. If you were gay, then Greenwich Village or Harlem were it, baby. The churches in Harlem weren't too tolerant, but the community as a whole mostly looked the other way. Of course, gays were discreet. Like Richard Bruce Nugent used to say, people didn't shout their business from the rooftops. They just did what they wanted to do. Nobody was in the closet.

If they had been, then that closet would have been mighty crowded, cause a whole lot of Harlem's best and brightest were gay or bisexual. There was Claude McKay, Countee Cullen, Alain Locke, and Wallace Thurman. There was the aforementioned Richard. Some would've put Langston Hughes on the list. Both men and women were in love with him. He just never let himself be seen with anybody and kept them all guessing. He was a beautiful, talented enigma.

The women were loving each other too. Bessie Smith, Alberta Hunter,

Jackie "Moms" Mabley, Mabel Hampton, Ma Rainey, and Ethel Waters: they all enjoyed female loving. I remember when Ma Rainey kept getting into trouble for making it with women. Back in '25, police cuffed her. Said she'd been having an orgy at home with women from her own chorus. Bessie had to bail her out.

You can't mention the scene without mentioning Gladys Bentley. That sister was two hundred and fifty pounds of gutsy talent. She used to get dressed up in a white tuxedo and top hat. Bentley was the heart and soul of the Clambake, a popular place for people "in the life." Like Queenie, Bentley was known for belting out double-entendre lyrics. She counted Tallulah Bankhead, Beatrice Lillie, Jeanne Eagels, Marilyn Miller, Princess Murat, Libby Holman, and Louisa Carpenter du Pont Jenney among her most fervent admirers.

You could say I had a little black book in my head of people who were in the life. I went through it now, trying to think of who else I could talk to.

There was Casca Bonds and Alexander Gumby. Casca ran house parties and Gumby did too, Gumby's being more like a literary salon that drew a certain crowd. Either one might've had the information I needed, but I was short on time and preferred a safer bet.

And that was Jack-a-Lee's.

Jack-a-Lee's party palace was in a class all by itself. It was essentially a brownstone on West 125th. The place was so infamous that Fats Waller and Count Basie wrote about it. Jack-a-Lee had a private party going on in every room, gangbangs and wife swapping, women pleasing each other and men working each other's pump. Anyone who wanted to could join in. As for drinking, Prohibition be damned, the liquor flowed. The folks poured gin out of milk pitchers, *crystal* milk pitchers, and smoked reefer like there was no tomorrow.

I got there just after midnight. From the outside, if your nose was sensitive, you could catch the whiff of something forbidden in the air, but all you could see were shadows moving behind heavily curtained windows. Once up the front steps and inside the door, you passed through a little vestibule and paid your fee. Then you were in a hallway. Turn right for the crowd; go straight up the stairs for private action. I turned right.

The party was in full swing. The air was hot and sticky. It reeked of sex, smoke, and booze. A piano player was pounding the ivories. Rouged men in flapper wigs and fringed dresses shimmied and shook. They were grinding each other, tonguing each other, and doing standing up what most folks do lying down.

No hypocrisy here. Violence, drugs, and liquor? Yes. But hypocrisy? No. And that was a relief after some of the stuffy society gatherings I often attended. I felt absolutely at ease with this crowd. Here, among all the costumes and flamboyant fakery, I still felt a greater sense of honesty than I did at a lot of the buttoned-up gatherings I wrote about.

I pushed my way into the packed parlor room. Eyes on every side gave me the once-over. Many in that thick, sweaty crowd knew me. They recognized me from mainstream parties, rent parties, social soirees, or the photo that accompanied my column.

Most also knew that I'd been interviewing the Black Orchid when he was kidnapped. What was I doing here now? Just having fun? Or was there another reason?

Jack-a-Lee saw me at the same time I saw him. He raised a chubby hand and waved. His full name was Jack-a-Lee Talbot and he was, as he himself put it, the *transvestite du jour*, the flavor of the day. Jack-a-Lee was arrogant and egotistic, but he wasn't stupid. He knew that fame is fleeting. So, while he had it, he meant to enjoy it to the hilt.

He was as broad as a barn and well past sixty, but his face was amazingly unlined and he had the verve of a man of twenty. He was wearing a bejeweled silver satin turban, a red satin robe, and gold-strapped sandals. His fingernails and toenails were painted fire-engine red. He knew everybody and everybody wanted to know him.

I cut through the crowd and, on his end, he pushed through to get to me. People were knocking into their neighbors to get out of his way. Jack-a-Lee had the bulk of an elephant and the energy to go with it.

He greeted me with two enthusiastic and *très chic* air kisses. Then he gave me the once-over with heavily kohled and mascaraed eyes.

"I'd love to say you look simply marvelous, dahling, but I can't. Not that I'd expect you to. Not after last night." He wrapped a fleshy arm around my shoulders, bringing me close and dropping his voice. Lights of greedy curiosity danced in his dark eyes. "I hope you're here to share all the delicious details. Come. Let's find someplace *très privé* and you can tell Jack-a-Lee everything."

We went up to the second floor. There were four doors along the corridor: three bedrooms—one in the front and two in the back—and a shared bathroom in between.

Jack-a-Lee started toward the door to the front, then hesitated. He put a finger to his pouty lips, shook his head. "No, I think Aimee's in there doing . . ." The rest got lost in a mutter, but it didn't matter. I didn't want to know.

He headed back to the two rear bedrooms. He opened the door on the right and stuck his head in. From inside came groans and grunts. Jack-a-Lee raised an eyebrow and pulled the door shut. He went to the next door. Same story. He put his hands on his ample hips, pursed his lips, and reflected.

"We could go upstairs, but I know it's busy up there too. Real busy, if you know what I mean. So there's only one alternative." He flipped a hand toward the middle door.

I sighed. Goodness knows what that bathroom would look like—and smell like—in the middle of a house party like this.

"*Après-vous,*" I said.

"No, m'dear. After you."

I took out a handkerchief and used it to turn the knob, or tried to. The door was locked.

This was too much.

Now that we were standing right outside the door, I could hear the sounds of intimate contact. I gave Jack-a-Lee a look. *What do we do now?*

Jack-a-Lee was a true diva. He had a notion he could get some of the most delicious gossip in the world out of me and he was being blocked from getting it. He was frustrated and embarrassed. This was his own house and he couldn't find a place to talk. He raised a fist and banged on the door.

"Whoever's in there, get out! Pull out right now, do you hear? I don't care where else you do it, but you can't do it in there. Get out of there fast. No screwing in the bathroom. Those are the house rules. I will not have someone pee on themselves while they're waiting for you to have your fun. You can do it downstairs in the middle of the dance floor for all I care, but not in my bathroom." *Bang! Bang! Bang!* He made the door shake in its frame. "And I mean now!"

There were squeals of terror, the sound of hurried dressing, and the shot of a little bolt being thrown back. The door was flung open and two half-dressed men, one with his pirate pants still open, the other trying to arrange his dirndl, stepped out.

"Well, I never—" began the one with the skirt.

"Yes, you did, but you'll never do it again, not in my place, if you take that attitude with me," Jack-a-Lee said.

He dismissed the two men with a wave of his hand, then grabbed my wrist and dragged me into the bathroom. Inside he looked around and wrinkled his nose with distaste.

"I guess I should be grateful they were just stirring chocolate. Sometimes, people leave such a funk in here." He looked at me and smiled. "Then again, I like it earthy, don't you?"

His wit was contagious. My lips twitched with a smile. I repressed it. It seemed wrong, under the circumstances, to be merry. So, I rolled my eyes and gave him a look that said loud and clear, *Be serious.*

He pouted. "Come on, honey. Where's your sense of humor?" When I didn't respond, he said, "All right, then. Be that way. Here," he flipped down the toilet lid. "Take a seat on my gracious commode and tell Mama all about it."

I perched on the lid and he squeezed his bulk right next to me. It was tight, but not unpleasant. It was like sitting next to a rather large, warm marshmallow.

I told him everything he could've read in the papers and not an iota more, but made it sound as though I had. He was thrilled.

"And you were right there? You actually saw the whole thing?"

"Sure did."

He put two plump fingers to a dimpled cheek and shook his head with feminine delicacy. "I'm so jealous. Nothing that exciting ever happens to me."

"The thing is, somebody saw Queenie being roughed up by an ofay like the one who took him last night. Broad, got light eyes. Said to be an enforcer. I need his name or who he works for."

"And you think I can tell you?"

"I'm sure you can."

Jack-a-Lee mulled it over. "Let's say I could. Why should I? Lay my life on the line and for what?"

I was prepared for the question. "You're going to the Faggots' Ball?"

"Wouldn't miss it for the world."

The Faggots' Ball was the largest drag ball of the year. That wasn't the official name for it, of course, but it's what everybody called it. A fraternal society, the Hamilton Lodge of the Odd Fellows, hosted it every February at the Rockland Palace Casino on Eighth Avenue and 155th Street. The event was set in Harlem, but folks came from all over and they weren't only colored. Thousands flocked to it. It was one of the largest, maybe even *the* largest, gathering of lesbians and fairies in New York City.

"I'll be there too, with picture-snappers," I said. "Suppose I promise to put your mug on the front page of the *Chronicle's* society pages?"

"*Moi?*" He put a hand to his chest and fluttered his long false eyelashes. "Little old me?"

"Jack-a-Lee, there is nothing little or old about you."

His face broke out into a smile, but then his eyes got serious. "Look, sweetie, that's a nice offer, but the ball's not until next Friday. A lot could happen in a week. And as nice as it is, a picture's not everything."

"What do you want?"

"The reward money, but it can't be seen coming to me."

I thought about it. "Okay."

"You can fix that?"

"If you give me the skinny and it works out."

"No ifs, ands, or buts. I want a guarantee. If I give you the information and you screw it up, I still get my money."

"You'll get it."

"All right, then. It sounds like a guy named Olmo, and he's not white. That motherfucker's one of us."

I thought about the accent, the bright pale eyes. "I never would've—"

"America's one-drop rule, baby. And he's got more than a drop. Mama's ivory, but daddy's ebony. He grew up in Stockholm. They call him the Velvet Swede."

"And who does he work for?"

He paused. "Stax Murphy."

The name fell from his lips like a brick. Stax was one of Harlem's most notorious policy bankers. He was also a loan shark of the worst ilk. The New York Police Department had at least three warrants out for him: murder, extortion, and blackmail. Blackie and his men had been searching for Stax for years, but they hadn't gotten close, not once. "He's like a ghost," Blackie had once told me. "This is a man who can practically disappear in front of your eyes. He knows every trick in the book and probably wrote a few."

"And Queenie owes him?"

"Big time. He's been losing at craps and running to Stax for help."

This was bad news, very bad news. I heard this with a sinking heart. If Queenie was in debt to Stax, then the singer's chances of survival were sinking by the second. Men like Stax tried to get their money by intimidation first. By the time they resorted to kidnapping, it meant they had given up hope of getting their money back, so they were out for a pound of flesh instead. I had seen the results of their henchmen's handiwork. It was never a pretty sight. I flashed on the memory of putting those handcuffs around Queenie's wrists and felt sick.

Someone knocked on the door.

"Go away!" Jack-a-Lee yelled.

"But I got to go bad!"

"Then get the hell outta my house and take it outside!"

There was plaintive grumbling and the sound of feet scurrying away. Jack-a-Lee turned back to me. His eyes were dead serious and he suddenly looked old. "If you're thinking about going up against Stax, don't. He'd kill you without blinking an eyelash."

I raised my chin and tightened my lips.

"Listen," Jack-a-Lee said. "I knew a man Stax killed just for stealing a loaf of bread. Name was Stone, Ralph Stone. He didn't even steal the bread, not really. He was a guest in the house and ate more than half of it. One of the other guests complained. Stax said he'd 'handle it.' A couple of days later, he did.

"He and Ralph were sitting in a car, down on 125th Street. They're drinking, doing a little reefer. Stax takes out his gun. Looks like he's just showing it off. And Ralph—now, he's easy to impress and wants to please—he asks if he could touch it. Stax gives him the gun, watches him admire it. Then Stax takes it back, says, 'You wanna see how it works?' Ralph nods. And that was that. Stax pumped two bullets in him. Shot him right in the face, up close and personal." Jack-a-Lee paused. "You go after him, you'll be dead before I ever get my face in the papers, much less that dough. Now, you know I can't have that."

"I get it, but . . ."

"You're still going after him."

"No, I'm going after the story and wherever it leads. Right now, it's leading to him."

"But baby, you've got no backup, no protection."

"You're beginning to sound like Sam."

At the mention of Delaney, Jack-a-Lee beamed. Some of his normal mischief returned to his eyes. "Honey, you got yourself a fine sheik there. Um-hmm. Hope you're giving it to him, nice and regular."

"That's none of your business."

"Of course it is. Cause if you don't, then I will."

"He doesn't swing that way."

Jack-a-Lee cocked his head. "Oh, you'd be surprised." He examined a fingernail, buffed it against his breast. "Trust me, if I gave him a taste of my sweetness, he'd never look back."

"Thank you for your advice." I leaned forward. "Now tell me: where do I find Stax Murphy?"

If Stax was behind Queenie's disappearance, then I wanted to talk to him—and do it fast, before the cops started a shootout and got everybody killed. The chances of convincing Stax to let Queenie go were probably next to nothing. I knew that, but I had to try. I owed it to Queenie. I owed it to myself.

Sam would've disagreed, and he'd be horrified at the thought of me hunting down Stax, so I wouldn't tell him. He'd find out soon enough.

My main worry was what I'd say to Stax. I didn't quite know what I'd say, but I was sure I'd think of something. Because I had to. Meanwhile, I was enjoying what my question had done to Jack-a-Lee's expression.

His heavily kohled eyes widened, his jaw dropped, and his voice went up half an octave. "Are you out of your mind?"

"Come on," I said.

"Lanie—"

"Tell Stax that he needs to talk to me—"

"*Needs?* Wha—"

"Yes, needs. Tell him that despite all the killing, I wasn't the only one to survive that massacre. I was down at that station house last night, Jack-a-Lee, and I can tell you—there were a ton of witnesses. That sketch artist was busy. Now, if I can connect him up to this, then the cops can too—"

"You're not going to say anything, are you? Or tell them I told you?"

"Of course not. But I don't have to. They've got those drawings. They're showing them around right now. Sooner or later somebody's going to slip or make a deal and say something. That's it. Stax is Olmo's boss, and he's already on the most wanted list, so they'll be hungry for him. I'd say another twenty-four hours, tops. If he wants to be smart about it, he'll talk to me and get his story out there, before the cops do it for him."

Jack-a-Lee thought about it, then shook his head. "Lanie, he'd kill me."

"Okay," I shrugged. "No help, no picture, no moolah."

He narrowed his eyes. "You're being cruel."

I tilted my head.

"Look," he said. "If I even *tried* to get that information for you, we'd both be dead in a minute. Stax doesn't want anybody knowing—"

There was another pounding on the door, which jumped in its frame.

"Hey!" a male voice yelled. "Is there anybody in there? Whoever you are, you'd better get the hell outta there! You don't and I'll get Jack-a-Lee. You know what he said about fucking in the—"

Jack-a-Lee yanked the door open. "Are you crazy! Banging and yelling like that?"

The man who'd knocked stumbled backward, tripping on his fake satin cloak. He would've fallen into the stairwell if the banister hadn't caught him.

"Oh, Jack-a-Lee, it's you! I didn't know. How was I supposed to know?"

Jack-a-Lee growled at him, glanced at me, and then turned back to his guest. "The lady and I are conducting business, very important business. Do you hear? You're just lucky that I'm in a good frame of mind. Or else I'd—"

"It's okay," I said. "We're finished."

Jack-a-Lee jerked around with a frown and a look of surprise. "Are you sure?"

"Are you going to give me what I asked for?"

"No."

"Then, yes, we're done."

I walked out and he followed. Downstairs, the crowd was applauding. A man stood next to the piano. On his head was a top hat; around his neck, a wing-tip collar and black bow tie. He was otherwise naked. As I watched, he lit a cigarette. But instead of smoking it, he balanced it end-up on the piano bench.

"What's he going to do?" I whispered to Jack-a-Lee.

"Just wait."

The man squatted over the bench and lowered himself onto the cigarette. The crowd hushed. Everyone was waiting for a cry of pain or the moment when the guy would chicken out. Neither came. The performer lowered himself until that cigarette disappeared into his rear end, bit by bit.

"Isn't he marvelous?" Jack-a-Lee gushed.

"He's something all right."

"One day I demanded he show me how he did it. I got down on my knees for a good, close look. He actually has such fine control that he can work that ciggy right up there and squeeze it out before it burns him. It was one of the most remarkable things I've ever seen."

I had nothing to say. Actually, I had plenty to say. I was just too polite to say it.

Jack-a-Lee, of course, knew this. He gave me a mischievous look. "Shall I ask him to give you a personal performance?"

I looked askance. "Thank you, but no. That's one repeat performance I can do without."

CHAPTER 11

I headed out of Jack-a-Lee's around one in the morning. It was a shock to leave the crowded warmth of his town house and step into the cold empty streets. I hurried to my car, careful not to slip on the ice. I got in, shut the door, and exhaled, watching my breath hang in the chilled air. Then I started the engine.

It was only fourteen blocks uptown to my house—a short distance to drive, but long enough to do some serious cogitating. The Black Orchid was into Stax Murphy for sums unknown. Stax sent the Velvet Swede to collect. Perhaps it became clear that Queenie didn't have the dough and never would, or maybe Stax got impatient, or even just plain greedy. Whatever. He decided to nab Queenie and squeeze Lucien Fawkes for the cash.

That scenario made sense. There was only one thing wrong with it. The ransom demand: it hadn't been made. Twenty-four hours had come and gone, with nary a peep from the kidnappers.

Now that was something to chew on.

Maybe, like Lucien said, the request was simply delayed for some reason. Or maybe Stax had something totally different in mind.

But what could that be?

I thought about it while sitting at a traffic stop and decided that the only thing I knew for certain was that Queenie had secrets. Maybe one of them had gotten him kidnapped, possibly killed.

There was also the Cotton Club angle, but Lucien himself didn't seem to put much faith in it and neither did I. I just couldn't see Frenchy needing to kidnap any songbird to put him in that golden cage.

The traffic light changed. Instead of going straight, which would've taken

me home, I pulled a hard left and drove west. I was thinking of the police station, but something else must've been on my mind, because I found
myself slowing down in front of Sam's place. His second-floor apartment
was opposite the police station and one block from the newsroom. He was
always on hand in case a major story broke, always there for an emergency.

Always there, period. He was my rock, stable and true and firmly in my
corner. I wanted to talk to him, tell him what I'd found out from Lucien
Fawkes, Morgana, and Jack-a-Lee. But that wasn't the only reason I went
there.

Over the past months, Sam had worked hard to show me that love was
still possible, that it was worth giving a chance. And what had I done but
push him away?

For the first time since my man died, I wondered if Hamp would have
been happy with the choices I was making. I was sure he would've been
proud of the way I did my job. I could even imagine him smiling down at me.

But since Sam had made his interest known to me, I'd had a different
image of Hamp, one of him frowning—not at Sam, but at me, with concern
wrinkling his handsome brow. Life was giving me a second chance at love
but I couldn't bring myself to grab it and I didn't quite understand why.

Hamp. God, I missed that man so much, I missed him in every part of
my being. For the longest time, I didn't even think about somebody else
touching me. The desire was just gone.

But that was changing because of Sam, who was patient, kind—and
good-looking. There was no denying it. He was single. He was fine. And he
wanted me.

Still I hesitated.

I glanced up the street. Beyond the next light, on the other side of the
road, was the newsroom where we spent most of our days working together.

Amend that.

As the paper's society reporter, I was out and about, running from one
function to the next. As its city room editor, he was a fairly permanent fix-
ture in the fishbowl of his office. So we couldn't actually spend that much

time together. Our roles precluded it. But like most in the newsroom, I thought of him as the paper's anchor. His was the first face I sought whenever I walked in the door, and I often sensed him seeking me out too.

Why was I hesitating?

Sam was waiting. But how long would he wait?

Selena Troy, our very pretty obit writer, wasn't waiting. She wasn't just the youngest member of our reporting staff, she was also by far the most ambitious. She'd made more than one play for Sam and no doubt would make plenty more. She would persevere until one day she got him, until she brought him down, like a lioness taking down her prey. Then she would make sure that everyone knew about her conquest. Subtlety and discretion were not among her concerns. Selena was one of those women who enjoy the hunt as much as many men do. Sam knew that. Maybe that's why he'd apparently found it so easy to resist her charms—so far.

I glanced up to see if his lights were on. They weren't, but instinct told me that he would be awake. Instinct and the dark circles he often had under his eyes said Sam went late to bed and maybe sometimes not at all. Without giving myself time to think about why I was there or what I wanted, I got out of the car, ran up to his front door, and rang the bell.

And waited.

There was no answer.

I raised my hand to ring again, then lowered it. Disappointed in a way I wasn't ready to admit, I ran to the car, hopped back in, and drove on.

CHAPTER 12

Ever since his divorce, Blackie had pretty much lived at the station house. He couldn't stand the thought of being alone. Once, when he'd been especially exhausted and sad, he'd been blunt: "The house is so empty without her. I don't know how you do it, Lanie, living in that big house all on your own. I only have two rooms and it's too much for me. Way too much."

So I thought it was likely he'd be at the station now, working the case, glad to have something to take his mind off his troubles.

He was in all right, sitting at his desk with a thick file open before him and stacks of papers on either side. His shirt was rumpled, his tie askew. The harsh light of the station house threw shadows that revealed worry lines I hadn't seen before and new streaks of gray in his black hair.

He was hanging up the phone as I walked in.

"So, you *are* here," I said.

"I belong here. What are you doing at this time of night?" His Irish brogue was heavy, thick with fatigue.

I shrugged, gave a half smile, and plunked down in the chair next to his desk. "You know how it is. Reporters . . . we don't keep regular hours either. We follow the story, like you guys follow the case."

"Actually, I think it's the other way around. We don't follow the case; it follows us."

"And when it catches you?"

"We're goners."

I chuckled at that and so did he.

"A bit of melodrama always helps, me ould da used to say," he added with a crooked smile.

"As if this case doesn't have enough."

His smile faded. He looked at the file before him, already two inches thick with notes and reports and photographs. "That Harvard boy's family, they're breathing down the mayor's neck. The mayor's breathing down the commissioner's neck . . ."

"And the commissioner's breathing down the captain's—"

"And the captain down mine. I feel like I've got a herd of bloody elephants on my back."

Despite his complaining, I knew that the Cinnamon Club massacre was the kind of case that Blackie lived for. It had clear, straight lines, just bad guys and good guys and no in-between. But the expectations that went with cases like this were crushing, from the public to City Hall, the brass, and on down. If you weren't careful, you could end up spending more time managing other people's expectations than actually working the case.

"So, you don't have anything?"

"Oh, I didn't say that. But it's nothing I can share."

"You working it alone?"

He shook his head. "We're putting together a task force. We'll announce it tomorrow."

"How many on the team?"

"Three. With me, it'll be four."

"Smart guys?"

He lowered his head. "You promise not to quote me?"

"I promise."

"Nice guys, but they're rubes. I wouldn't have picked them."

"You mean it's for show?"

"You promised not to quote me."

"I won't."

"It's a bunch of malarkey."

"When's the news conference?"

"At noon."

I made a mental note of it, then pointed to the open file before him. "Sure there's nothing in there for me right now?"

"What for? Your paper won't come out for another week. You don't work for a daily, remember?"

"Even so. I like to stay in the know."

He paused, studying me. "You ever regret leaving the *Harlem Age?*"

"No. Why? It's not a daily either."

"But it seemed closer to what you like to do."

I shook my head. "I'm fine where I am." I glanced at the stack in front of him. "So, what's up with the file?"

"Let's see. What've we got here? Well, for one thing, we've got a confession."

I straightened up, all ears. "You have a confession and you weren't going to tell me?"

"Hold on." He raised a hand. "I admit that no, I wasn't. But since you're so insistent, I might share a few details."

"Please."

"One question."

"Yes?"

"Which confession would you like to hear about?" He flipped through the pages. "We have a least a dozen. It's your choice. I'll give you everything but the names."

I sat back. "Very funny."

"Some of it, yeah. In short, what we've got here is a whole lotta nothing: crazies who want a minute of fame. At least fifty people claim to have seen the Black Orchid since the kidnapping. As far north as Poughkeepsie, as far south as Dixie. I don't know how they heard about it down there, but evidently they did. Most of it don't mean a thing, but we've got to follow it up, all of it. And no doubt more will come in. Ever since that boy's family announced the reward, the phones have been ringing off the hook."

I listened to the silence of the station. "It's quiet now."

"Thank God."

I shifted topics. "I heard that you guys went through Queenie's dressing room."

"So, you were over at the club, were you? Trying to sniff things out on your own? Now, you know you're not—"

"I went to interview the club owner. Part of the regular follow-up." I leaned forward. "What were you looking for in the dressing room?"

"I could ask you the same thing."

"I didn't say I was in there."

"Were you?"

"Of course."

"Why?"

"To get a sense of him. You know, for the column."

"Of course . . . the column." He gave me a cynical smile.

"So, what did you find?" I repeated.

"Nothing in particular. Actually, nothing at all."

That jived, when I thought about it, with what I'd found. A strange sense of nothing at all.

"Look," he said, "there is one thing I can tell you."

"And what's that?"

"Another one died today."

My smile faded. "Another victim?"

"I was taking the call as you walked in. She was twenty-five. Took a shot in the throat."

"Oh God," I murmured. After a moment, I took out my pad and pencil. "What's her name?"

He shook his head. "Family's asking us not to release it."

"Also rich, also—?"

"No, they won't be bothering us. The father said she was better off dead than to be doing what she was doing."

"Which was?"

"Sinning with the sons of Ham."

"He actually said that?"

"He's a preacher. Has very firm ideas about blacks and whites and how ne'er the twain shall meet. It's in the Bible, don't you know?" He rubbed his eyes and shook his head in disgust.

For a moment, we both fell silent. Then my gaze drifted back to Blackie's file. I was usually good at reading documents upside down, but the type was too small and my eyes too tired.

"What're you guys thinking?" I asked.

"You know I can't tell you that."

"Come on, give me something. I've got to keep the story moving. And given the pressure you're under, so do you."

"Keep it moving, huh?" He narrowed his eyes. "Maybe it's me who should be asking: What have you been up to? What have you found out?"

I smiled. "Don't you think I'd tell you if I'd found out anything, anything useful?"

He guffawed. "Hell no! Of course you wouldn't. I like you, Lanie, but I know how you are, how you all are. When it comes to you guys, what's yours is yours and what's mine is yours."

"Do I hear the pot calling the kettle black?"

"But seriously, Lanie, what've you got?"

"Who says I've got anything?"

"You always got something. Every cop knows that. You always got something."

I paused, then leaned on his desk and said, "Okay, supposing you're right. Maybe I turned over a rock and found a worm or two, maybe even got a name. Why should I share it with you before I share it with Sam?"

He shrugged. "Cause I'm the cop who can put you in jail for obstruction and withholding evidence?"

I nearly burst out laughing. "Wrong answer."

"It's always fun talking to you, Lanie."

I glanced at my watch. The clock was working its way well past two. "Time for me to take my leave, kind sir." I got up to go. "Get some sleep, Blackie. That's what I'm going to do."

"Back to that big empty house of yours, huh?"

"It's not empty to me."

"Full of memories, right?"

"Good memories."

He sighed. "You're too young for that to be enough."

CHAPTER 13

It was long past Christmas. That was my first thought upon seeing the paper-wrapped parcel. It had been left leaning against my front door, illuminated by the spill of light from the lamps overhead.

Big things come in small packages. That was my second thought, and it caused a ripple of anxiety.

The rectangular package was about eight inches long, five inches wide, and maybe two deep. The sender had wrapped it in plain brown paper and secured it with yellow twine. When I picked it up, I found that it was hard and the contents had heft. It smelled strongly of cigars.

A mistaken delivery?

Maybe. There was no way to tell: The wrappings were blank. There was no address—not mine, not the sender's. Nothing. Just wrapping as plain as plain could be.

I turned it over gingerly and gave it a little shake. I had a fleeting thought that it might be a bomb. *Schhwwwwuush.* Something shifted softly inside.

I tucked the parcel under one arm and went inside. I left it on a side table in the vestibule with my purse and hung up my coats, the one I'd worn and the one I'd retrieved from the Cinnamon Club. Then I took the package into the parlor and sank down on the sofa. I couldn't undo the knot in the twine, so I went downstairs to the kitchen, fetched a butcher knife, and slit the string. The paper fell away to reveal a wood cigar box.

Hmmm.

La Imperial Habana was etched into the top cover. A strip of olive-green labeling that wrapped around the edges bore the words *Grandfrabrica de Tabacos, 1925*. A washed-out Henry Clay tax stamp appeared on the lower right-hand corner.

I lifted the lid. A heavier smell of old cigars—and of something else, something slightly foul—wafted out. The protective separation paper that would've normally covered the cigars was still in there. A white envelope lay on top. The envelope was ordinary; you could get one like it at any stationary store.

The good news was that it was addressed; the bad news was that it wasn't to me: 534 West 139th Street. I was at 543.

That alone didn't necessarily mean that the package wasn't intended for me. Mixing up house numbers happened all the time, especially with a typed address like this one. But this envelope included the name *Bernard*— a family that lived across the street, the one whose light had been burning when I arrived home the night before—and that clearly meant it wasn't for me.

Perhaps I shouldn't have done what I did. An inner alarm bell certainly told me not to. But I've always been curious. I set the envelope aside and removed the separation paper.

Even as I recognized it, suspected what it was, I wanted to deny the sight of it: why would anyone wrap a cigar in a bloody handkerchief?

I used the handle of a spoon to nudge back the flaps of stained linen and reveal what truly lay within.

It was somebody's finger, his or her ring finger. Despite being slightly shriveled from blood loss, it looked rather fresh.

I dropped the spoon, covered my mouth with my hand, and turned away. I had suspected something terrible, but seeing it, actually seeing it, was different. Chills ran up my spine. I told myself to toughen up. *Calm down. Take a deep breath and focus. You can only help Queenie if you focus.*

The digit had been cut cleanly at the base. Though grayed from the loss of blood, the skin on the finger was clearly brown. The fingernail was polished and feminine, but the size of the finger was distinctly masculine. It wore a ring, a thick gold-colored band with a large yellow diamond surrounded by clear crystals.

There was no mistaking it. Queenie was inordinately proud of that yellow diamond ring, which I could now see was fake. He wouldn't have parted from it without violence.

An image flashed through my mind. Of men restraining Queenie, shoving his hand against the edge of a table, extending his ring finger while pressing down the other digits. Of a meat cleaver being raised and then—*bam!* He struggles, screams, and realizes with horror that it's too late. The deed is done.

The image was so strong and swept across my mind with such force that it took my breath away, left me feeling dizzy and sick.

I had seen incredible things done to the human body. While covering the police beat for the *Harlem Age*, I'd reported on shootings, stabbings, strangulations, even state electrocutions. I was there when the cops found corpses infested with maggots or swollen beyond recognition after being pulled from the river. I'd witnessed enough to inspire nightmares for the rest of my life. But none of it got to me the way the sight of that finger did.

With all the others, there had been distance. They were strangers. I'd never heard their laughter, seen their smiles. This time, I had. This time, I knew the victim.

Had they sent me the finger of a corpse?

The kidnappers wanted to sell Queenie. They knew it would be best to keep him alive, at least for a while, in case people asked for verification. But they were also willing to maim him to prove they meant business.

I glanced back down at the finger, felt a wave of anger, and dropped the lid on the cigar box.

Get a grip. You've got to believe that he's not dead, not yet.

Question: why would the kidnappers send this to that nice, conservative family across the street?

The Bernards were prominent and well-to-do. Alfred Bernard was a much-admired pediatrician, known for his generous donations of time and energy when it came to tending to orphans and street children. He was the main force behind local efforts to stem the spread of tuberculosis, a leading cause of death among our young.

Phyllis Bernard was a former nurse, a Phi Beta Kappa alum of the University of Chicago, a prominent clubwoman active in the 135th Street YWCA, the Movement, and the Charlotte Spokes Day Nursery. She had founded the Gifted Ladies Club, a housing initiative for young working women.

Despite all of this community involvement, the couple rarely entertained. And when they did, they invited only a chosen few, the best of the best. The very distinguished Bryan Canfield, head of the Movement, was one such example; and George Ramsey, my managing editor, was another.

I had once been among that select group. It was because of Hamp, who had been a highly respected surgeon. He'd worked with the Harvard-trained physician Louis T. Wright, the first black surgeon for the New York Police Department, the first black physician to join the staff of any New York hospital, and the first black clinic director at Harlem Hospital. Through Wright, Hamp and I had come to know the Bernards. The three men had sat on several medical committees together.

After Hamp's death, I had slowly distanced myself from this particular circle. I don't think I did it consciously. In retrospect, I can only say that I had a strong need to forge new social ties, ones that weren't based so predominantly on my role as a doctor's wife, especially now that the doctor was gone. In short, I don't think I wanted their pity.

For a moment, I was caught in that past. I came back to the present with a shiver. Did I know anything about the Bernards that would explain why they'd be the recipients of this ghastly package? No, nothing that I could think of. They wouldn't have been caught dead in a place like the Cinnamon Club. I wouldn't have dreamed they knew of Queenie Lovetree's existence.

It was time to open the envelope.

I raised the lid, found the letter inside. Like the envelope, it was typewritten. The message was brief and brutal:

Here is the proof you asked for. We want $20,000. Unmarked bills, used tens and twenties. Numbers should be nonconsecutive and authen-

tic. When ready, place ad in personal classifieds of the New York Daily News. Sign it Margie Winthrop. Expect ad Wednesday. Pay and keep your mouth shut. Or you'll be picking him up in pieces.

It was the ransom letter that everyone had been waiting for—and it had been sent to the Bernards, not Lucien Fawkes.

I read the note again. It was standard fare, with all the usual ingredients: the warning against going to the police, the demand for payment, instructions about the money itself; but nothing about the time, place, or method of delivery. The kidnappers would get to that later.

Nothing unusual there. The twist wasn't even the severed finger, which, as horrid as it was, wasn't all that surprising. After all, the kidnappers had to prove they were serious. Neither was the twist in the letter. Instead, it was in the delivery of the letter to me and the addressing of it to the Bernards.

Here is the proof you asked for.

This suggested that the kidnappers had already communicated with the Bernards at least once, and that the family had balked. It also meant that the kidnappers remained confident that the Bernards would pay if confronted with this grisly "proof" of their victim's identity.

But why did the kidnappers believe that the Bernards would care enough about Queenie Lovetree to pony up twenty grand? Then there was the more immediate question: if the package was intended for the Bernards, why had it ended up on my doorstep?

Could the kidnappers have simply reversed the house numbers by accident? As for the fact that I lived across from their intended target, in a kidnapping that I'd also witnessed—it was one of those odd coincidences that could happen from time to time.

However, I didn't believe in coincidences, not of that degree.

The kidnappers wanted me in on the case. They were still making me an accomplice. I didn't like that idea, but I was also intrigued by the possibility. Sooner or later, they would miscalculate and the access they were giving me would become a weapon I could use against them.

The delivery of the box not only granted access but conveyed information. The kidnappers were trying to tell me something, and I thought I knew what.

I read the ransom note again. Apparently, the Bernards hadn't definitively said no, and clearly hadn't reported the demand to the police. Instead, they had asked for proof. So the Bernards not only knew Queenie, but had a vested interest in his well-being.

Obviously, he was related to them. The thought took some getting used to, but it made sense. For one thing, it explained Queenie's secrecy and maybe even the Bernards' reclusiveness. But just how closely related was he?

He was the right age to have been their child, but the wrong sex. The Bernards had only one child, as far as I knew, and that was a rather plain daughter. Up until a few months ago, I hadn't even realized she existed. She was a prim and proper girl in her early twenties, demure and soft-spoken.

I had lived on the block for four years and in that time had never seen the girl, not until one day the prior October, when the Bernards were all out walking along West 139th Street. They usually just gave a nod and strolled past—but that day, I tripped over the uneven sidewalk and spilled my groceries. Even though they knew me, the older Bernards didn't break their stride. But the young woman with them stopped and started to help me gather my things. It was only then that the others, including the young man with her, jumped in.

Introductions followed. I was stunned to learn that she was their daughter, Sheila; the fellow, her husband, Junior Holt. The couple had moved back six months earlier, after graduating from Howard University, Dr. Bernard said. Sheila was homesick after spending four solid years away in Washington, D.C., with nary a visit home. She'd always been too busy to come back on holidays and had spent summers in Europe, Mrs. Bernard added. Traveling was fine and good when you were a student, but when studies were done, it was time to grow up and take on the mantles of responsibility. So Sheila and Junior had moved home to New York, where they could find work.

It was Dr. Bernard who did most of the talking. He was in his sixties, tall and handsome, about six-foot-two, with salt-and-pepper hair, beautifully groomed and elegantly dressed. He had a reputation for being gruff and controlling with medical staff. But when he considered himself among social equals, he exuded charm and wit. Clearly, he was a well-educated man used to influencing people.

As for Phyllis Bernard, she was the perfect Strivers' Row matron: from the top of her gray-streaked hair, dressed in finger waves, to the tips of her black kid shoes, she was perfectly made up and attired. She was the type of woman who follows her husband's every lead. Like a politician's wife, she gave polite nods or made small interjections to accentuate what he said, but rarely came out with a comment of her own.

Alfred and Phyllis Bernard always conveyed an impression of longstanding marital happiness. Despite whatever troubles they might have faced along the way, they were still deeply in love. It was there in the way he took her hand and gave her a glance or a smile every now and then, as if seeking her affirmation about what he said.

I remembered feeling a pang at seeing their silent communication. This was the kind of enduring marital love I'd hoped for. I'd had the right man; we could've gone the distance. Then death got in the way.

But now I resolutely put such thoughts aside. It was important to recall everything I could about that October meeting. It was the one and only time I'd seen the Bernards all together.

Sheila resembled neither of her parents, at least not at first glance. The most striking thing about her was her sweetness, gentleness, and apparent deep love for her husband. She had a distinct though faint Southern lilt to her speech.

What about Junior? He'd said so little. I could summon up only a vague image of a tall, slender fellow with dark, sad eyes. I recalled the truism that girls always marry their father. He showed none of Dr. Bernard's polished confidence, but he did have that same sense of physical grace about him.

Meeting Sheila and Junior had cleared up one mystery. In the months prior, I'd often heard music when walking past the Bernards' residence.

Someone in that house was an accomplished pianist. He or she loved to play Chopin and Brahms. Someone sang opera too. Sometimes I heard Enrico Caruso playing on the Victrola, most often his recording of sacred music by Rossini. I would also hear the pure, thrilling live voice of a young, male tenor singing along. It must've been Junior and Sheila: he singing and she at the piano in accompaniment.

It all made for a pretty picture: fine, upstanding parents. A plain but obedient daughter, properly married, and a respectful, dutiful son-in-law. Queenie wouldn't have fit in. Queenie must have been the secret son, the prodigal they never saw, never spoke of.

Hmm.

I recalled the night before, seeing the lights burning in the Bernards' window. I had wondered why they were awake when all others on the block were asleep. To think I'd envied them. They'd probably already heard from the kidnappers. They were probably terrified.

And now I'd have to deliver this box to them. Once more, I'd have to act on the kidnappers' behalf.

I narrowed my eyes. The kidnappers. Who were they? How would they have known to contact the Bernards? Surely, not many of the family's friends knew about Queenie. So were the kidnappers from Queenie's past, privy to his secret? Or were they simply desperate strangers who'd lucked out? Had they terrified Queenie so badly that he'd told them his true identity?

One thing was sure: the kidnappers had been busy. While everyone had been waiting for them to contact Fawkes, they'd brutalized Queenie and gone after his family.

And then, by accident or intent, they told a reporter about it.

I used the spoon handle to flap the handkerchief back over the finger, replaced the paper separator, and slid the letter back into the envelope. Then I went back upstairs, taking the obscene package with me. I left it on the parlor room coffee table and went to the phone. I reached for the receiver and glanced at the clock.

It was 3 a.m. Would Sam be home?

I dialed his number and let it ring five times. It occurred to me that maybe Sam shouldn't be involved. He would insist that I take the box to the cops. I wasn't sure I wanted to do that, not yet. I was about to hang up.

Too late. His voice stopped me.

CHAPTER 14

Forty minutes later, Sam and I were sitting over coffee in my parlor. The cigar box sat closed on the table before us. I wasn't sleepy and neither was he, so we didn't need the java, but it provided familiar and comforting qualities to help us in light of this unusual and disquieting delivery.

I told him about my talks with Fawkes and Morgana and Jack-a-Lee. I mentioned that I'd stopped at the station to talk to Blackie.

"Did you tell him about Olmo?"

"No, I wanted to check with you first."

"Good." His gaze dwelled on the box. "Do we agree that it wasn't an accident, or mistake, it landing on your doorstep?"

"You think it's a trap?"

"I don't know."

"But what kind?"

"Again, I don't know. But the best way to avoid falling into it is to take a step back—and get help." He sipped his coffee. "We need to decide what to tell the police."

"Don't you mean *whether*? The letter states that the police are not to be involved."

"Kidnappers always demand that."

"Normally, I'd say, 'So what?' But this time we're dealing with someone's life."

"You're always dealing with someone's life in a kidnapping."

That was true. I hesitated. "You're saying we have to take this to the cops?"

"Are you actually suggesting we shouldn't?"

"I'm saying . . . that maybe we should let the family decide. Or, at least, not do anything until they've been informed." I paused. "I'm asking for time."

"Do you actually want to be the one to give them this?"

He had a point.

"No," I said, "but . . ."

He sighed, set his cup aside. "I don't know. We'd be taking an awful gamble." He got up, moved to the window, and peered out. Worry puckered his forehead. "We should take that damn box to the cops. Let them handle it."

I went to him, put my arms around his waist, and rested my head on his back. He hugged my arms to his sides and lightly drew his fingertips over my clasped hands. I closed my eyes and took a deep breath. He radiated such a sense of comforting warmth. He smelled faintly of herbs and tobacco. Lately, he'd taken to smoking a pipe.

"Looks can be so deceiving," he said.

I could feel his voice rumble through his chest. I raised my head. He nodded toward the Bernard house.

"You can read the address that clearly from this distance?" I asked.

"No, I took a walk past the house before coming here." He sighed. "Looks so peaceful. God only knows what they're going through."

The house was dark and still. It was a stately redbrick building, three doors down from the equally elegant McKay house, which had been the scene of two very inelegant murders.

"You're sure you don't want to go to Blackie with this?" Sam asked.

"Not until I've talked to the Bernards. Telling the cops, that's their decision to make."

He hugged me close. "But you know what they're going to say."

I rested my face against his chest and nodded. "No cops."

"We'll be sitting on a ticking bomb."

"I know."

The room was so quiet we could hear the sound of our own breathing. His heart beat steadily beneath my ear.

"All right," he whispered into my hair, "we'll try it your way. No cops. For now."

CHAPTER 15

While I lived in a limestone town house on the south side of 139th Street, the Bernards lived in one of the Roman redbrick houses on the north side. Many people loved the sunny yellow limestones, designed by Bruce Price and Clarence S. Luce, but the stately redbrick homes caught most of the accolades. They were designed by Stanford White, one of New York's leading architects, and they were eye-catching.

Like its neighbors, the Bernard home was beautiful and manicured, but unlike the others it was also shrouded in shadow that Friday morning. I told myself it was merely an accident of foliage: a large tree stood just east of the front door. It filtered most of the early-morning sunlight, and, with its wide expanse of branches, blocked most of the afternoon's too.

It was around nine when I rang their bell and waited expectantly, the cigar box tucked under one arm. I'd rewrapped it in the brown paper and found some fresh twine for a simple knot. From the corner of my eye, I caught a flash of movement: that of a curtain being drawn back, then quickly let go. That didn't bother me. It made sense to check who was at the door. But as the seconds ticked by, it did begin to frustrate me that someone was home, knew that I was out there, and still wouldn't answer the door.

A moment later, the Bernards' neighbor Gladys Cardigan stepped out from next door, dressed in slippers and a flowery pink housedress. She was about seventy years old and small. She appeared to fit the textbook definition of a cute, little old lady, but she was tough and sinewy. Her eyes were bright and shrewd. She'd buried two husbands, along with two sons who died on the battlegrounds of France.

Mrs. Cardigan was a retired teacher and now volunteered at the New

York Public Library. She assisted librarian Ernestine Rose in setting up the monthly poetry readings and book discussions at the Harlem branch on West 135th Street, just off Lenox Avenue. To me, Mrs. Cardigan was an inspiration. To most everyone else, she was simply an inveterate snoop.

She stood on her threshold, half in, half out, and gestured toward the Bernards' front door.

"You'll be waiting there for ages. They're home, I'm sure of it. But if they didn't invite you to come over, they're not going to answer the door."

"Oh, really?"

True, the couple of times I had visited the Bernards' house it had been by invitation. I had never before just stopped by. In a brutal sort of way, it made sense to apply that attitude to certain types of strangers. It was clearly an effective way to avoid panhandlers, religious zealots, salesmen, and a motley crew of drifters who would happily waste your time if you let them. I didn't think it right, however, to extend that attitude toward neighbors.

Mrs. Cardigan glanced at the package under my arm, her eyes curious, then smiled at me. "Why don't you come over here for a minute or two? Have a cup of tea?"

Hmm. A chat. So she could pick my brains.

I could turn the invite down, make enough of a nuisance out here to convince the Bernards to let me in, or . . . maybe it would be wiser to hear what Mrs. Cardigan had to say about our neighbors.

She had a lovely, frilly house, overstuffed with decor. There were lace doilies and china dolls, brocaded furniture and fringed lamps. The overall effect was slightly suffocating, but I enjoyed it. It reminded me of my maternal grandmother, Great Nanny Belle. There were pictures of Mrs. Cardigan's lost family everywhere.

Like Nanny Belle, Mrs. Cardigan provided her company with butter cookies and tea. She kept glancing at the box but bided her time. I'd decided to let her take the lead. Once we were settled in the parlor, she did. She sat across from me, sipping her tea. She darted her eyes at the parcel, which I'd placed next to me on the parlor sofa.

"A present for the Bernards?" she asked.

"A mistaken delivery."

"Oh," she smiled. "That does happen, doesn't it?"

"Sometimes."

"I don't see an address on it," she said. "How do you know it's theirs?"

My, she had good eyes.

"Did you open it?" she asked.

"Well, I had to."

"And?" She waited.

"And," I shrugged, "it's theirs."

"You're sure?"

"Very."

She pursed her lips, evidently disappointed, then reluctantly dragged her gaze away from the box. She took another sip and looked at me. "You used to go over there a lot, didn't you?"

"Sometimes, when my husband was alive."

"How did they seem?"

"Normal," I said, intentionally downplaying my interest.

She gave a snort. "I guess normal is as normal does."

"Why? You don't think they're—"

"They almost never go out. Never have company."

"True, but—"

"I've been trying to get that woman to join my poetry readings for years. At first, she'd open the door and speak politely, but she always stood firmly in the entrance. Now she won't even do that. Never once invited me in for coffee or tea. Nothing."

"You don't say."

Warming to her story, she leaned forward and lowered her voice to a conspiratorial whisper. "I used to know them before they moved to Strivers."

"Where from?"

"Brooklyn. My baby sister Lucile went to school with Phyllis. It was just co-incidence that we ended up on the same block. Strange how that can happen."

"Fate," I said.

Mrs. Cardigan nodded, lost to her memories. "I remember how, when Sheila was a little girl, they used to dress her up. Fine outfits. Everything fine. Always had to be the best. Only they didn't call her Sheila then. Her name was . . ." She frowned in thought, then snapped her fingers. "Janie. That's right. They used to call her Janie. She was a pretty little thing. Too bad she didn't stay that way."

"What do you mean?"

"Well, she was rather light-skinned back then. And pretty, real pretty. They'd get her all dolled up in ruffled lace dresses and Mary Janes. The whole nine yards. They'd parade her up and down DeKalb Avenue like she was the finest thing since hot cocoa."

"There's nothing wrong with that, is there?"

"Oh, I'm not saying there was something wrong with it. But it was a bit odd, I think, how they just up and sent her away."

I cocked my head. "What? Did something happen?"

"I don't know. I remember seeing Phyllis on the street and asking about her. She got this funny look on her face. Then she said something about sending the child down South to stay with her sister. I was so surprised. They doted on that child. She must've been around eleven or twelve at the time. I couldn't imagine them sending her away."

"Did you ask them why?"

"They wouldn't say." Concern wrinkled Mrs. Cardigan's brow. "You know, you couldn't ask for nicer-looking people. But they're strange, Lanie. Strange. And nice-looking people aren't always nice."

"'Tis true."

"Why, I was just reading the other day about that doctor in Chicago. He killed five women. Married them for their money, then killed them all dead. They had his picture in the paper. You couldn't wish for a better-looking man. But he's evil."

"No, you can't judge a book by its cover." I took another sip.

"I think it's been ten years now since they sent that child away. One day, she was here; the next, she was gone. Just like that. You didn't see hide nor hair of her."

"Is that right?"

"Of course, the child was so moody."

"You mean sad, or temper tantrums?"

"Kind of hard to say. Sometimes, she'd be so quiet, you'd think she was scared to talk. But then she'd get right smart and sassy. She'd say things that would make you blink."

"How so?" Recalling the Sheila I'd met, I found that hard to imagine.

"Knowing, like a little adult. She had a keen intuition, and when she got like that, it was almost—almost, mind you—as if *she* was the one in charge. She'd say something and Phyllis would get this expression, like she was . . ." Mrs. Cardigan frowned, searching for the word.

"Angry?"

"No, scared."

"Of her own child?"

"That's right. And that's why I used to think they'd gone and made that child disappear."

"Disappear?"

"Mm-hmm. I was so glad to see her when she moved back. I don't want to tell you what I thought they'd really done." She gave a delicious shudder. "Anyway, years went by. I'd see them and ask about her and they'd give me some vague answer. Never said nothing about her coming back, and when I mentioned that they must miss her, they'd just glance at each other and then give me the same old smile. I'm ashamed to admit it, but I used to wonder if Janie was even theirs, if they'd perhaps kidnapped her."

I nearly choked on my tea. "Seriously?"

Mrs. Cardigan waved her hand. "Oh, I was being a fool. She looked just like them back then. But I used to love to pretend. It just irked me that . . . well, that they're so mysterious."

"Some people like to keep to themselves."

"Maybe."

I frowned as though I'd had a sudden thought. "Is Sheila their only child?"

"Oh, yes. For sure."

"No son?"

"No. Why?" Now she frowned too, intense with curiosity.

I shrugged. "Just wondering." I took another sip. "When was the last time you stopped by to see them?"

"Yesterday. I went over to ask her about sharing a monthly subscription to a magazine I thought she'd like."

"And what happened?"

"Dr. Bernard answered. He slammed the door in my face."

"He didn't!" I tried to make light of it. "Well, you'll just have to polish your approach. There's always one hard nut to crack. I guess they're it, for you." I glanced at my watch, saw that some twenty minutes had passed, and reached for the package. "I'd better go now. But thank you. It was good to see you."

"Yes, it was nice having you over. You must come again," Mrs. Cardigan struggled to her feet and took a firm hold of my forearm. "Here, let me lean on you."

With exaggerated slowness—she'd certainly moved faster when she let me in—Mrs. Cardigan escorted me to the door. She reached to open it, but then paused and put a wrinkled hand on my wrist.

"I like you Lanie Price. Always have. Quite bluntly, you're the daughter I wish I'd had—not that I was unhappy with my sons, but they're gone now. All I have left is memories, wonderful memories to be sure, and some people would be content with that, but not me." Her grip on my wrist grew stronger. "You're here, you're now, and so am I. We've got to make the best of it. We have to stick together and help each other whenever we can. Understand? I can help you keep an eye on things. And no one need ever know, no one but you and me." Mrs. Cardigan put a trembling index finger to her lips. "Shh," she said, and smiled. "Partners?" She extended a hand.

I was totally charmed. "Partners," I replied, and shook on it.

CHAPTER 16

I t was Sheila who finally answered the door. Her complexion had a pallor that had grayed her skin. Her lips were drawn, her dark eyes quick and nervous.

"Oh, hello," she said in a short, breathy voice. She sounded as though she'd raced to the door. She was about my height, quite thin, and more plain than pretty. Her eyes were red and puffy, and she was gripping a handkerchief so tightly that her knuckles gleamed under her skin.

I identified myself, just in case she didn't remember me. I explained that I needed to see her parents.

She fingered her handkerchief. "I . . . I don't know." She glanced over her shoulder. "They're really busy right now and—"

"Sheila?" a loud male voice called from within. "Who is it?"

Dr. Bernard emerged from the parlor. He wore a pale blue shirt under a V-neck navy-blue cashmere sweater, and pale gray pants. His black leather shoes were polished to a soft gleam. He came up short when he saw me. He looked not only surprised, but irritated. Then he seemed to make some inner mental adjustment.

Sheila willingly stepped aside to let him deal with me. He blocked the door; his attitude was polite, but it was clear that he wanted to get me away from the house as quickly as possible. There was no sign of the charm I remembered.

I decided to preempt him. "Dr. Bernard, I'm sorry, but I have news."

"I'd love to invite you in," he answered, "but I don't have time."

"You do for this." I tapped the box under my arm. His gaze slid to it and lingered for a moment. Then he glanced back at me, wary and puzzled.

"I don't understand."

"You will."

His eyes met mine for an instant. He gave a tight-lipped nod, then turned away and headed back down the hall. I stepped inside. Sheila closed the front door.

"This way," she said, and showed me into the parlor.

The room was Spartan. The largest piece of furniture was a shiny black baby grand piano that sat near the front windows. The keyboard lid was down. A cluster of gilt-framed family photographs, set on a large white crocheted lace doily, decorated the top. I squinted at them. The photos hadn't been there the last time I visited. But then that had been a couple of years ago.

An antique scrolled writing desk sat in one corner. Bookshelves banked an adjoining wall, covered with rows of leather-bound books, some of whose titles appeared to be in German.

Phyllis Bernard perched on the simple sofa, crocheting, her legs neatly crossed at the ankles. Her back was ramrod straight, her glasses resting on the tip of her nose. She was shaped like a pear and a bit plumper than I remembered. Her eyes widened when I walked in. It wasn't just surprise; it was alarm. She smiled, but it took obvious effort.

"Oh, Mrs. Price," she said, rising. "What a surprise."

"She says she has news for us," Dr. Bernard explained. "Something to do with that box." He gestured toward it.

"It was left on my doorstep," I said. "Sometime late last night."

Phyllis Bernard's gaze met her husband's.

"The package wasn't addressed, so I opened it," I continued. "Once I did, I realized that it was meant for you."

I could've told them the contents. I nearly did, but I wanted to see their reactions. I didn't feel good about not warning them, but I did think it for the best. I held the parcel out to Dr. Bernard, but he made no move to take it.

"What's in it that made you decide to come here?"

"A letter."

His face showed indecision, fear, and resentment. And why not? He was caught up in a bad game against players who'd stop at nothing to win.

"Dr. Bernard?" I prompted.

"Alfred," his wife said. "Go on."

He accepted the box with an expression of distaste and held it at arm's length. Did he already have an inkling of what was inside? He eased down on the couch, his wife and daughter at either side. They looked sick with fear.

Dr. Bernard balled his hands into fists and sucked in his breath, like a man about to dive into dark, deep, and icy waters. His fingertips grazed the lid of the box, then lifted it. He removed the letter, read it, and glanced at me. "You shouldn't have read this."

He hadn't even questioned why someone should address such a letter to him. Clearly, he knew what it was about from his lack of surprise.

"The box was on my doorstep," I said. "No address, no nothing. I assumed it was meant for me. There was nothing to change that assumption. Until I saw the letter. By then, it was too late. I'd already seen what it covered."

Their gazes returned to the box. Dr. Bernard pushed the letter aside, removed the separation paper, and revealed the stained linen. He grabbed a pencil and used it to flip back the corners.

Sheila cried out and Phyllis Bernard shrank back with a sob. Dr. Bernard, the clinician, took a long, hard look at the disarticulated member and then slammed the box shut. For a moment, he sat perfectly still, his jaw working, his eyes full of cold rage.

"I'm sorry, Mrs. Price, that they've gotten you involved in this. No one . . ." He swallowed. "No one deserves . . ." He blinked, his voice so thick that he couldn't finish, then closed his eyes and took a deep breath.

"Do you recognize it?" I asked.

He shook his head and waved me off. "No—please. No questions. I am so sorry that you had to see this, but please, I can't say any more."

"So you do know Queenie Lovetree," I said.

"Queenie who?" Phyllis Bernard asked.

"Queenie Lovetree," I repeated. "It's his finger."

Her face remained blank.

Now I was confused. "He's a drag queen, works down at the Cinnamon Club. Some people know him as the Black Orchid."

Phyllis Bernard shook her head. "I don't understand. What's—"

"Queenie was kidnapped the other night. You must've heard about it," I said.

No answer.

I stared at each of them in turn. They maintained a noncommittal silence.

"He was wearing that ring," I said, "or one just like it."

"A coincidence," Phyllis Bernard said.

"Not likely."

I waited for them to respond, but Sheila turned away and Phyllis Bernard lowered her gaze. Dr. Bernard was the only one to hold steady. His eyes were as hard as stone. No answers there.

"Junior," I said. "It's Junior, isn't it?"

The tension in the room, already bad, jumped another notch.

"Why would you say something like that?" Sheila said.

"Because it makes sense. He's the right age, and he's apparently not here. Furthermore," I gestured toward the family photographs on the piano top, "those pictures, the man at your side. I didn't remember much about him, but the instant I saw that picture, it hit me that he looked extraordinarily familiar."

"Of course he does. You've met him."

"Yes, I have. Two nights ago, at the Cinnamon Club, before he was kidnapped. That picture. That's exactly how Queenie would look without makeup and dressed as a man."

"How dare you!" Sheila was indignant. "To suggest that—"

"I'm not suggesting. I'm stating that it's your husband they've got. He and Queenie Lovetree are—"

"No, please! Please don't say that!"

"Why not? Because it's true?" I paused. "Are you telling me that it's not? Honestly?"

Sheila blinked like a deer caught in headlights, then shot a frightened glance at her father. His look clearly said, *Keep your mouth shut.*

"You just wouldn't understand," she murmured. Tears slipped down her face in rapid succession.

"Try me."

"It's not my husband," she said. "It's his brother."

She gestured toward the piano. "That's his picture over there. They look very similar." She glanced at her parents again. "It's Billy who sings at the Cinnamon Club, Mrs. Price. The family's not proud of it. So, we—we don't talk about it." She'd balled up her handkerchief. She couldn't bring herself to look at me.

Her father stepped in. "I didn't want her to tell you, but now that she has, I can see in your face that you don't believe her."

I didn't know what to believe. "Well, then, where is Junior?"

"On a business trip."

"Does he know what's happened?"

"We've been in contact. He's on his way back."

I peered again at the photograph.

"What you're seeing is a family resemblance," Dr. Bernard said. "When we first met William, my wife and I, we thought he and Junior were twins. They're not. William is a year younger."

I walked over to the piano to take a closer look. There were two black-and-white pictures of what appeared to be the same young man, one of him alone and one of him standing next to Sheila. "Which one is William?"

"Neither," Dr. Bernard said. "They're both of Junior."

I reached for one of the pictures. "May I?"

"Of course."

I picked it up, studied it for several seconds, mentally applying Queenie's makeup to the face, adding the wig and the costume. It definitely worked. There were also marked differences, however. There was something about the eyes that I couldn't quite figure out. Overall, Queenie's face was leaner, the cheekbones higher, the lips fuller than that of the man in the photo. But those changes could've been the result of expertly applied makeup, or lighting, or simply that the photo's subject had lost weight. I set the picture down.

"How do you tell them apart?" I asked.

"The eyes. Junior's are dark. William's are light, almost golden."

Yes, that's what I'd sensed in the photo. Even if I didn't have a picture of William, I had a mental one of Queenie and knew that one of his most stunning characteristics were his golden eyes.

"But the main difference is in their personalities," Dr. Bernard said. "They're like night and day. You can't mix them up. Junior is calm and dependable, a man of taste and discernment. William, on the other hand . . ." He made an exasperated sound meant to cover the rest. Then he gave me a cynical smile.

"Mrs. Price, I do understand. The idea that a transvestite might be our son-in-law is just too plump a duck for you to resist. But believe me, that's not the case." He paused. "Naturally, we don't entertain William or his kind in our home. But he's related by marriage, so we stand by him. For the sake of our daughter and her husband, we will do whatever's necessary to ensure William's safe return."

I had to admit it: Dr. Bernard was right. I'd really liked the idea that the flamboyant and outrageous transvestite known as Queenie Lovetree was married to the only daughter of Strivers' Row's most conservative pair. The idea that it was Sheila's brother-in-law who'd been kidnapped was a whole lot less sexy, but it certainly made more sense.

"Okay," I said reluctantly. "So you're saying that Queenie is part of the family—but only to a degree?"

The three of them nodded.

"Then why did the kidnappers contact you instead of Junior's family?"

Sheila answered: "My husband and his brother, they don't really have any family left, and what there is . . . well, they wouldn't be able to meet the kidnappers' demands. Understand?"

I could accept that. "When did you first hear from them?"

"A telephone call that night," Dr. Bernard said.

"It was so late," Phyllis Bernard said. "They told us they had William and they demanded money."

"We didn't want to believe them," Sheila added.

"You know how it is," Dr. Bernard went on. "That could've been a prank call. It could've been from anyone."

"And so we refused," Phyllis Bernard said. "God help us, we—" A sob broke from her. "Oh, Alfred, we're responsible for this, don't you see? If we'd just gone ahead and paid, then—"

"We didn't know, Phyllis. We just didn't know." Dr. Bernard turned back to me. "Please, let us handle this. Please—don't tell anyone about this. We know now that they'll kill him. We'll need a little time to get the money together, but we will, and then we'll pay and they'll let him go."

I sensed that he said this more to reassure his family than to convince me.

"I beg you not to put any of this in your column," Phyllis Bernard said. "Alfred and I . . . we're so sorry you had to be brought into this, but we'll take it from here."

"But that's exactly what you shouldn't do, try to handle it on your own."

"We'll deal with it," Dr. Bernard repeated. "It was some horrible mistake that this package arrived on your doorstep."

"I'm not sure it was."

"What?" Dr. Bernard's lips parted in surprise. His family stared.

"I'm not sure it was a mistake," I said. "I was there when he was kidnapped. Now a package containing his finger just happens to land on my doorstep, and I just happen to live across the street from you."

"What are you saying?" Dr. Bernard asked.

"That I think the kidnappers want my involvement."

"But why?" Phyllis Bernard looked both horrified and stunned. Sheila just stood there with her mouth open in a state of fear and shock.

"I don't know," I replied. "Most kidnappers like to work in secret. Obviously, this one doesn't."

"But the letter, the phone call . . ." Sheila started.

"Both times, he said not to tell anyone," Dr. Bernard said.

"Naturally. But look at what he's done. Kidnappers usually nab their victims in secret, but this guy chose to do it in a crowded nightclub, before a slew of witnesses, right in front of a reporter—"

"He couldn't have known you'd be there," Dr. Bernard said.

"He didn't have to. He knew the club would be packed."

It was hard to tell if my words were sinking in. The Bernards seemed shell-shocked.

"Even if he didn't know who I was that night, he must've found out since then. The package on my doorstep then becomes an incredible coincidence. At first, I tried to tell myself it was a house number mix-up. But I don't buy it. I believe the kidnapper, or kidnappers, left the box there intentionally. Whoever is behind this wants the story covered."

The worry on the Bernards' faces deepened.

"Pardon me, but your explanation's more than a bit self-serving," Dr. Bernard said.

"When do you expect your husband back?" I asked Sheila.

"Tomorrow. We hope." Sheila glanced at her father, looking for help, or confirmation, or both. He gave a barely perceptible nod and she continued. "Junior will be horrified when he . . ." Her eyes went to the box. "When he finds out what they've done to Billy."

"Junior wanted us to pay," Dr. Bernard said. "He begged me, but I held out. And this box is the result." He took a deep breath. "We can't take another chance on doing the wrong thing."

Guilt and fear were driving their decision and that was never a good thing, but it was to be expected. What could I do about it? I had promised myself that I would abide by their wishes, at least for now. Perhaps I could help them in another way: get them thinking.

"I know you'd like to be alone," I said, "but I'd like to ask you one more question." I looked at each of them, trying to make eye contact. "Who else knew William's secret?"

"I don't know," Sheila said. "I've been racking my brains since this whole thing started. Billy's a good man, a really great guy. I know he's a little different, but I don't see why anyone would want to hurt him—I mean, not because he'd done anything to them, for sure."

"You misunderstood my question. I'm trying to figure out if the kidnappers knew who they were taking. If we know that they were aware of Queenie's identity beforehand, then we can narrow down the number of people who might be responsible."

"The fact is, we can't say when they found out," Dr. Bernard said. "All we know is that they did. That's what's important. Furthermore, my wife and I, we don't really know all that much about William, his friends, or what he does. We were totally surprised when the kidnapper called us. We didn't even know that someone named Queenie Lovetree existed, or that she'd, I mean he'd, been kidnapped. Not until we heard it on the radio. Normally, we just don't have anything to do with those kinds of people. You understand?"

"Yes," I said, "I think I do."

A clock chimed the hour somewhere deep inside the house. Time was a-moving.

I pressed them: "Are you absolutely sure that you want to try to take care of this yourselves and not take it to the police? You do realize that the kidnappers are counting on you to refuse the kind of expert help you need, right?"

I could have saved my breath. The Bernards remained resolute. Dr. Bernard got to his feet with a polite little smile that just about telegraphed what he'd say next.

"We appreciate your help. We really do. But we will take care of this on our own. Now I don't mean to be rude, but I have to ask you to go. We don't have much time and we've got plenty to attend to."

He started to show me out. Then the telephone rang and everyone froze. All eyes went to the receiver, which sat on a small table lamp next to the sofa. Dr. Bernard strode back across the room and put the candlestick phone to his ear.

"Yes?" His body stiffened and his eyes shot over to me. He made a waving gesture, indicating that he wanted me to leave. I stayed put. Irritated, he half-turned and lowered his voice. "Yes, I received it . . . No, there was no problem with the delivery. No one else has seen it."

Again, he glared back at me and tried to shoo me out. I ignored it. I was going to listen till there was nothing left to hear. As he grew increasingly frantic, Phyllis Bernard started toward me, obviously intending to usher me out, but an exclamation from Dr. Bernard stopped her in her tracks and riveted all attention back on the conversation.

"Twenty-five thousand!" he roared. "But that's five thousand more than—" His hand tightened on the receiver. Beads of sweat popped out on his forehead. "I don't have that kind of money—"

I moved closer, trying to listen in—Dr. Bernard was too upset to even attempt to stop me—but I couldn't hear the kidnapper's voice clearly.

Dr. Bernard turned away and hunched over the phone; his voice was desperate. "And then what? What do I do? . . . But— . . . No, you can't! You can't just—"

There was a click. It was so loud, even I heard it. The line had gone dead.

Bernard stared at the receiver, then slowly lowered it back to its cradle. For a long moment he stood there, looking down at the phone. Finally, he raised his eyes to me, their expression bitter.

"So now you know. You have all the confirmation you came for. What are you going to do with it?"

Sheila stood in the center of the room, wringing her handkerchief, tears glistening in her eyes.

So much love for her brother-in-law. Under other circumstances, I would've wondered whether she was having an affair with him. But if I was confident of anything, it was that Queenie only slept with men.

Then again, Queenie might've swung both ways. What did I know?

I started to say something, but changed my mind and turned to go. Sheila followed me out and opened the front door. As I exited the house, she whispered, "Please, you won't write anything or tell anyone, will you? You won't do anything that'll get him killed?"

I tilted my head. "One last question."

"Yes?"

"Did people ever call you Janie? Is that your middle name?"

Sheila frowned. "No. Why?"

"Oh, nothing. It was just a thought."

CHAPTER 17

It was around eleven when I got to the newsroom. The place was bustling. I glanced down the main aisle between the cluttered desks and saw Sam at his, work piled high on either side, his office door open. I dropped my coat in my chair and went over to him. He spoke without looking up. "Close the door."

"Why?"

"Just do it."

I did, but I wasn't too thrilled with the tone of his voice. I was about to let him know it when . . . well, something about the way he put his pencil down and rose from his chair made me hold my tongue.

He rounded his desk and came up to me. Then he reached around my waist, closed the blinds that covered the glass panel of his door, and took me in his arms. "Because," he said, "I want to do this."

His kiss was luscious. It was so hard, so probing, that it left me dizzy. Then he released me, stepped back, and reopened the blinds.

"Now," he said, "let's get down to business." He gestured for me to take a seat and perched on the edge of his desk. "How'd it go with the Bernards?"

I summed up their reaction to the cigar box.

He was thoughtful. "So the Black Orchid really is related to the Bernards by marriage. Well, well, well."

Then I described the phone call from the kidnappers.

"I don't like it." He rubbed his chin. "The Bernards are in over their heads."

"They're terrified we'll go to the police—"

"We have to."

"What?"

"I went to see Ramsey."

"Oh." I suddenly felt ill. Ramsey was the executive editor. What he said went, and he was no fan of mine. "What did he say?"

"Bottom line is we have to tell the police what we know."

"Shouldn't we put the family's wishes first? We don't have the right to make this kind of decision on our own."

"By keeping mum, we could be doing them more harm than good. And we could be setting ourselves up for charges of obstruction." He paused. "I'm sorry."

"All right. But can I at least warn them?"

"That's up to you. And you will tell Blackie about the box and the letter in it."

"The letter! But—"

"You don't need to give the name of the family or individuals to whom the letter was addressed. Okay?"

"I don't like it."

"You don't have a choice."

"No," I said slowly, "I don't." I eyed him as if he were a traitor. "The Bernards will be furious."

"I'll accept that."

"*You'll* accept it? I'm the one who'll have to deal with them."

"If you can't handle them, just send them my way."

All I could do was shake my head. "You're stirring up a hornet's nest. And for nothing!"

"I'm looking out for this paper."

"We'll upset the Bernards. They won't talk to us anymore."

"They're not 'talking' to us now. They only let you in because of that damn box. It's the kidnapper who's cut you in, not them."

He was right.

"Fine. But what about Blackie? He'll demand to know our sources."

"You just don't tell him. Simple."

"Yeah. Simply impossible." I gave him a look of utter exasperation. "So, when's this little interview supposed to take place?"

"Whenever we can arrange it. The sooner, the better."

"Like tomorrow?"

"Like right now." He leaned over his desk and pushed the phone to me.

I looked from the phone to him, quietly fuming. "I gave the Bernards my word."

"The decision's been made."

With obvious reluctance, I picked up the phone and held it in my lap. I cranked it up and stuck the black horn-shaped receiver to my ear, leaning forward and shifting slightly away from Sam as I did so. Then I lightly rested my thumb on the drop hook—cutting off the connection—and started dialing.

"Detective Blackie, please," I said, talking into the dead mouthpiece. "This is Lanie Price of the *Harlem Chronicle* calling."

Sam went back to sit behind his desk.

I went on: "He's not there? . . . Working the Cinnamon Club massacre. . . . Yes . . . Yes, I know, but . . ." I glanced at Sam to see if he was listening. He was sitting in profile, staring at a map on the wall.

My imaginary conversation continued. "Mm-hmm, I see . . . Yes, I understand, but . . . Well, would you at least take a message, please? . . . Yes, a message . . . All right, I'll just—"

I stopped abruptly, stared at the bell-shaped mouthpiece. "Would you believe he hung up on me? Said Blackie was too busy to talk to nosy reporters."

Sam swiveled back around. "I thought you knew everyone down there."

"Yes, well, there's always a new one." I replaced the receiver, set the phone back on Sam's desk. "You see? I tried. They don't want to hear from me."

"Try again later—and next time, take your finger off the hook."

The phone suddenly rang. He reached for it and I got up to go. But he raised a finger for me to wait.

There's more? I wondered. I dropped back down in the chair and prepared to wait, worried and fidgeting.

He kept the call short, hung up, and paused in thought. Whatever he had to say, I was not going to like it.

"Given what's happened," he began, "I've decided to put out a special edition. It'll—"

"Sam, no!" Memories of the Todd case, when one of my articles inspired a killing, shot across my mind. "This is a man's life we're talking about. Telling the police is one thing, but printing it is another."

He held up a hand. "We'll only report on the news conference. We won't mention the cigar box. That make you happy?"

Happy wasn't quite the word for it. Relieved, though. "Thank you." I moved toward the door. "I'll get to work on the story, right after the news conference."

"No, Lanie, you won't." His voice stopped me.

I turned back, puzzled. "Excuse me?"

"You're off the story."

I blinked. "What?"

"You heard me."

I felt as though I'd been punched. "I . . . I don't understand. Why?"

"Journalism 101. You don't report on a story when you're part of it. And you are definitely part of this one. Whether you wanted to be or not, you're knee-deep in it. And it's affecting your judgment."

"No, I—"

"Decision's made."

"But I'm objective."

He gave me a sorrowful look. "No, baby. You're not."

"Don't *baby* me. I'm a professional, just like you. And I do my job, just like you."

"I know that."

I threw up my hands. "I don't believe this! Who are you giving it to?"

He nodded to a point past my shoulder. "Selena."

"*Selena!* You can't, she—"

He raised a hand to hush me. "Now, I know you don't like her."

"Oh, and you do?"

"Lanie, don't go there."

"Not possible. I don't like her. I don't trust her. And neither should you."

"Why not?" He met me eye-to-eye. "Fact is, Selena has never done anything to undermine my trust. And, unlike someone else I know, she has never done anything to endanger this paper."

Another reference to the Todd case. It stung. "That's not fair."

"But it's true. You don't like her. Fine. To do your job, you don't have to."

I forced myself to swallow my anger. While I had lost the fight to keep my story, I sure meant to have a say over who got it. I tried to sound reasonable: "Sam, please. She hasn't earned the right to cover a story like this. Why not George Greene?"

"Greene's good, but he's distracted. His wife is expecting a baby any minute. I need somebody who's going to give this story his all—just like you would—and that person is Selena."

"But—"

"I repeat: decision's made."

We stared at one another for several long seconds. How could we have moved so quickly from a warm kiss to the coolness of this decision? He'd known what he was planning to do when I entered the office. He'd already been planning to take my story away when he held me in his arms. I felt so betrayed.

There was nothing left to say. I went to the door, grabbed the knob. "Blackie's news conference starts in ten minutes. I'll talk to Selena as soon as I get back."

"You'll talk to her now, and you'll take her with you."

Stung once more, I turned back. "This is wrong, Sam. Wrong."

"It's done."

It took all my strength not to say what was on my mind. I left. Even did so without slamming his door. I was proud of that.

I strode past Selena's desk. "Get your stuff. You're coming with me. Now!"

CHAPTER 18

I hurried over to my desk and grabbed my hat. I was just swinging my coat over my shoulders when the telephone chirped. Although I was in a hurry, my hand went to it automatically. Before I could even say hello, a big voice boomed in my ear.

"Hello, dahling! *Comment ça va?*"

"Jack-a-Lee?" I was surprised to hear his voice. It wasn't even noon yet. Like many denizens of the night, he rarely went to bed before five a.m. and usually slept his days away.

"I know, dahling. I'm stunned myself. I just couldn't sleep."

"No?"

"No. You see, ever since our little tête-à-tête, I've been wondering. How can I help Lanie? Hmm? Dear, sweet Lanie. And then it came to me. So utterly simple. And so appropriate."

Selena sauntered over to me, her dark eyes furious at the way I'd spoken to her. She opened her mouth to say something but I held up a finger to shush her, then spoke into the phone. "I have to go. I have a—"

"Don't rush me, dahling. Let me savor it. It isn't every day that I get to help you, a star reporter, break a major case that not even the New York Police Department, with all of its frigging detectives, can crack."

I covered the mouthpiece with my hand, held it away, and spoke to Selena: "Blackie's starting a news conference over at the station. It's about the Black Orchid kidnapping. You can go on over and I'll meet you in a minute."

Her eyes widened in surprise. "You mean, I—"

"Yes. Go!"

She gave me a smirk and a knowing nod. "Finally, Sam realizes that you can't cover shit."

"And you'll be deep in it if you don't get going."

She turned up her nose and trotted away with an air of self-importance.

As soon as she was out of earshot, I removed my hand from the mouth-piece and put the phone back to my ear. Jack-a-Lee was still prattling on.

". . . It's so obvious they don't know their asses from their elbows. But you, m'dear, are sharp as a ta—"

"Jack-a-Lee, what is this all about?"

"Why, I told you. I'm going to help you break this case wide open. And when you win whatever awards you people win, I want a front-row seat and my name featured prominently in your little acceptance speech."

"You have thirty seconds. Then I'm hanging up."

"Patience, dahling. I just want to confirm our little arrangement for next Friday's ball. It'll be a front-page photograph, hmmm? Just like you prom-ised. I have the most luscious outfit. I'm sure to win top prize. You'll die when you see it. Trust me, this'll be one costume they'll remember. I've just about outdone myself."

"I'm hanging up *now*."

"All right! All right!" He gave an exasperated sigh. "I've done what no one else could do, would have even dared think to do." He paused dramatically.

I said nothing.

He sucked his teeth. "I tell you, Lanie. You are turning into a—"

"Jack-a-Lee! One, two, three—"

"Okay, okay! I have set up a meeting between you and . . . guess who?"

I straightened up. "Olmo? You've found Olmo?"

"Hell no! Much better than that. I've set you up with the man himself."

"Stax Murphy?" I dropped down in my chair and lowered my voice to an intense whisper. "You got me an appointment with Stax Murphy?"

"I sure did."

"How did you . . . ? You said—"

"I'm a miracle worker. What can I say?"

"Oh, Jack-a-Lee, thank you—"

"Save the gratitude for later. You've got to get a move on."

"Why? When is it?"

"Now."

"*What?*"

"He's sending a car for you. Look for a black Packard. It should be pull-ing up downstairs in front of your office building door . . ." he paused and hummed, "in exactly two minutes."

"But—"

"Like I said, no need to thank me, dahling. I know I'm wonderful. Get going. If you're not there when they pull up, they won't stop. Play nice, have fun, and toodle-loo. I'll see you at the ball."

Then he was gone. I hung up and sat for a second. Was I going to do this? Was I really going to meet with Stax Murphy? On my own, with no backup? My gaze roamed around at the newsroom, not really seeing anything.

Yes, I was.

I grabbed a sheet of paper, thinking I should type a note. But words failed me. If this didn't work out, they wouldn't know where to find me any-way. Meanwhile, I could be missing my ride.

Ignoring the elevator, I slammed through the door leading to the stair-way and rushed down the stairs. I really should've left a message, told some-one what I was up to. But there was no time.

No time.

They had planned it that way. Timed it so that I wouldn't be able to no-tify anyone or set up an ambush. Timed it so I wouldn't have time to think.

Then again, if I had said something, Sam wouldn't have let me go. I put thoughts of him aside.

Why did Murphy want to see me? Was this a trap? Had he heard that I was looking for him and now considered me a danger? Did he want to silence me? Why hadn't I asked Jack-a-Lee what he'd told Stax Murphy?

No time, that's why.

My heart was pounding when I got downstairs. I sprinted across the lobby just in time to see a black Packard ease past the front door. It was the kind of large, ostentatious car that told the world you had dough. I caught up to it and banged on the front passenger window. The man inside glanced up and the car slowed to a stop.

I stepped back as the door flew open. A heavyset man emerged. He wore a long, black coat and a fedora pulled down to one side, obscuring most of his face.

The build, the clothing: his resemblance to the kidnapper was so strong that bolts of fear shot through me. But there was a sense of exhilaration too. I was on the right track. This wasn't the Black Orchid's kidnapper, but he wore his uniform.

He was a branch from the same tree.

CHAPTER 19

He forced me into the backseat. Another large man waited inside. Within seconds, I was cuffed and blindfolded. The cuffs were heavy. They weren't tight, just cold, and at least they'd cuffed me with my hands to the front.

"Where are we going?" I asked.

They said nothing.

"Are we going far?" I asked.

They said nothing.

Suppose this *was* a trap? Was Jack-a-Lee really just a convenient go-between, or was he working for Stax? He'd given me Olmo's name. He wouldn't have done that if he'd been working for Stax, would he? Maybe that's it. He'd asked around, gotten too close, and now Stax had him. Maybe he'd made the call under duress. But no, he hadn't sounded nervous. He'd sounded just fine.

I tried to clear my head. These men who picked me up had not been rough, simply efficient and silent. Their demeanor revealed nothing about Stax's intent.

If Stax meant to kill me, then what would I do? What *could* I do? Panic surged through me once again. What in the world had I been thinking? Getting into a car with some strange men, heading off to see a kidnapper—a killer—with no word to Sam or the newspaper. Yes, Jack-a-Lee knew, but if something went wrong, he wouldn't open his mouth.

There was nothing I could do about it now. And truth be told, I would have done the same if I had it to do all over again.

Stax could have only two possible motives in wanting to meet—to find out what I knew and then kill me, or to find out what I believed and then persuade me otherwise.

The car swung sharply to the left and I swayed in the other direction. After a series of sudden turns, I gave up trying to keep track of the rights and lefts; there were too many. I couldn't tell how long we drove in any one direction, either. I tried to listen for indicative sounds, but the windows were rolled up, sealing out everything but my own breathing. All I could say with certainty was that the drive wasn't long, no more than five minutes or so.

We rolled to a stop. I heard the front passenger door open, then mine. The dank smell of the river hit me.

"Get out!" a rough male voice said.

I stumbled out of the car. A chilling breeze slapped me in the face. It scissored around my ankles and I heard the rumble of metal doors opening. Strong hands gripped me by the elbow on either side. Hard voices warned me of steps, then dragged me up five metal stairs. I tripped over an iron bar on the floor at the top, in what must have been the doorway. They caught me and led me inside, then the doors closed behind me with a hollow clang. I sensed that I was in some expansive, empty space, a warehouse, perhaps. But with the blindfold, I could see nothing.

The hands guided me forward a few steps before one of the men said, "Hold it."

I heard another door open. There was a bang at my feet. A disgusting smell, of fecal matter, of rot and mildew, wafted up.

"The stairs are right in front of you," a voice said. He was to my left, behind me. "There's about twenty of them. One of us is already in front. I'll be in back. Go slow and you won't trip."

"Can't you take the blindfold off?"

No answer. Just a light but firm pressure at the base of my spine, the prod of a gun muzzle. Tentatively, I put one foot forward, seeking that first step. I found it and eased down. Every step felt as though I were hanging out into the middle of nowhere. I would take a step with my right foot and then bring my left foot down next to it. I managed to get down three stairs this way. Then my right heel caught and I pitched forward. The henchman in front caught me and straightened me up.

By this time, I was terrified. "Please, undo the blindfold. It'll take forever for me to get down otherwise."

No answer. Then came a voice that seemed to float up from the pits of hell, strong, vibrant, echoing: "Take off the cuffs."

"But—"

"Uncuff her, I said."

There was a pause, then my hands were yanked around. A hand gripped one wrist while another inserted a key. The cuffs fell away and I rubbed my wrists with relief.

The voice below me said, "There is a railing to your right."

The man behind me gave a little shove and I grabbed for the railing. I made my way down, and I counted: *one, two, three* . . . When I got to twelve, my nose had gotten used to the smell, somewhat. But now I felt it on my skin, a dirty thickness in the air.

I heard two sets of footsteps going back up the stairs and then a heavy thud, the sound of the trapdoor being latched. An animal presence, watchful and potentially lethal, moved around in the dark. Was I was now alone with Stax Murphy, a man that not even the NYPD had been able to track down? I could hear the pattern of feet treading on the gravel floor in front of me.

"Mr. Murphy?"

"Yes?"

"May I remove the blindfold?"

"Yes."

I pushed it back over my head, blinked, and rubbed my eyes. I was definitely in some kind of warehouse basement, probably over by the Hudson River. It was cavernous and mostly empty. I took it in before turning my attention to my host for the evening.

He was tall and well-dressed in a dark gray cashmere coat, his silver hair brushed straight back in a perfect conk partly concealed under a fedora. A banker in the world of organized crime, he actually resembled a banker from

Wall Street. His features were chiseled, lean, and clean-shaven. He was in his fifties, had a strong, bent nose, fleshy lips, and nearly black almond-shaped eyes. Familiar eyes. The same eyes that had stared at me from behind the barrel of a gun.

"Do I measure up?" he asked.

"To what?"

"Your expectations."

"I didn't have any."

"Of course you did."

He leaned against a pillar, his arms folded across his chest, and observed me carefully. "According to the paper, you were there," he said. "At the kidnapping. You saw everything."

"You already know that. Your man must've told you."

"Forget about him—"

"So you admit that you—"

"I admit nothing." He straightened up, put his hands behind his back, and walked in a slow circle around me. "I want you to tell me everything, every detail you can recall, about what this kidnapper said and did."

This wasn't what I'd expected, not at all. "You don't know? But you sent him."

"I said, tell me what you saw, what he said."

And so I did.

He listened without interrupting, then asked another question: "The police, they have a portrait: they did it with your help?"

"Yes."

"And is it accurate?"

"Very."

He stared hard at me. He found another chair, dragged it across the floor, turned it backward, and straddled it.

"I had nothing to do with it, any of it," he said.

So this was the "persuade otherwise" option. I felt certain relief. Not much, but some.

"All right," I said slowly.

"You don't believe me?"

I smiled faintly.

He chuckled. "Of course you don't. Why should you? I'm a man of my word, but you don't know that." He became thoughtful again. "You've been asking about a man named Olmo."

"I've heard that he works for you."

"Who gave you his name?"

"You know I can't tell you that. Reporters, their sources and all that."

"You're not afraid of dying?"

I tried to muster my courage. "Should I be? Is that what this is all about?"

He paused. "Not today, no."

Not today? I ignored that part, and simply said, "Well, then."

My little effort at bravura earned a faint amused smile.

"I've also heard," I continued, "that the Black Orchid owes you, and that he wasn't paying the debt to your satisfaction. Did you send Olmo to teach him a lesson?"

He shook his head. "Whoever took this singer, it wasn't me. I don't conduct my business that way. And you must be wrong about Olmo."

"I'm not."

"I told you—"

"And I'm telling you: he did it. If you had nothing to do with it, then he did it without you. You're worried and you have good reason to be." He cursed under his breath and I decided to play a hunch. "He's your blood, isn't he? Your son?"

"No." He eyed me, then shook his head. "My sister's." He looked bitter.

I said nothing.

"She wanted me to do something with him. He's not very bright, but he's ambitious."

"Enough to want to impress you? Or steal from you?"

"Steal from me, no. But impress me, yes . . . He'd do something—maybe."

His candor surprised me. It hinted at desperation. I recalled what Fawkes had said, that the kidnapper had been brash and stupid. Apparently, the kidnapper's uncle agreed.

Stax stood up and kicked back the chair. "Damn!" His voice echoed off the walls. "I can't believe he would go behind my back, do something like this. When I find him—and I will—I'll kill him."

"When was the last time you heard from him?"

He turned to me. "You've got to tell the cops I had nothing to do with this. I heard that you're in good with them."

"When was the last time you heard from Olmo?" I repeated.

"The day of the kidnapping. I've had my men out looking for him ever since."

"And what have they found?" I asked, but I could see the answer in his eyes.

"Nothing."

The worry in his voice suggested he was telling the truth. Still, I remained cynical. "If Olmo's such a boob, then how could he outsmart you?"

He took a step toward me, his right hand tightening into a fist. "I didn't bring you here to—"

"You brought me here to plead your case. If you want me to take it to the cops, then you have to give me something to work with."

"Buy me time."

"And say what? That you didn't do it? They'll laugh me out of the station house."

"You can make them believe."

"I can't make them do anything. They're cops. And I'm just a reporter, a colored one at that."

"You're telling me I'm going to have to rat out my own flesh and blood?"

"Your nephew made too big a splash, killed too many people—and the wrong kind—for all this to die down. Because of him, they're coming after you."

"They've been after me for years."

"Not like now."

He shook his head. "I'm not turning him in."

"Then I can't help you."

He spat on the gravel floor. "You've got nerve."

I didn't answer, but I didn't look away, either.

"All right, but you've got to promise me something," he said.

"What?"

"Carry the message and print the truth."

"That I'll do."

He yelled out to his boys: "Take her back!"

CHAPTER 20

When I walked into the newsroom, the first person I saw was Selena. She was at her desk, typing furiously, her face intent. She paused to check her notes, bit her lower lip, and then went back to pecking away. She was working hard; I had to admire that. And maybe she did deserve her chance at a solid story. It just shouldn't have been this one.

Nevermind. Whatever she was writing was going to turn into a sidebar once I told Sam where I'd been.

I peered down to his office, caught him watching me. He seemed anxious and angry. *Now what?* I'd given her my story, just as he'd told me to. I'd even let her cover the news conference. Well, whatever he was stewing over now, it would have to wait.

He waved me over and instructed me to sit down. "It's nearly two o'clock. Where have you been? Selena said you never showed up at the news conference."

"No, I—"

"Blackie's already got that picture of Olmo out and—"

"Sam, please listen! I have been cuffed and blindfolded, and—" I moved in closer, "I've been to see Stax Murphy."

His jaw slackened. That was very satisfying to see. "You what?"

"I said," I paused, "that I just interviewed Stax Murphy."

He was speechless. Then he gathered his wits. "You just— How in the world— What did he say? How did you get him to talk? How'd you find him in the first place?"

Ah, this was more like it. This was the way it should've been, with Sam listening and not judging or scolding.

"I was on my way out when my phone rang. It was a source. He said he'd set up a meeting with Stax. He claimed it was to do me a favor, but now I think Stax put him up to it. Either way, I was told that the meet had to happen right then and there."

"And so you went?"

"Yes."

"Without informing anybody."

"Well . . . yes." I felt an increasingly familiar sinking sensation in the pit of my stomach, and prayed, *Please, Sam, don't ruin this.*

"Go on."

"Well, I don't have to. Not if you don't want to hear it."

His eyes flared and he pointed a finger at me. "Lanie, don't start. I gave you direct instructions—"

"Which I followed."

"Barely. And then you ran out of here, telling no one where you were going." He leaned on the desk and stared down at me. "You could've been killed."

I held his gaze. "I was doing my job."

"Part of your job is to keep in contact with me." He swallowed hard. "Look, baby, I don't want you taking chances like that."

"Do you want to hear what he said or not?"

"Let me guess: he said he didn't do it."

I was losing patience. I was very tempted to quit—both him and the paper. "I don't know how much longer I can work this way. Most times, you and I, we get along like greased wheels. But every time a story comes up that's even a little bit risky, you go all . . ." I tried to find the right word, "*protective* on me."

"I just don't want anything to happen to you."

"I don't want anything to happen to me, either."

He looked doubtful. "Really?"

"Yes, really." I'm not sure how Sam knew it, maybe he'd sensed it, but there had been times in the wake of Hamp's death when I hadn't cared all that much about living or dying. But that was then; I had changed.

"Now, I knew meeting Stax might be dangerous. But it was a chance I had to take . . . And yes, you're right, I should've told you. But I just didn't have time."

He looked at me and threw his hands up. "All right. It's done."

"Listen, I got it on the record that the main man accused of doing the Black Orchid job is denying all involvement."

He dropped back heavily into his chair. "That's worth something, sure. I just don't think it was worth risking your life."

"Sam."

He was not happy. "Look, I'm glad you got it on the record, but you've got to admit, there's nothing surprising about it. Don't you agree?"

"Not necessarily."

He leaned back, put his hands behind his head. "All right, you got me. What's so special about *this* denial?"

"For one thing, it makes sense."

"Come again?"

"Stax has survived as long as he has by being neat, efficient. He's a pro, and pros only do what's needed to get the job done. He never would've gone into that club and shot it up the way this guy did, like a cowboy."

"I'm listening. Go on. There's more, I hope."

I explained about Olmo being Stax's nephew, and how Stax thought Olmo might've done the job on his own to impress him.

"Stax is worried, Sam, worried sick. Says he's been looking for Olmo and can't find him."

Sam remained silent for a moment. "You did good," he finally said. "I'll give you that. But you took a foolish risk. And you knew damn well that I would've stopped you."

I stayed quiet.

"Give Selena what you have."

My chest tightened. "What?"

"I'm telling you to take a step back. No more talking to gangsters and wanted men."

This couldn't be. I started to choke up. "So we're not just talking about this story."

"No."

"You said I could cover crime."

"I meant in the courtroom."

"Where it's nice and safe and all wrapped up."

"Exactly."

I bit back a response. The words were right there, on the tip of my tongue. *This is not going to work. Ever.*

He indicated the newsroom. "Go out there and talk to her. Whether you believe it or not, she's determined to do a good job."

"Is she?"

"Yes, she is—and she will, with your support."

I actually felt dizzy. And I wondered why I wasn't walking out, permanently. Was it because this job was all I had? If I gave it up, what would I do?

I'd find something else, that's what. I could go back to the *Harlem Age*, for example. John Baltimore would take me back in a second. So it wasn't fear of losing my sense of identity, of self-worth, that was keeping me here. It was something else.

It was Queenie.

His kidnappers wanted me in on this story, I was convinced of that. What I wasn't sure of was why. Regardless, I didn't want to mess things up by walking out. After this was over, I'd figure out my future plans.

"All right," I said. Without another word, I got up and moved toward the door.

"And Lanie?"

I stiffened. "Yes?"

"I promise to make sure Selena does a good job. If you don't trust her, then at least trust me."

I didn't look back, just nodded and went out.

I headed toward Selena's desk, then found myself walking past it. I felt her eyes follow me and I ignored her. I sat down at my desk, slid a fresh sheet of paper into my Underwood, and went to work. I typed without pause for a good twenty minutes. The interview with Stax Murphy rolled out straight and clean. There were no embellishments, no shortcuts either. It came to six double-spaced pages.

I read it through once, twice. Made a minor adjustment. Then I got up, headed back down the aisle past Selena's desk. Again her eyes followed me and again I ignored her. I went straight to Sam's office without knocking and slapped the typewritten sheets on his desk, right on top of the pages he was editing.

He looked up.

"This is the Stax Murphy interview," I said. "It's all here. And it's done right. You want to give it to Selena, then you do it. You want to strip my name off, then you do it. But if you do, I'm out of here."

Queenie or no Queenie, I meant it.

Then I turned around and marched out.

CHAPTER 21

It had been a long day. I hadn't had lunch, so I was hungry and tired. I decided to go home. On the way, I stopped at a grocery store between 142nd and 143rd Streets on Lenox Avenue, just over from the Savoy Ballroom. A big sign above the store entrance announced, *Aaron's Own, Grocery and Delicatessen*. Large, alternating black-and-white diamond tiles decorated the façade. The windows were stocked with goods. Hand-painted signs advertised milk for six cents a gallon and Pepsi-Cola for five cents.

Inside, there were the usual tin ceilings and hard maple wood floors. Blue tiles on ivory spelled out the words *Fish* and *Fruit*. Toward the back was the deli counter.

I picked up corn flakes, a dozen eggs, some coffee, bread, and chicken. Prices were going up all the time, but at Aaron's they were still relatively affordable—a dozen eggs for fifty-nine cents, a pound of chicken for thirty-nine. I loaded up, then dropped back over to the Renaissance Pharmacy on West 138th to collect some hair products. At the time, I was wearing my hair in a bob. I was loyal to Madam C.J. Walker's hair products. Unfortunately, they were out of Glossine, so I reached for Apex's Glossatina. For a moment, I considered Plough's Pluko hair dressing; according to an ad I'd seen, Josephine Baker loved it. But I was skeptical—how did I know she wasn't just paid to say that? I went with the Glossatina instead. I ignored the skin lighteners—hated them, thought they were bad for your skin and worse for your self-image—but I did pick up a bar of Walker's complexion and toilet soap. As a matter of fact, I got two. Usually, they sold for twenty cents a large bar. They had a sale on, two for thirty, so I went for it.

Then I started home. Halfway there, I realized that I had no interest in cooking, so I stopped off and bought a chicken potpie. I tensed up when approaching my door and wondered whether I'd find another gift from Queenie's kidnappers. When I saw the empty doorstep, I heaved a sigh of relief.

Once inside, I grabbed the letters that had been slipped inside the door slot and were lying on the vestibule floor. I hung my coat up, tossed the mail on the parlor sofa, then went downstairs to the kitchen and put my groceries away. Back upstairs, I pushed the mail aside, stretched out on the sofa, and closed my eyes.

For the last hour or so, I'd enjoyed some normalcy. My mind had been free of the Black Orchid kidnapping and my fight with Sam. But the minute my eyes closed, it all came back.

Splintered images of the couple that lay slumped over the table, of the Ralston girl's face, of the kidnapper's grin all flashed behind my eyelids. I saw the finger again, smelled that faint foul odor. Then, in a rush, came Sam's face, Stax's face, and the image of Selena pecking away at her typewriter.

I turned over on my back, rubbed my forehead to assuage an oncoming headache. I suppose I should've been calling the Bernards and contacting Blackie. I would do neither.

In Blackie's case, I needn't do anything. The special edition wouldn't report on the cigar box, but it would mention the Stax Murphy interview. Once Blackie saw it, he'd be on the line, calling me.

As for the Bernards . . . I got up, went to my parlor window, parted my curtains, and looked out. It was around dinnertime. You'd think they'd be home. But all of the lights were out. Hmm. No lights didn't mean they weren't home. I could imagine Sheila, for example, sitting in her gloomy room, waiting and worrying.

I closed my curtains and leaned against the window. There was nothing I could do to help them. Not right now. This was always the worst part of any case, but especially a kidnapping: the waiting.

My gaze fell on the mail. I flipped through it quickly. An invitation from A'Lelia Walker. She was having a soiree at her town house three blocks down, on West 136th Street. A'Lelia was the daughter of Madam C.J. Walker.

She'd inherited her mother's wealth but, as far as I could see, not necessarily her business acumen. Instead of making money, A'Lelia was making a name for herself as a patron of colored artists.

When A'Lelia threw a party, you could be sure it would have a mixed crowd: journalists, painters, gamblers, writers, actors, and Pullman porters. Sometimes, she even had European royalty.

I knew people who would've sold themselves to get one of A'Lelia's engraved invitations. I knew others who wouldn't have anything to do with her—including one of my best friends, Grace Nail. Grace said she would rather do the Black Bottom on Lenox Avenue than cross A'Lelia's threshold. Grace was married to the renowned James Weldon Johnson. So folks thought she turned up her light-skinned nose at A'Lelia because A'Lelia was dark-skinned and the daughter of a washerwoman who'd made good by selling hair-care products.

But that wasn't it at all. Grace said, and I agreed with her, that A'Lelia's parties required a strong stomach. They had a reputation for looseness. A lot of the talk was exaggerated, but, like they say, where there's smoke, there's probably some fire.

"Honey, I've got nothing against A'Lelia," Grace once said, "but her parties? Sometimes, they get a bit too-too." Then Grace frowned, looked at me, and continued. "But you go to Jack-a-Lee's parties, don't you? If you can stand his, then I guess you can stand hers."

"I'll go anywhere for a story," I replied. "A'Lelia's parties, like 'em or not, make good copy."

I noted the date and time on A'Lelia's invitation, saw that it was actually for an after-party on the night of the Faggots' Ball. I'd probably end up going then. I tapped the invitation in my hand. The ball. I still had to get together a costume for that. It was one of the biggest events of the social season, so I'd have to look good.

I hoped this thing with Queenie would be settled by then, that he would be free and fine. The ball was the kind of affair that Queenie would love. He'd shine at it. It was made for personalities like his.

At that thought, all my worrying about him rushed back. Where was he? Were the Bernards getting the money together? What would happen next? Another note? Another demand? Another bit of Queenie in a box on my doorstep?

I tried to ease my mind by sorting the rest of the mail. I put the invitations on one side and the bills on another. Then I made myself check my diary, jot down the social dates. Even if I wasn't writing the articles on the Black Orchid kidnapping, I still had my column, *Lanie's World*, to find fodder for. Finally, I turned to writing out checks to pay the bills. Through it all, concerns about Queenie hovered on the edge of my mind. Sam too.

Would he really take my name off the Stax Murphy interview? My feelings toward him kept changing. Sometimes, I loved him so much. Other times, I could've . . . well, shaken him. What he'd done was just plain wrong. And if this was a sign of how it was going to be, then . . .

No, I told myself, *don't go there.*

He and I had both been tired and worried. He was upset about me disappearing like that, and maybe he was right to be.

But still.

My gaze went to the telephone. Sam and I didn't often disagree, but when we did, it was bad, and the reasons were always the same: my work at the paper. Usually, after fights like this, Sam would phone to see how I was doing, maybe even to make up. But, apparently, he wasn't going to call this night.

Well, I certainly wasn't going to call him.

I tried to read. I picked up *The New Negro* by Alain Locke, but put it down again. It was too dry to hold my attention. I went back to my bookshelves and ran my fingertips over the titles. G. K. Chesterton's *The Incredulity of Father Brown*, Wilkie Collins's *The Moonstone*, Arthur Conan Doyle's *The Adventures of Sherlock Holmes*, Jessie Redmon Fauset's *There Is Confusion*, Zora Neale Hurston's *Their Eyes Were Watching God*, D. H. Lawrence's *Lady Chatterley's Lover*, Robert Louis Stevenson's *Dr. Jekyll and Mr. Hyde*, *Cane* by Jean Toomer, Walter White's *The Fire in the Flint*. I floated back to

Zora Neale's book; it was one of my favorites. I'd read all of these books at least once, but hers, I'd read three times already. It always distracted me and lifted my spirits.

But not that night.

That night, my worried thoughts kept returning to the Black Orchid. I tried listening to the radio. I switched channels between *The Eveready Hour*, *Rambling with Gambling*, and the Boston Symphony Orchestra. Eventually, I turned it off. Even the classical strains of the symphony were just an annoyance.

I took a bath and ended up going to bed early. Although I fell asleep as soon as my head touched the pillow, I woke in the middle of the night. My clock on the fireplace mantle was lit by the moon. Two a.m.

On impulse, I got out of bed, went to the window, and peeped out. Across the street, at the Bernard house, the lights were on in a second-floor window and a shadow paced back and forth.

I watched for several long seconds, trying to figure out who it was. Soon, however, I just returned to bed, but I couldn't fall asleep again.

CHAPTER 22

The special edition hit newsstands at five that Saturday morning. My phone rang nine minutes later. It was Blackie, and he was angry. He didn't even say good morning, just started firing questions, one after the other.

"I want names, names and places! And I want them now! How did you find Murphy? How did you contact him? Who helped you do it? Where'd you meet him and when?"

"Blackie, you know I can't—"

"Of course you can! And you know something? You will. I want you down here, at the station, in fifteen minutes flat."

"I—"

"I'm not asking—I'm sending a car to get you. And you'd better be there when he arrives."

I started to call Sam, then reconsidered. If I told him Blackie was bringing me in, he'd want to be there. If Sam was there, one of two things would happen: he'd get upset and mention the cigar box; or he wouldn't get upset, but still mention the cigar box.

Either way, he'd make things worse. Either way, I had to do this on my own.

Twenty minutes later, Blackie had me in a back room of the precinct. He was pelting me with questions, and I was giving him just one answer.

"I can't say . . . I can't say . . . I can't say."

His brogue thickened as he became more upset. He alternated between anger and pleading. "Don't be like this, lassie. You're biting the hand that feeds you. Don't do it."

"I'm sorry."

"Don't you understand? I got a multiple homicide and you're sitting on information that could solve it. I can't let you outta here. Not unless you give me something."

I was silent.

He went on: "And you shoulda come to me. You shoulda done it before the paper hit the stand. We coulda worked together. Now you've made me look like a fool. Can't you see that? I can't help you. I can't afford to be nice. The brass won't let me. What were you thinking, girl? What was *Sam* thinking?"

I had nothing to say to that.

"Speaking of which, where is he? I would've thought he'd be here with you." Suspicion lit his face. "You didn't call him, did you? And why not? Because he doesn't know what you've done—or not done." Blackie squinted at me. "He told you to tell me, didn't he? You disobeyed his orders and that's why you're here and he's not. Well, well, well. It's nice to know that somebody over at that paper of yours has some sense."

Blackie paced back and forth. He ran a hand through his hair. "I'm sorry, Lanie. You're gonna have to be our guest for a little while. I got no choice, I got to hold you."

"On what charge?"

"Obstruction of justice."

He gave me a chance to call Sam. I declined. "And please, don't you do it."

He didn't answer. Instead, he had me booked and fingerprinted. Then he put me in a holding cell at the precinct. The cells to the immediate left and right were empty. So was the one directly opposite. It was a Saturday morning; they should've been full from Friday night. I wondered if he'd shuffled prisoners around for my sake. The ones who were there were a fairly quiet bunch. Hours passed. It wasn't so bad, I knew it could get much worse.

He checked on me after lunch. "Changed your mind?"

I shook my head.

"Sorry to hear that." He started to walk away, then turned back. "Lanie, please, you can stop this. Right now. Don't make me take the next step."

I didn't answer.

He gripped the bars and stared at me. For a moment, he looked more like a prisoner than I was.

"The next stop is Harlem Jail, Lanie. Trust me, you don't want to go there."

I could guess what his superiors were saying. I could guess how much pressure he was under. "Do what you have to do."

He paled. There was nothing left for him to say, so he just walked away.

I felt sick. He was right: horrible things happened at the Harlem Jail. I didn't want to go there. I wanted to go home. But I couldn't, not if it meant telling him what he wanted to hear. I wasn't being brave, just stubborn. And it was easy to be stubborn. Because I felt no fear. I felt nothing. I felt numb.

Technically, it was the 5th District Prison. It stood on the corner of East 121st Street at Sylvan Place, between Third and Lexington Avenues. It was built in 1885 and resembled a castle, with a fairy-tale tower and a stone, brick, and terra cotta façade. Depending on the sunlight and time of day, the exterior shifted from red to pink.

I'd visited the place many times in my police reporting days. It housed courtrooms, offices, and jail cells. There were three gated entrances. The main courtroom had stained glass windows, a sculptured barrel-vaulted ceiling, and intricate woodwork. A gold, black, and red balustrade spiraled up to an octagonal tower. There were cells right next to the courtrooms. But the real jail area, the one they took me to, was upstairs.

The officers led me through a dimly lit corridor to a heavy metal door, which revealed a bare room. Electrical pipes snaked across the ceiling and connected to a signal box above the doorway, probably some kind of alarm bell.

There were five tiers of back-to-back cells. Forty cells in all. Walls of mesh wiring, iron bars, and pipe railing ran along the passageway. Guard posts stood at either end.

Each cell had a number over its threshold. Dirty yellow paint covered the cell's brick walls. The cement floor was dank, the stench unbearable. A stained oval sink jutted from one corner. Two metal folding bunk beds were attached to the wall by chains. A seatless toilet stood tucked mere inches from the head of the lower bed. At first, I was appalled at the placement. Then it occurred to me that at least this way the partial cover given by the bed conveyed a modicum of privacy. I was grateful that the cells had natural daylight. And my cell and the one next to it were empty.

So far, I had felt no sense of fear or panic. I was as calm as I would've been if registering at a hotel. The slam of the cell door, the turn of the key closing the lock: neither bothered me more than a noisy hotel neighbor. I don't think I was being brave. I do think I was in shock.

I closed my eyes and imagined I was back in my parlor. But instead of seeing my home, I saw the Bernards' house. I started thinking about Sheila and Junior and William. I remembered my interview with Queenie, and I could see him laughing; I could hear his husky voice.

Then I reflected that the kidnapper must have known Queenie's true identity; I thought about the box that had landed on my doorstep, but I didn't reach any conclusions.

Hours passed in isolation.

I grew hungry, but the food, when it came, was terrible. I put it aside, wondering how long before hunger drove me to eat it. I was thirsty too, but I refused to drink. Not only did the water look foul, but I didn't want to risk having to use the facilities.

Blackie came to see me. It was late afternoon by then. Actually, more like early evening. The sky through the windows across from my cell was a charcoal gray. Blackie didn't enter my cell, just stood outside of it. He looked more miserable than I felt.

"You got anything you want to say to me?" he asked.

"No more than I did before."

"Just thought I'd ask." He stood there, still hoping.

"Good night," I said.

He gave a sad half-smile, then tipped his hat. "Good night, Lanie."

More hours alone. A deepening darkness. I curled up on the lower bunk, closed my eyes, tried to collar a nod. I heard the other inmates talking—some talking, some arguing—followed by the clang of a door. Then footsteps. Another door boomed open and a woman shrieked. The reality of my surroundings hit me. I had to get out of there.

Two days. That's all. Two days. You can do that. They can't hold you longer than that.

Where did I get that idea? Don't know. It was wrong, and I knew it. Blackie could hold me as long as he needed to. But once the idea was there, I clung to it.

You can do this. You can do it.

The footsteps grew closer. The sight of a man's shoe came into view, then a dark gray pants leg. Then the man himself.

I followed the leg to the hands that gripped the bars, up the arms to the broad shoulders in the dark coat and the worried face that topped them.

Sam. It was Sam.

CHAPTER 23

An hour later, I was home. I was curled up on the living room sofa with a cup of hot tea, shivering.

Sam was pacing back and forth. "Why didn't you call me? Why didn't you let me know?"

Because you would've found out. You would've known that I didn't tell them about the cigar box. You would've known that I defied you. I looked away, at the fireplace. "I didn't want to bother you."

"Bother me," he repeated. "Woman, I've done everything I can to prove to you that I want to be there for you. Why won't you let me?"

I didn't know what to say. "Thank you" was all I could manage.

He sank down next to me, took my hand. "When I got that call from Blackie, when he told me what he'd done . . ."

"I know." I closed my eyes and was embarrassed to realize that I was crying.

"Oh, baby." He gently wiped the tears away. He had these incredibly broad thumbs. They were large and scratchy, even calloused, like he'd done a lot of hard labor. They always reminded me of how little I knew about Sam, how full of contradictions he was. He had the intellect and bearing of a man with a lot of education. But he had the hands of a laborer.

"How'd you get me out?" I asked.

"I did what you should've done. I lied."

"You *what?*"

"I said that Stax kidnapped you. That he knew you were working the story and grabbed you right off the street."

"Blackie believed you?"

"He let you go, didn't he?"

Obviously.

"There was only one hitch," Sam said. "He wanted to know exactly when Stax grabbed you."

I frowned. "Why?"

"Think about it. If you met with Stax before or during the news conference, then that means Stax knew he was under suspicion—before his name was even released."

Understanding dawned. "So, Blackie's also worried about leaks in the department."

"He's been worried about it a long time. He'd have to be. He'd have to figure someone was tipping off Stax. No other explanation for how the guy keeps getting away."

Made sense. "So what did you say?"

"I told him that Stax knew there were survivors, and that they'd give a description. Common sense said the cops wouldn't wait for the news conference before showing that drawing around. So Stax decided to take the initiative."

"Good." It was essentially the same argument I'd used on Jack-a-Lee. *Great minds think alike.*

"Lanie?" he said.

"Yes?"

"You didn't tell Blackie about the cigar box, did you?"

A moment went by. Then I shook my head. I was prepared for an explosion; it didn't come.

"I figured as much."

I could hear the disappointment in his voice, and it cut to the quick. Somehow, lately, I was always disappointing him. Perhaps now was the time to say what had been on my mind.

"Sam, I appreciate what you did today, getting me out of jail and all, and I want to thank you for running my story on Stax."

"It was a good piece."

"Yes, but . . . everything I write is good."

He raised an eyebrow, but didn't argue. The hand caressing mine slowed.

I hesitated, searching for the right words. "The thing is, ever since we got together, you've been . . . well, overprotective. I don't think you would've reacted the same way, when you heard about Stax, if we weren't involved. And I don't think you would've taken my story away, told me to stay off this case, if we weren't involved."

His expression was unreadable. "Is that all?" he said finally.

"It's not that I don't love you or appreciate—"

"Do you?"

I blinked, puzzled. "Do I what?"

"Love me?"

"Well, I . . . Yes, of course."

"Of course?"

"All right, yes, I do."

"Then do you want me to love you?"

I shook my head. "No, Sam, that's not what this is about."

"That's exactly what it's about, what it has *always* been about—whether you're ready to let me love you. Whether you're willing to let someone inside that hard shell you crawled into after your husband died."

"I—"

"You keep running off, taking chances that could get you killed. You act as though you don't matter to anyone but you. Well, you do. You matter to a whole lot of people." Before I could answer, he held up an index finger. "That's number one. Number two is that I am your boss, Lanie. It is my *job* to know your whereabouts. Your welfare—the welfare of everyone in that newsroom—is my responsibility. Do I make myself clear?"

I could feel my temper rising. "Staying safe is not why I got into this business. Do you think I became a reporter just to cover parties?"

"I assume it was because you wanted to help people."

"I wanted to tell the stories that no one else would tell. Ida B. Wells and Nellie Bly, they're my heroes. I wanted to be like them: do important work, cover significant stories. But the fact is, I'm a coward. I don't have Ida's guts to fight lynching or Nellie's courage to go inside an insane asylum."

"But you do."

"No, I don't. Every now and then I just find a story that I do have the guts to cover. A story that could make a difference."

"And you think this is one of them?"

"Yes, I do."

"Why?"

"I can't say. But there's something awfully wrong here," I nodded toward the window, "about that house. Please, Sam, let me have this one."

He was thoughtful, his brow creased with concern.

"It's not just what you do. It's *how* you do it."

"Look, you're right about me running off. I was wrong about that, and I'll try not to—"

He cut me off with a glare and I amended myself.

"I promise not to do it again. But if I do that, will you promise me something in return? To give me the freedom to follow the harder stories, no matter where they take me?"

"Lanie . . ."

"Please."

After a moment, he drew a deep breath. "All right," he said. "But you have to keep your half of the bargain too."

"I will."

He smiled skeptically. "Sure you will. Until the next phone call."

"You don't trust me?"

"Oh, I do. As far as I can throw you."

"I'm sorry," I whispered.

"No, you're not." He put two fingertips under my chin and lifted it, so my gaze met his. I closed my eyes and felt his lips press gently against mine. Parting my lips, I squeezed my body to his, felt his embrace tighten. The kiss grew long and hard and hungry, but after a while he held me away. His eyes contained desire—and doubt. "I don't want to, if . . ."

"No, please. I feel so cold inside. Ever since the night of the shooting, I can't get warm." I moved closer. "Warm me, Sam. Do whatever it takes to warm me."

He cupped my face with his hand. "Are you sure?"

In answer, I turned my face into his hand and kissed his palm. At that point, he swept me off my feet Valentino-style. I nuzzled my face in the curve of his throat.

"You're so silly," I whispered. "I am not a damsel in distress."

"Aren't you?"

He stayed that night. He was there most of Sunday too. I sent him home right after Sunday dinner. We spent part of the time strolling around the neighborhood; otherwise, we watched the Bernard house. We sat in the bay window of my parlor room, taking turns, not really sure what we were searching for. We saw no one enter or leave it.

Monday and Tuesday were also quiet. I did my usual running around, went over to see Grace. Checked in on Mrs. Cardigan. Attended the weekly meeting of the Women's Auxiliary at the Young Women's Christian Association. Dropped in on a planning meeting for the Faggots' Ball and listened to panel members worry about the weather, how it might affect attendance.

Nothing new vis-à-vis the Black Orchid. Blackie left me alone. My phone at work was oddly silent too. It was as if we were all waiting for the other shoe to drop.

On Wednesday, it did.

CHAPTER 24

I spent that morning on the phone, double-checking the names of people at two social gatherings I'd missed. A couple of sources also phoned in with information about an affair between the married director and unmarried in-génue of a play . . .

Then I took a call from the manager of the Savoy Ballroom. He wanted to give me an update on their bathing beauty ball and contest. This would be the second year in which the Savoy held the events. The previous year had been a rousing success, and this year's looked like it would be too. They were turning the dancehall into a jungle, to bolster the atmosphere. More than two hundred woman had already entered the contest, I was told. Starting in late July, and every Saturday night in August, some forty to fifty young women in bathing suits would parade up and down before an audience. The whole thing would culminate in a ball in early September. Prizes included up to five hundred dollars in cash.

I hung up the phone thinking that everybody was running a beauty con-test these days. They were guaranteed moneymakers, almost always pulling in large crowds. More significantly, they served the social benefit of reaf-firming the beauty of colored women, something that had been ignored and disparaged for way too long.

I finished typing up the column and handed it in. Then I set about doing what was really on my mind.

I ran downstairs to the newsstand on the corner and bought a copy of the *New York Daily News*. I headed out without my coat, thinking I wouldn't need it for a two-minute errand. But the short spell in the frigid wind was enough to chill me to the bone, and the building lobby was unheated.

By the time I returned to my desk, my teeth were chattering so hard my jaw hurt. I flipped the paper open to the personal classifieds and ran an index finger down the columns. At the top of the third column, two ads down, I found what I was looking for: *We are ready. Signed, Margie Winthrop.*

I closed the paper and thought about it. If I told Sam, he'd probably just ask me to share the news with Selena. Despite our little talk and reconciliation, I still felt the need for caution.

Speak of the devil. I glanced up and saw her walking past, holding a coffee cup. She must've sensed me looking at her, because she slowed down, turned, and retraced her steps to my desk. She peeked down at the newspaper and asked, "What've you got there?"

"A newspaper."

Her eyes went from me to the paper, and back again.

"Is there something in there I should know about?"

"How about everything?"

"You saying you think I'm ignorant?"

"Oh no, Selena. I would never *say* that."

She put a hand on her hip. "If there's anything in that paper that's got to do with the Black Orchid, then it's got to do with me."

She had good instincts, I had to give her that.

"I'll tell you what," I said. "If you think there's something in this paper about the story, then you find it." I handed it to her. "I've got better things to do."

I smiled politely and waited for her to go away. It took her a moment, but she left. Then I happened to glance down Sam's way, felt his eyes on me. I smiled at him and gave a nod, as if to say, *Don't worry, I'm playing nice with her.* Apparently satisfied, Sam nodded in return, then returned his attention to whatever was on his desk.

Selena was back at her desk, nose deep in the newspaper. *Excellent instincts. If only she'd use them to dig up her own stories instead of waiting for Sam to toss her one of mine.*

Certain that the coast was clear, I picked up the phone and put a call through to the Bernards. Unfortunately, but not surprisingly, Dr. Bernard was in no mood to talk. He said he wanted to keep the lines clear and hung up. I was disappointed, but didn't argue.

For several minutes, I sat there wondering how to proceed. The ring of my phone brought me back to reality.

It was Sheila. She was excited and frightened. "Mrs. Price, another letter arrived just now. This one's addressed to you and me."

"Me?"

"Yeah. They want us to go to the Mercer Hotel. You know it?"

"The one on 145th Street?"

"Uh-huh. We're supposed to register there at six o'clock tonight. And sign in as Anne and Alice Martin. Then we're supposed to wait for them to contact us." She paused. "There's something else, a note. It's from Billy, written by him. I'll read it to you."

"Okay."

"It says, *I am alive, but they know about me. They say they don't like people like me. My hand hurts. They say they'll do other things to me, then kill me, if they're not paid. So, please do what they say.*"

"You sure it's him?"

"I recognize his handwriting."

"What does Junior say?"

"Junior?" Sheila repeated. "Oh, yes! Well, he's not back yet. But he called today. He's—he had trouble with his train."

"What does your father say?"

She paused before answering. "He doesn't know."

I leaned on my desk and dropped my voice. "Doesn't know?"

"They were out when it came. I just happened to be here."

"And you're not going to tell them?"

She was silent a moment. "I can't."

"Why not?"

"Please, don't make me explain. Just trust me. You can't say anything, not to anyone. Not to them and not to the police—especially not the police."

"Sheila, I have to."

"Please!" Her voice became a ragged cry. "I'm begging you. Don't say a word. Just do this with me. Come and don't say a word."

I thought about it. "I'll have to tell my editor."

"No, you—"

"Sheila, it would be foolish to run off and do this without letting someone know where we are or what we're up to."

"But what if he—"

"Don't worry. He won't."

There was a pause and then a long sigh. "All right."

"What about the ransom?" I asked.

"I'll get it. Just be there, tonight, alone."

"I will."

There was soft click and she was gone.

"Who was that?"

I straightened up to find Selena standing behind me.

Her eyes narrowed with suspicion. "Did that have to do with the Black Orchid kidnapping? I bet it did, didn't it?" She took a step toward me and wagged a finger under my nose. "Sam told me you'd try to sneak something past me."

"He did no such thing." Pointedly ignoring her, I pulled open a drawer, fetched a fresh steno pad, and slipped it into my purse. "Just because Sam gave you the Black Orchid story doesn't mean you have the right to watch everything I do." I shrugged into my coat. "Now, I suggest you go do your job and let me do mine."

Before she could answer, I grabbed my purse and walked out. I had a bag to pack. I was a block from my home when it hit me: I had forgotten to leave a message for Sam.

CHAPTER 25

The Mercer was one step away from being a flophouse—one very short step. The place was a magnet for every hoodlum, hooker, dealer, and otherwise shady character within a one-mile radius. There had been a couple of murders at the Mercer, but I hadn't caught the stories when I was covering crime. A converted three-story brownstone, it sat on the northwest corner of Lenox Avenue and 147th Street. That was just two blocks north of the gracious Hotel Theresa and less than ten blocks north of genteel Strivers' Row. Not far in physical distance, but worlds away in atmosphere.

In short, it was the perfect setting for a shakedown.

I drove my car and met Sheila in front of the hotel promptly at six. She was outwardly calm, but her troubled eyes revealed the same scared kid I'd seen before.

"It's going to be all right," I said.

She took in the Mercer's shabby, downright evil appearance, grabbed a deep breath, and set her thin shoulders. I put a gentle hand on her elbow and we walked in together.

Given what we'd seen outside, the lobby was no surprise: uneven walls covered in grimy green wallpaper, a tattered red carpet underneath, a battered wooden elevator to one side, and a scarred wooden reception desk set straight ahead, with a mean-looking sister behind it. I knew her by reputation.

Ida Mercer, the widowed wife of a saxophone player, ran the show. She'd had very little experience with the finer things in life, but she knew how to manage a flophouse. She was a large woman with narrow black eyes in a wide, fleshy face. She wore her thick hair parted down the center and braided into two pigtails. It was a child's hairdo, but there was nothing childish about Mercer. She was in her mid-to-late fifties and, from the weariness in her eyes, her soul must've been a hundred.

Mercer smirked knowingly when we asked to register. "One room or two?" She had a low, husky voice.

"One," Sheila said.

"Two," I said.

We'd spoken together.

Mercer talked to me, but glanced sideways at Sheila. "Sounds like girlfriend here is the type to get cold at night."

Sheila gave me a panicked look. "Please, I don't want to stay alone here."

Mercer smiled as though Sheila had just proved her point.

"All right," I said.

"How many nights?" Mercer asked.

"Just one."

If we were lucky, we would make the drop and be out by midnight. We wouldn't even have to sleep here. We might even be on our way to pick up Queenie if everything went smoothly. Realistically, I didn't think so, but a girl can dream, can't she?

We signed in and paid up-front, using the names Anne and Alice Martin, just as we'd been instructed.

"Here's the house rules," Mercer said. "This is a righteous, God-fearing Christian establishment. I don't put up with no drinking or whoring. You two look like nice ladies, but you can never tell. So I repeat: No drinking or men in the room. And no stealing neither. Iffin' you steal something, I'll find you and make you pay for it. Iffin' you break something, I'll do the same. Got it?"

I nodded to make her happy and put out my hand for the key.

The stairs were creaky and uneven. I had one small bag and Sheila had two, which we carried ourselves. Our room was on the top floor, which had six small rooms set along a narrow corridor with a stairway to one side and a communal bathroom to the rear. The accomodations were unexceptional: minimal cleanliness, a queen-sized cot with a thin, sagging mattress, a splotchy blue blanket and gray sheets, a single overhead light, a battered table and chair.

Worse than I would've liked, but much better than I'd feared.

The room was on the corner, so it had windows on two walls and you could see the lights from Lenox Avenue stretching far south. It was a nice sight; it was enough to give you hope. Going to sleep or waking up to a view like that, a person could think that maybe this wasn't the end of the road.

Then again, not everyone might react that way.

Sheila walked to the middle of the room and just stood there, taking a long, hard look at her surroundings. Then she sagged down on the edge of the bed, bent her head, and wept.

I gave her a moment, then sat next to her. I put an arm around her shoulders and let her have a good, long cry. When she was all sobbed out, I passed her a handkerchief. She dabbed her eyes, sniffed, and thanked me. But she refused to meet my gaze.

After a pause, I whispered in her ear: "Now that we've come this far, don't you think it's time you told me the truth?"

She froze. "The truth?"

I could just about see the shiver that rippled down her spine. "It's time to stop the lying."

"I don't know what you're talking about," she said in a low voice.

"Yes, you do. And now's the time to talk."

"I have no idea what—"

"The kidnapping, Sheila. It's a fake, isn't it?"

Her head snapped up. "No! Of course not! What are you talking about?"

"I'm talking about the fact that the kidnapper contacted the Bernards instead of Queenie's boss."

"So?"

"It was a tell. An insider pulled this job, someone who knew Queenie's true identity."

"No. They tortured Billy. They—"

"Stop it!" I snapped, almost savagely. "The kidnapping was an act. At least, it started out that way."

"How can you say that?" she said in a horrified whisper. "They cut off his finger. They—"

"That's what happens when you partner with gangsters."

She shrank back. "You're wrong, just so wrong."

"I wish I were, but you know I'm not. There have been too many coincidences: first, the kidnapping. It wasn't luck that it happened when I was there. I was meant to see a performance, one that had nothing to do with singing."

Sheila swallowed but said nothing.

"Then there was the cigar box," I continued. "It was hand-delivered to my doorstep. Another coincidence? I don't think so."

"But that doesn't— I mean, maybe the kidnapper felt he had a tie to you somehow, because you were there that night."

"Yeah, and that tie is Queenie. If you're a publicity-hungry performer, like Queenie, what better way to keep a reporter in the loop than by leaving that box on her doorstep?"

She rubbed her brow. "No . . . Maybe Billy gave the kidnappers the wrong address on purpose, as a cry for help."

"It's possible, but I doubt it. Queenie was behind that box coming to my house, but he didn't send it as a cry for help."

Sheila's eyes widened. "Why then?"

"Whoever put that box on my doorstep wanted me to know about the connection between the Bernards and Queenie. Whoever did it knew that the minute I saw it, I'd start asking questions. Not just why me, but why you? Why your family? What was the tie between Queenie, or Billy as you call him, and the nice family across the street?"

Sheila opened her mouth again, but no words came out.

I went on: "You say you didn't know about the finger? I'll buy it. I can believe that it wasn't part of the plan. I can even see things from your point of view. All of a sudden, there I was at your doorstep. Carrying that box.

Asking questions. You had to think on your toes, and you did. I have to give it to you: you can lie without batting an eyelash."

I said it hard, said it fast. I wanted her to feel as though I'd slapped her. She winced as though I had. But she remained silent. Despite my harsh words, I thought she was a good kid, a decent kid, inexperienced with lies. Maybe she had a natural talent for faking it, but I didn't think so. I could see it in her eyes. She was trying to come up with another fat one, but I wouldn't give her the space.

"You people did tell the truth about one thing, didn't you? That the family wants nothing to do with this kidnap victim. Nothing at all. And maybe that's the key to this whole thing."

She seemed to shrink inside her skin. She offered no defense, just cowered under the onslaught. Her face was growing paler by the second. I felt bad for her, but I had to get through. Now was the time to do it. Later would be too late. And so I went on, relentless and showing no mercy.

"There is no Billy, is there? There's only Junior. Junior *Bernard*. He's Queenie. He's your husband. And *he's* their kid, not you."

Sheila went very still. For a moment, she even stopped breathing. Then she closed her tear-filled eyes. "Oh God, I'm so sorry. How long have you known?"

"Since I brought the cigar box."

She raised her head, stunned. "But how?"

"Let's just say you're a little too brown."

"What?"

"A source told me the Bernards' little girl was pretty light. Plus, you said that nobody ever called you Janie."

"I don't understand."

"The day I brought the cigar box, I asked you if anybody had ever called you Janie. You didn't know what I was talking about."

"But who is Janie?"

"It's the name Junior went by when he was a child."

"But . . . that's a girl's name."

I nodded. "Exactly."

"Oh." Her eyes widened. "So you already knew when you left the house."

"I had a suspicion, but it doesn't matter. What does matter is that your husband's life is on the line. If we're going to save him, then you have to tell me the truth."

"I didn't want to do this pretend kidnapping. But Junior said I had to. He said it was the only way." She swallowed, bit down on her lower lip. "He promised me he'd be safe, that nothing bad could happen, cause he knew somebody."

"Who?"

"I don't know. Somebody he met at the club. All he said was that this guy would know what to do." She clutched her shoulders. "I don't believe this. It wasn't supposed to be this way."

"How was it supposed to be?"

"Simple. Real simple. Junior made it sound so easy."

Kids playing with fire. "What was he thinking?"

"He said it was the only way to be free."

"Of what?"

"Of *them*." Her tone turned vehement.

"His parents?"

She nodded. Straightening up, she wiped her face and sniffled. Her expression had turned bitter. "You want to know why we did it? I'll tell you why. There's no reason to hide anything anymore—and that includes the truth about those vipers, my in-laws." She balled her hand into a fist. "They control us. They control *him*. He couldn't make a move without getting their approval. Neither one of us could."

"But then how could he be singing at the Cinnamon Club?"

"They didn't know. They didn't want to know." She took a deep breath. "But I guess I should start at the beginning."

Chapter 26

I got her some water. There was a glass, relatively clean. The sink was dingy but the water ran clear. She accepted it gratefully, and drank like a woman coming in from the desert. Then she set the empty glass on the floor and launched into her story: "Y'see, I didn't know anything about all this—this kind of living—when I met Junior. This thing about men dressing up like women and even loving each other? I hate it." She shuddered slightly. "It sickens me and I don't believe it's right before God. But there's a whole lotta worse goings-on in this world, and I'm no one to judge anybody. Furthermore, I love Junior. I really do, and nothing's ever gonna change that."

She paused, reflecting.

"I guess I should be ashamed to say that. Maybe I am. Maybe I'm a fool of a woman for loving a man like this, but that's me. That's how I feel."

She glanced at me with a sad, bleary smile. I gave her an encouraging nod.

"We met at Howard," she continued. "We were in the same class, both first-semester seniors. I'd just transferred in and was lonely. He was the handsomest, gentlest man I'd ever met. I sensed a sorrow in him and that drew me to him too. I liked the fact that he wasn't a lumberjack kind of guy. I'd been out with those types before and I didn't want to ever again. Junior made me feel loved and cherished. I fell head over heels for him. My parents took to him immediately. It was great.

"I guess you could say I was sheltered," she explained softly. "Daddy was a preacher, and Mama . . . well, she was a farm girl. I had two older brothers, Lynn and Wallace. But a woman shot one and the other died in a train accident. After that, my parents got real protective. Nothing bad was going to happen to their baby girl. And when they met Junior, they just knew everything was going to be all right." Her expression turned grim. "Like I said, Daddy was a preacher and Mama sewed clothes. Neither one of them finished high school, but they believed in education. They were so happy when I got that scholarship to Howard. And when I came home and told them about Junior . . . well, you can imagine. They were thrilled. Baby girl had done good, real good."

They got married in secret ("Junior insisted") and spent the next month on campus, then moved up north. She'd so anticipated graduating and moving to New York. That dream included them having a place of their own.

"But Junior said it would make more sense to move in with his mom and dad at first. We'd have a nice place to stay and could save money."

They'd been married for nearly seven months now, and six of those seven had been spent at his parents' house.

"Things went wrong from the moment I stepped into that place. Junior couldn't be with me anymore. He just couldn't . . . if you know what I mean. Everything had been fine up until then. But from that first night on . . . he couldn't do it." She shook her head.

"At first, he kept making excuses. And I bought 'em. I mean, I really thought he was sick or tired or had a headache or something. Then one day I came home and found him moving all of his stuff into a separate room. No warnings, no discussions, nothing. I asked him if I'd done something wrong. He said I hadn't, but he refused to move back to our room and would rarely let me step foot in his."

"When did that happen?"

She thought about it. "Back in September." Soon after Queenie appeared on the scene. "He was going out most every night. He said it was with friends, but Junior didn't have any friends, no one but me. So I knew then that—"

There was a knock at the door. Sheila and I exchanged glances.

"Yes?" I called out.

"It's Mrs. Mercer. Open up."

I went to the door and Mercer handed me an envelope. "Taxi driver brought it," she said, mounds of flesh jiggling on her hips as she walked away.

I shut the door and ripped open the missive.

"What is it?" Sheila breathed at my side.

"Another note from the kidnappers." It was typewritten on the same plain paper as the other ones. *Take the money and drive to Mount Morris Park. Enter on the north side and look for a stake with a white cloth attached to it in the northeast corner.* I looked at Sheila. "Are you ready to do this?"

She nodded.

"What about the dough?" I asked.

Sheila grabbed the satchel and yanked it open. "It's all here." She handed it to me. The bag was full of bundled bills.

"Did you count it?"

Sheila shook her head. "I saw Dr. Bernard counting it."

"How did you get it if you didn't tell him about the letter?"

"I saw where he hid it—in the piano bench."

I had a bad feeling about this. "Are you sure you don't want to bring the police in?"

"Oh, no! We can't do that. These people are crazy. Look what they've already done. And now they say they're gonna do worse."

"That's all the more reason for you to call in the cavalry."

Sheila's eyes looked sorrowful. "I'm afraid you're all the cavalry we've got."

CHAPTER 27

M ount Morris Park was a small square of greenery surrounding an im-
posing rock. It interrupted the north-south run of Fifth Avenue, from
120th to 124th Streets. I parked the car on the northeast corner of 124th and
left Sheila locked inside with the satchel carrying the money. The park was
dark and shadowy and a cold wind cut through my clothes. The wind was
uncomfortable, but it turned out to be a good thing. Without it, I might've
missed the white fluttering cloth tied to the stake.

Under the cloth was a tin can; inside the can was another note. This
time, the instructions said to drive east to 124th Street and Park Avenue.
There we'd find another white cloth.

I hurried back to the car. It was just as cold inside as out. Sheila was
shivering when I returned.

"What happened?" she asked, with chattering teeth. "Did you find
anything?"

As I started the car, I told her about the note. There was no traffic at
this time of the night, so it only took a minute to get to the next piece of the
puzzle. The cloth was tied to an iron railing in front of a brownstone. We saw
no note or other form of communication. I steered us to the curb, then left
the window cracked and the engine running to keep us warm.

"What do you think will happen now?" Sheila asked.

"I guess we'll get more instructions."

"But how?"

"I don't know." I noticed a pay phone on the corner. "Over there?" I
pointed. "Maybe they'll call us on that."

"But how'll they know?"

"They're probably watching."

She studied the telephone. "If it rings, will we hear it?"

I had wondered about that too. I rolled my window down a bit more and a blast of arctic air hit me in the face.

Next to me, Sheila shivered. We settled into silence, preoccupied with our private worries.

"We've been sitting here a long time," Sheila said after a while.

"I know." I glanced at my watch. "Fifteen minutes already."

"You think they're just testing us?"

"For sure."

"To see if we called the police?"

I nodded.

Sheila turned to me. "I mean, you *didn't* call them, did you? You didn't tell anyone?"

How I wished I had. I shook my head.

"Good," she exhaled. "We don't need to worry then—about the police messing things up, I mean."

I studied her profile. She was so very young and naïve and terribly, deeply in love.

She must've felt me staring at her, or maybe even read my thoughts, because she just started talking, picking up where she'd left off.

CHAPTER 28

Alone in her marital bed at night, Sheila often felt an overwhelming urge to cry. What had she gotten herself into? Was this how it would be for the rest of her life? She would allow a couple of tears to slip down her face, but then impatiently swipe them away. What was done was done.

The man she'd married was gone, if he'd ever really existed, and now she was stuck with a stranger. The man she'd married didn't smoke or drink, but for the past few days she was sure she'd smelled both, not just on her husband's breath, but his clothing as well.

Unable to sleep one night, she glanced at the clock on the fireplace mantel and saw that it was ten minutes past two. Her gaze went to the window. Where was he? What was he doing out there?

And who was he doing it with?

Her mood shifted from anger to fear and back again. She went to her bedroom door and set it ajar. She would be able to see him when he came up the stairs, but he wouldn't be able to see her sitting there, watching and waiting for him in the dark.

She climbed back into bed, kept her bathrobe on, and drew the sheets and blankets up to her chin. The robe was bulky under the linens, but she didn't care. She needed the extra warmth. Her hands felt cold, her feet felt cold. She felt cold inside as well as out. Her eyes sought out the clock again. She could barely discern the hands in the dark. No matter, she could guess what time it was: not even five minutes later than the last time she checked.

Crazy thoughts swirled through her mind, thoughts about losing her husband, her marriage; about the Bernards and their sweet smiles, but worried eyes.

Had they known this would happen?

The idea of moving to New York City, to Harlem, and to a big, fine town house on one of the city's most graceful blocks, had thrilled her. She'd been nervous about finally meeting her in-laws, but their reception made her feel warm and welcome.

Sheila paused in her memories. Her voice was steady, but her hands were trembling. She smiled grimly. "Mr. and Mrs. Bernard . . . they made a big to-do over me, talking about how happy they were that Junior had found me, had met someone like me. And that they were just overjoyed when Junior told them I'd agreed to marry him.

"Hmph. I should've known right then and there. First of all, Junior and I had kept our wedding secret. He said he hadn't told his parents. So somebody was lying, them or him. But why lie over something like that? And then, I kept thinking, what mother is ever happy—I mean *that* happy—to see her only son come home with a bride? Something had to be wrong somewhere. That woman wasn't just happy. She was grateful, and now I know why."

Sheila looked down at her wedding ring, twisted it on her finger. "Mrs. Bernard, she was always watching. At first, I thought she was watching me. But she wasn't. She was watching Junior. His father was too. Meanwhile, they were being real nice to me. Anything I wanted, I got. At first. But then the questions started. Mrs. Bernard would delicately ask me about how things were going between Junior and me, and I'd tell her things were fine. Again, I didn't think anything of it, not initially. But when Junior and I were sitting at the dinner table, I would catch them cutting glances at us, like they were waiting . . ."

The first time Phyllis Bernard had introduced her as their daughter, Sheila had seen it as a sign of them taking her to heart. She'd considered herself lucky and blessed. So many mothers-in-law rejected the woman their son married and did everything to undermine their relationship. Not Mrs. Bernard. She was everything you could wish for in a mother-in-law. And Daddy Bernard, he was wonderful too. So caring, so protective. So . . . attentive.

In her room that night, understanding dawned. Sheila saw matters much more clearly. They wanted her to be happy all right. They needed her to be.

"They wanted me to spy on Junior, to keep him in line," Sheila explained. "At the time, I didn't know what for, but I soon found out. I thought he was having an affair, had a little something-something stashed away on the side. I wish it had been that simple."

"You followed him," I guessed. "Or had him followed."

"I did it myself."

He led her to the Cinnamon Club. It was a place she'd never heard of, a lifestyle she'd never conceived of.

"I wasn't prepared for what I learned that night. Not at all." Her voice cracked. "When I saw all those people, I . . . well, at first, I still didn't know what was going on. I knew it was a sinning place, like the juke joints we had back home. I'd never been to one, never wanted to, 'specially not after what happened to my brother Lynn. He used to hang out in them kind of places. That's where he met that woman who shot him. Him being killed like that, it gave me a righteous fear of bars and speakeasies.

"When I walked in that door, the first thing that hit me was that this was a place of happy people. Real happy people. They were laughing, jiving, having fun. It may sound strange, but it was the first time I realized just how miserable I'd been. For months, I'd been making excuses, rationalizing things. Standing there in that club, I actually envied those people.

"And you know what's really crazy? I can't believe how naïve I was. I must've been out of my mind, cause for the longest time I just stood there refusing to accept what I could see. That it was women with women, men with men, hugging and kissing and making out.

"I started looking for Junior. I kept wondering why he hadn't taken me there. I could understand his need to escape that house, but I couldn't understand why he hadn't brought me with him. Maybe he thought I wouldn't like that kind of place. That could be, but . . . we were married. We weren't supposed to be keeping secrets from each other. Not unless . . . Maybe he just didn't want me anymore. Maybe he wasn't just trying to get away from that house, but away from me too. And that's when I started really search- ing that crowd for his face.

"It wasn't until he strutted out on stage, all dressed up, that I made the connection. Lord knows, I didn't want to. He's a pretty man, Miss Lanie, don't you think?"

"Yes, he's very attractive."

"Pretty," she repeated. "Like Rudolph Valentino. That's what they used to call him at Howard. The colored Valentino. All the girls were after him. Another reason, I suppose, why I was so glad, so grateful, when he picked me." She closed her eyes for a moment. "I know I'm not exactly what men call attractive. Just passing, as Mama used to say. So I never expected, I didn't dare hope that a man like Junior would . . ."

"Ever have eyes for you?"

She nodded.

"So when he showed interest, you were happy."

"Thrilled," she whispered. "Stupid fool, I was thrilled. I remember when I introduced Junior to Mama and Daddy. Mama took me aside later and she repeated something she'd always said, but I'd never really heard before. She said that a woman should never marry a man who's prettier than she is. And you know what? She was right."

"Sheila—"

She waved me off. "It's okay. I don't need, or want, any false comfort. I made a big mistake, and then I went and made it even bigger. I stayed for the show. Junior is a good entertainer, I have to give him that. And it was obvious that he belonged up there."

"You really do love him, don't you?"

"Yes, I do."

"Even after finding out about his double life?"

"You don't just stop loving a person because of something like that. Well, I couldn't. He was still my husband—and I know it sounds crazy to say this—but hurt as I was, it still felt real good to see him up there enjoying himself. I kept thinking, *This is the real Junior. Not the man you married, and not the man you've been living with.*"

"And of course it helped to know that he wasn't with another woman." She nodded.

"But Sheila, you must've realized that just because he didn't have another woman didn't mean he didn't have a man." I didn't intend to be mean. I simply needed her to be honest. We all needed her to be honest, Junior most of all. If he had started a relationship with someone, then that might well be the person we were looking for.

Sheila stared vacantly out the window at the dark, cold, empty streets and pressed her lips together. "I made sure he didn't see me. It wasn't that hard. The place was packed. Obviously, everybody knew about it—everybody but me. I watched most of Junior's performance. Then I went back to the house and sat up for a long time, thinking. I couldn't make up my mind what to do, but when he walked into the house just before dawn, I took one look at him and I knew.

"I didn't say anything to him right then. I wanted to, but a voice told me not to. He came on up the stairs. The makeup was gone and he was back in his regular clothes. And I could see that he was in a good mood, humming to himself. He went straight to his room and closed the door."

"Did you ever confront him?"

"The next evening, right after dinner. I told him I knew, that I'd followed him, that I'd seen him perform and I knew."

"How'd he react?"

"He denied everything, said he'd been sleeping in his room the whole night."

"Was he playacting?"

She hesitated and then shook her head. "That's the funny part. I don't think he was. At first, I was furious. I thought he was lying. But then I could see that he really didn't remember. I told him again that I'd been there, that I'd seen him, so he could just stop with the charade."

Sheila tensed. "Then his attitude changed. He got all self-righteous.

How dare I follow him! A woman is supposed to trust her husband, and so on. Now that, I think, was the act."

"What do you mean?"

"Well, I don't think he cared about me following him. I think he cared about what I saw. There was this fear in his eyes and I think he was a little stunned. Anyway, I just let him talk. After a while, my silence got to him. He quieted down and asked me what I was going to do. Was I was going to leave him? That's what it all boiled down to. Goodness knows, I had plenty of reason. The answer should've been obvious. But it wasn't.

"I told him I didn't know. I'll never forget the look on his face when I said that. He sank down on the edge of our bed, and all that beauty, all that joy I'd seen in his eyes when he was performing, it just went away. He aged right before my eyes, and that's when I knew. I knew why he'd married me, and I knew that none of it mattered—that I was going to stay."

"I don't know many women who would've made the choice you did. I'm not sure I would've."

"I'm so ashamed."

"Don't be." I put a comforting hand over her clenched hands. "You've got to be one of the most generous women I've ever met."

Her eyes full of gratitude, Sheila managed a smile. "Thank you. But me, generous? I don't know about that. I love him. It would've been harder to leave than to stay. Leaving him meant facing my people. I felt sick just thinking about it. I chose the easy way out." She paused. "At least, I thought I had. But it didn't turn out to be so easy, did it? After that, I thought I understood his parents better, why they'd watched us so closely. They knew he had a problem. They knew this could happen."

"Did you try to talk to them about it?"

"I didn't know how . . . No, I was afraid to."

It turned out that the Bernards had their son under tight-fisted control. During the day, at least, he couldn't do a thing without their permission, or spend a dime without their say-so.

"But they must have known that he was tipping out at night."

"Not specifically, no." She hesitated. "I think they suspected it would happen. Maybe they didn't realize when it did."

I found that hard to imagine. How can you not be aware that your son is slipping out of your house every evening? Junior had to be at the Cinnamon Club by eight o'clock at the latest. The Bernards would've still been up at that time. Surely, they must've seen or heard him leaving. I pointed that out.

"You're probably right. Like I said, I didn't have the nerve to talk to them about it. And, to be honest, something about them frightened me. I thought I might lose Junior if I said something. They'd secretly hoped I could fix him, keep him home at night. Well, obviously, I hadn't done that. I know it doesn't make sense, but I was scared."

Actually, I could understand.

"They clamped down on us," Sheila said. "At first, it was subtle. Then it grew more noticeable—or maybe I just became more aware of it, more willing to believe what my senses were telling me."

"So, the kidnapping, it was supposed to be the solution?"

She nodded.

"Whose idea was it?"

"Junior's. Believe me, I never would've come up with something like this on my own. But Junior's smart and, well, one day he decided he just couldn't take it anymore."

"Did something specific happen to tick him off?"

"It had been building for a long time and one morning, he woke up and the plan was just there, fully formed in his head. He didn't mention it to me right then, of course. Only later, after he'd walked around with it, turning it over, polishing it. As a matter of fact, he said he didn't intend to tell me at all. He wasn't sure I'd go along with it, and he was afraid I'd give him away. But then he realized he'd need my help."

"You mean, he didn't trust his parents to follow the kidnapper's orders. He wanted someone on the inside who could tell him what they were doing."

She gave a wan smile. Junior also figured they needed an expert, some-one who could make the kidnapping seem real. "He knew somebody. Called him Olmo. No last name. Funny name for a black guy. Always made me think of somebody Swedish or something."

The plan was simple, she said, or started out that way. Junior was supposed to just disappear. He didn't want a big show of violence, of him being grabbed and pulled into a car, for example, because then there would be witnesses, and witnesses would call the cops.

"How did that evolve into what really happened?"

"I don't know. No one was supposed to get hurt. No one. It was all supposed to be clean and quiet. We'd get the dough, pay Olmo, go off, and be free." Her voice was heavy with regret. "It all seems so stupid now, stupid and naïve."

I couldn't disagree with her there. "How much did you offer this character?"

"Two thousand."

"And you were going to touch his parents for twenty? Didn't you two figure that this guy might pull a double-cross, make a grab for more, if not the whole thing?"

"We just didn't think. And it was Junior who set the numbers, not me."

"His parents, his plan, his numbers."

"He said his mom and dad could well afford it. I mean, two thousand doesn't sound like a lot compared to twenty. I give you that. But Junior felt like he'd earned that money. This whole thing was his way of forcing his parents to give him his inheritance early."

"And then you two were going to run off together?"

She nodded. "I know. It was dumb. Real dumb."

I could've said a lot of things, but chose not to. She was punishing herself enough already. "The important thing now is to locate Junior, because your fake kidnapping has become very real. Did you ever meet Olmo?"

"Nope, never did. The night it happened, Junior kissed me and left the house. He said the next thing I'd hear or see of him would be the ransom note. Olmo would be arranging the drop and I was to carry it out."

"And where was Junior going to stay?"

"He wouldn't tell me. He said it was best if I knew as little as possible, sort of like in the military. Everybody on a mission only knows their part."

"But suppose something went wrong. Didn't he think about you having enough information to back him up?"

"He didn't think anything would go wrong. Said that if he started thinking that way, he might lose his nerve. And he trusted this guy Olmo."

"Did he mention contacting me, or that he'd decided to have a big, splashy kidnapping instead of a small, quiet one?" I failed to keep the sarcasm out of my voice. Sheila flinched and I could've kicked myself. The last thing this child needed was to be judged.

"No," she mumbled. "He didn't say anything about it, nothing at all."

"All right," I sighed. "So the kidnapping goes down. What was supposed to happen next?"

"He was going to let a couple of days go by, just long enough for his parents to start getting worried. Junior had fairly regular habits: he'd stay out late every night but he'd always come home in the morning."

"So when he didn't show up, they would notice."

Sheila nodded.

"How did you hear about what really happened?"

"The radio. It was on the news. I couldn't believe it. All those people killed. I kept thinking, *My Junior can't be behind that*."

She decided that Olmo must've talked Junior into staging the kidnapping in public to scare his parents and make them take it seriously. But the killings went beyond that. The killings convinced her that something had gone really wrong.

The first call came early. Instead of two days after the kidnapping, it came that night.

"I didn't take the call," Sheila said. "Phyllis Bernard did. You could see the shock on her face. Dr. Bernard yanked the phone away from her and took it himself."

The plan was for Olmo to demand the money and give them a deadline for getting it together.

"Junior always said that all his parents would need was two hours at the bank, and that he didn't want to give them more than that. We needed to keep up the pressure, he said. But then something else went wrong: Dr. Bernard refused to pay. How did he know if they really had his son? Mrs. Bernard was horrified. I was stunned. I'd never thought— It never occurred to me that he wouldn't pay."

I supposed it hadn't occurred to Junior, either.

"Dr. Bernard demanded proof," Sheila continued. "He told them that he wasn't going to move until that proof arrived."

And it had, the next night, on my doorstep.

I grimaced at the memory. Sheila and Junior had made a bad mistake, hiring a gangster and thinking they could control him. I just hoped Junior would survive.

Sheila had talked herself dry. We settled down to wait.

When I think back to that night, that's what I remember: the wait, the hours going on forever, sitting in that car, freezing. The telephone on the corner never rang and no one approached us. Only two souls walked past; neither one paused or seemed to give us a second thought. So, at the stroke of midnight, we returned to the Mercer Hotel. We hoped that Olmo would still contact us. Fearing the worst, we avoided talking about what the kid-napper's silence meant.

Once in our room, Sheila became increasingly nervous. "Miss Price?"

"Yes?"

"When all this is over, when Junior comes home, what do you think will happen? With the police, I mean. It was that other man who killed all those people. You don't think the police will blame Junior, do you? They can't do that. He didn't even know the man was going to do that, else he never would've followed through with it."

I tried to keep her calm. "It's better to just focus on the here and now, on getting Junior back."

"Oh Jesus," she whispered. "How could this happen?"

I didn't know what to tell her. "Try to . . . try to keep the faith."

"What do you think Olmo's doing to him?"

I remained silent.

"If only I could take it all back!"

I sat down next to her, put an arm around her, and drew her to me. I rocked her as she cried. Eventually, she fell asleep. I tucked her in and tip-toed toward the window. The cold night air was clear all the way down the avenue, and I could see the twinkling lights of moving cars. Junior was out there. Somewhere.

What would we do in the morning? Sheila wouldn't want to leave. She'd want to wait for word from the kidnapper. I could understand that. If I were in her place, I'd wait too.

My thoughts circled back to that last set of instructions. Why weren't they there? Why hadn't Olmo left them? Suppose he had. Suppose someone else had found them, mistaken them for garbage perhaps, or a kids' game, and removed them. Olmo wouldn't know that. He'd think we ignored him. If that was the case, then Junior could be paying the price for it right now.

I forced myself to settle down. I'd probably have to stay with Sheila in the morning. Sam would be worried sick, so I'd have to get a message to him. By now the Bernards were probably up in arms as well. They had to have realized that Sheila was gone with the money. They might have even surmised the truth. Or worse, jumped to the conclusion that Sheila, the stranger, the interloper, had simply taken the money and run.

What a mess.

I don't know how long I sat there worrying. My thoughts went in circles. I reached no conclusions, just went over the same territory again and again. I slept lightly, fitfully. In the hours before dawn, I awoke to the sound of Sheila weeping softly. There was no more sleep for me that night. While she cried, I gazed out the window, wondering.

What next?

CHAPTER 29

I watched the sky lighten and turn gray. I glanced at my watch. Eight o'clock. Sheila was still in bed, curled on one side, the worn blue blanket drawn to her chin. I got up and stretched. Man, I felt stiff. Everything ached, especially my lower back, from hours of sitting in the cold and nodding off in the chair.

Yawning, I grabbed soap and a towel out of my suitcase, then left the room and headed down the hall to the bathroom. Most of the denizens of the hotel were still sleeping. You could hear them snoring through the thin doors.

The bathroom was cold. Frigid air rushed in through an open, narrow window. Despite the fresh air, the bathroom stank of urine and clogged pipes; the once-white tiled floors were grimy, and a fat water bug crawled lazily along one wall. The toilet lacked a seat and the bowl carried some substantial flecks and stains. I decided not to use it.

Outside, someone treaded heavily down the hall. There was a knock on a door, sharp and insistent. Some sleepy female guest, sounding puzzled and dazed, answered. Whatever passed next was lost to me as I turned on the water, waited for it to go from rusty brown to clear, and dipped my hands in it to wash my face. As I cleaned up, I tried to figure out what Sheila and I should do.

One thing I had to do was call Sam. That was for sure. Perhaps Mercer had a phone. And I had to get a message to the Bernards.

Throwing my towel over one shoulder, I made my way back to the room. I could see from a distance that the door to our room was ajar. My heart sank.

"Sheila?"

I ran the last couple of steps, kicked the door wide open, and rushed inside. The bed was unmade and empty. Sheila's small weekend bag was there, but she was gone and so was the satchel carrying the money.

A slip of paper rested in the folds of the sheet. This note was typewritten and smeared with blood: *Ditch Price. Come downstairs. Bring the dough. Now.*

I pounded down the stairs and out the hotel's front door. No sign of Sheila. No cars parked out front with a passenger. No sign of a struggle. Nothing.

I ran back inside. Mercer herself was on duty. I slapped the note on the desk and shoved it under her nose. "Did you deliver this?"

Mercer arched an eyebrow as if she just knew I hadn't spoken to her in that tone. "Maybe."

"Who gave it to you?"

She shrugged. "Can't say. Got a bad memory, you know? Gets that way with the stress and strain and all. So many people. So many probl—"

"Yes, yes, I get it!"

I raced upstairs, realizing to my horror that I'd left the door wide open. I prayed that my purse was still there. It was. I snatched it up, returned to Mercer, and pulled out a fiver. I grabbed her fat hand and pressed the bill into it.

"Now, tell me."

Mercer unfolded the bill, scrunched up her mouth in disappointment, then shrugged and pocketed the money. "It was a gentleman. Very nicely dressed. Said he'd wait for her outside, and he did. She come right down fast after getting that note, so she must've wanted to see him, don't you think?"

Shit. "You got a pay phone?"

"That'll be a quarter up front."

Highway robbery, but I paid. She dragged a phone from under her desk, put it on the counter, and shoved it toward me.

I moved the phone a bit further away, turned my back on her, and made the call.

Sam answered on the first ring. "Delaney."

"It's me."

"Lanie! Where have you been? Blackie and I have been looking all over for you."

In short, terse sentences, I filled him in on the letter Sheila received, the further instructions, her confession that the kidnapping was a fake, and what had happened that morning.

"She's gone," I concluded. "And she took the ransom with her, all of it."

"Shit."

I braced for what I knew would come next.

"Why didn't you tell me what you were doing?" I started to answer, but he cut me off. "Don't bother. It's obvious."

"I've got to call Blackie," I said. "You were right. I should've done that to begin with."

"Let me take care of it. You go home."

I took another step away from Mercer and forced myself to lower my voice. "I can't go home. I have to get over to the Bernards and explain everything."

"You'll do no such thing. Lanie, you're too close. You said the Bernards don't even know about the second letter. By now they must have realized that Sheila's vanished, but they don't know why. And they know the money's gone too. Last thing we need is for you to arrive and tell them what's happened."

"I'm the best person to make them understand—"

"Understand what? That you let Sheila walk into a trap?"

"I *let*—"

"That's how they're going to see it. They're going to blame you, maybe even hold the paper responsible. They're certainly not going to talk to you."

"I'm the one person they might talk to."

"Only to call you every name in the book." His voice was hurried, intense. "Anything they might say will be colored by their reaction to you personally. Go home."

"But—"

"Back. Off."

CHAPTER 30

Strivers' Row appeared to be an oasis of tranquility in the seething urban sea around it. But that was only an appearance. There was one household, at least, where nothing was quiet, where emotions were in turmoil and the occupants clinging to their sanity. The news I had to deliver wouldn't make it any easier.

By the time I returned to Strivers', I'd calmed down somewhat. I understood Sam's motives. His instinct was to protect me from the pain of the Bernards and the fury of the police. But it was wrong to hide. I had walked into this mess knowing the danger, and I wasn't going to leave it to someone else to clean up.

The good doctor must've been watching the street. He opened the door before I could even knock.

"Where is she?"

"I don't know."

"But she told you something, didn't she? She likes you."

"I like her too."

He was furious and disgusted and obviously tempted to slam the door in my face, but common sense prevailed. He stepped aside and let me in.

Phyllis Bernard was sitting on the living room sofa, in pretty much the same spot I had last seen her. She even wore the same dress, an indication perhaps of her emotional state.

I started with Sheila's call, relating that she'd gotten another letter. I told them everything except Sheila's admission that the kidnapping was a fake. I suspected they already realized this, but I wasn't ready for them to know that I also knew.

"I suppose you've told the police," Dr. Bernard said.

"They're being informed as we speak."

His voice was cold with repressed fury. "Thank you for doing everything possible to destroy our last chance of saving our so—" He caught himself.

"Your what? Your *son?*"

There was the faintest change in his eyes.

"It's time to stop the pretending," I said.

"I don't know what you're talking about."

"Sure you do."

Telling lies was a reflex in this family. He even managed to make his eyes flash with righteous anger. "You want to talk about pretending?" He wagged a finger at me. "How about pretending that the money's not all gone. All of it. Every single mother-loving dime. How about pretending that the girl wasn't in on it."

"What?"

He advanced toward me. "And while we're at it, let's pretend that you're not in on it either."

I don't want to admit it, but he got to me. He got to me so bad I wanted to smack him. Me, a peace-loving person. I put a fist on my hip.

"I'm not even going dignify that nonsense about me, but I will say this: I know you're not talking about Sheila. That girl loves your boy. Yes, your boy. Don't give me that look. I know all about it. It was your boy behind all this. He lied and faked his own kidnapping—and got a whole lot of people shot while doing it."

I've got to give it to him: he didn't back down. He was one of the most committed liars I'd ever met.

"Leave," he hissed. "Get out. Right now, or else I'm—"

The doorbell rang and we all jumped. Then came a hard, rapid knock. Dr. Bernard strode to the window and peeped out. I could've told him not to bother.

"It's some white guy," he said.

"Probably a salesman," his wife said.

"More likely a cop," I said. "They always show up at the worst time. You can ignore him, but he's not going away."

The knocking came again, harder this time, insistent. Dr. Bernard cursed under his breath and went to answer. Phyllis Bernard and I were suddenly alone. We studied each other with wary eyes.

From the hallway came the sound of Dr. Bernard and the Irish brogue that told me it was Blackie. There was the sound of a door closing, but no footsteps came down the hall. The two men must've stepped outside.

In the parlor, the silence between Phyllis and me stretched out. Then it occurred to me that I hadn't said one of the most important but useless things one can say in a situation as dismal as this.

"I'm sorry," I said, "very sorry, that these things have happened. But there's still hope—"

"Sheila." Her voice was merely a whisper, but it was heavy with loathing. "That little tramp. I knew she was trouble the minute I laid eyes on her. I knew it."

I blinked. "Excuse me?"

She pounded her knee. "We could've handled him. We could've worked it out, but no . . ." She shook her head. "She had to go and put the notion of a kidnapping into his head. He wouldn't have gone and done something like this on his own. Only someone like her would think we're rich. Shows you the kind of people she's from."

While I never fully bought the image of the kindly, genteel doctor's wife, I had never suspected this. Not this.

She caught my expression. "You've got to understand something. My husband and I . . . we have scraped and scrimped our whole lives to get what we have. And we're this much away from losing it." She held up a thumb and index finger barely an inch apart.

"We had to mortgage this house to raise the money. My husband didn't want to. This house represents just about everything we have, so no, he didn't want to do it. He hoped the kidnappers would be happy with what cash we had. But they weren't, so I pushed him."

She shook her head. "Damn Junior for getting involved with crooks and gangsters. How could he have been so stupid? First to marry that little wench, and now this!" She drew a deep breath. "We should've stuck to our guns. We were going to let him stew in his own juices, but after that horrible package arrived, we—I just couldn't. I had to do something. So, I pushed Alfred to go to the bank, and now . . ." She burst into sobs. "It's gone. Everything we have. Gone."

She was weeping over the lost money, the lost house, not the lost son. I disagreed with what Junior had done, but now I had an inkling of why he'd done it.

The front door opened and a cool breeze swept down the hallway. Seconds later, Dr. Bernard came in, Blackie right behind him. The detective paused at seeing me. Annoyance and frustration flashed across his face. Then he donned that professional mask again as Dr. Bernard introduced his wife.

"I'm very sorry to hear what you folks have been going through," Blackie told her. "I know from speaking to your husband that Miss Price here," he flicked a lethal glance at me, "has informed you of what's happened, that both your daughter and the ransom money have disappeared." He gave me another frosty glare, one that clearly said to keep my mouth shut. Then he continued to speak to them. His voice stayed moderate, his tone sympathetic, but an edge crept into it. "I wish you'd come to us, but I understand why you didn't."

"We were so frightened," Phyllis Bernard said, sounding sweet and vulnerable again.

Blackie nodded. "Yes, well, why don't you start at the beginning? Tell me—"

"Excuse me. I don't mean to be disrespectful," Dr. Bernard said, "but we don't have time for talking. Somewhere, somebody out there has got all our money. I need to know what you're going to do about it."

"I assure you," Blackie said, "we're already on it. You'd be helping us by sharing what the kidnappers have said to you." He paused. "And I'd like to see the box."

"The box?" Dr. Bernard repeated.

"Yes, the cigar box . . . with *everything* that was in it."

Dr. Bernard shot me another furious look. Clearly, he did not want to comply, but there was no getting out of it. He slowly stalked out of the room.

"Poor Sheila," Phyllis Bernard said. "Why would they take her?"

My lips tightened at her hypocrisy. It took all of my restraint not to say something.

"As extra insurance," Blackie replied, "in case something should go wrong."

"Something like what?" she wailed. "They got their blood money. We've given them what they asked for."

"Trust me. We'll know soon enough," Blackie said.

Dr. Bernard returned with the cigar box and handed it to Blackie. The detective lifted the lid, glanced at the severed finger, then opened the letter, keeping his face devoid of expression. He spoke without looking up.

"Dr. and Mrs. Bernard, when did you realize that the kidnapping was a fake?"

Bless Blackie. His question hit home. Dr. Bernard looked as though he'd been punched. He glanced at me, as if I were to blame for all their troubles, before turning to his now silent wife.

Dr. Bernard composed himself. "From the start, but we were wrong."

Blackie peered up. "I'm listening."

"My son, Junior, he's been after us for his money, his inheritance. I told him he couldn't have it, that he'd have to wait. Then all of a sudden this kidnapping happened. It was too much of a coincidence. So, when the kidnappers called, I told him them we weren't having it, that we knew it was a hoax, just Junior trying to get his money. Later I changed my mind."

"This cigar box did that?" Blackie said.

Dr. Bernard nodded.

Suddenly, the shrill ring of the phone cut through the room. Blackie pointed to the receiver, then said, "If it's him, get him to talk. Make friendly."

Dr. Bernard snatched up the telephone and Blackie moved in close to listen in. From where I was standing I could pick up that it was a male voice, but I couldn't catch any words. Next thing I knew, Dr. Bernard had handed the phone to Blackie.

The detective listened intently. Whatever he was hearing made him turn toward me.

"I'll be there," he said, and hung up. "Dr. Bernard, I have to go, but I'll be back to—"

"Was that about Sheila?" Dr. Bernard asked. "Or the money?"

"I'm sorry. I can't say more. Miss Price, you'll come with me."

I could feel Phyllis Bernard's eyes on my back as I left the room. She stayed in the parlor as Dr. Bernard came up behind us. He didn't exactly escort us to the door, but he most certainly slammed it behind us.

CHAPTER 31

Blackie held the door for me and I slid into the front passenger seat of the unmarked car. Then he went around the other side, started the engine, and pulled into traffic. All without saying a word.

"Where are we going?" I asked.

"You'll see."

"Come on, Blackie, tell me."

"Pipe down, Lanie. You're on thin ice already."

Okaaay. After a minute, I started counting backward. "Ten . . . nine . . . eight . . . seven . . ."

"What're you doing?"

"Counting down till your explosion. It's due any second now."

He started to answer, then swallowed it. But when we stopped at a red light, he couldn't hold it in anymore. "You should've known better!"

I didn't try to defend myself. Deep down, I agreed.

"I know you feel sorry for the Bernards," he began. "But they're not the only ones who've got a stake in this mess. There are other families—and I don't just mean the Harvard kid's either. I mean all the folks of the people who got blown away." He rubbed his chin. "Shit!" He pounded the steering wheel.

I dared pose a question. I knew it was bothering him because it was bothering me. "Are you going to tell the victims' families that the kidnapping was a fake, that their people died because of a family feud?"

He didn't answer right away. "Eventually. Maybe. But right now, I got something else to do."

The intersection of West 135th Street and Lenox Avenue formed a wide quadrangle, with two-way traffic flowing both north-south and east-west. Some people called this vehicular nexus the heart of Harlem. Maybe it was. If so, its arterial flow had come to a halt.

Hundreds of onlookers crowded the sidewalks, held back by police officers with truncheons. The focus of their attention was a huddled mass in the middle of the intersection. Newspaper photographers jockeyed for position. Reporters screamed out questions. Seeing me, more than one yelled, "Hey, how come *she* gets to go up close?"

Blackie ignored them all. He half-knelt by the small figure lying in the middle of the road, his face expressionless. I stood next to him.

"Is it her?" he asked.

"Yeah," I answered, "it's her."

Sheila lay on her right side. Her face and chest were bloodied, her legs splayed. One arm was thrown back and bent at an impossible angle. Her skirt was caught up around her hips, her stockings ripped and dirtied. She looked exposed and vulnerable. I reached out to draw her skirt down, but Blackie stopped me with a hand on my wrist.

"Not yet. Not till the M.E.'s done and the photos are taken." He observed me curiously. "What's the matter with you? You're not acting like yourself."

"Please. It's not necessary to take pictures of her like this."

After a moment, he relented.

I arranged the skirt to restore modesty. "She deserved better." I meant that she deserved better help than I'd given her, but he took it otherwise.

"Yup. Looks like she was a sweet kid." Blackie let his gaze roam among the crowd. "Olmo, oh Olmo, where are you now, you crazy son of a bitch?"

The left side of her face was swollen and bruised. Someone had worked her over, then pushed her out of a moving car and kept on driving. But that wasn't what killed her. It was being kissed in the head by a .38.

"He put the gun right up against her skin," Blackie said.

The star-shaped hole in her forehead looked like a third eye, the skin around it puffed and blackened.

"Why'd he kill her?" I asked. "He had his money."

"Did he?"

Blackie extended his hand and a uniform who had been standing nearby passed him a bag. It was the satchel Sheila had taken from the hotel.

"He threw it out with the body." Blackie yanked the bag open.

I looked inside and saw bundles of money. "I don't understand."

He took out a bundle and rifled through it. The first layer was a genuine twenty all right, but the rest was newspaper.

"Oh no!"

"Bernard signed her death warrant when he did that. Did you know he was going to do something that stupid?"

I shook my head.

Blackie cursed under his breath. "Un-effin'-believable. Just how selfish can one man be?"

I thought of Phyllis Bernard and how she'd bewailed the loss of all their money. Was she that good an actress, or had she really not known what her husband was up to?

Blackie was also still thinking of the Bernards. "I've got to tell them," he said. "You can go back to your newsroom for the time being, but I'm trusting you to keep mum about the fake dough."

Seemed like the deeper I got into this story, the less I could write about it. "Sure. Fine."

Even though I agreed to do as he asked, something about my tone must have set him off.

"Just answer me this: what were you thinking, not saying anything about the cigar box and going up to that hotel by yourself?"

"I was thinking about doing my job."

"You're not a cop. You're a reporter."

"And a damn good one. If—"

"It never would've come to this if you'd been straight with me."

"I gave them my word."

"Well, you had no business giving it. They say the road to hell is paved with good intentions. And you just proved it."

I shut up. He was right. If I'd followed the rules and gotten backup, then Sheila wouldn't have been able to sneak out of that hotel. Someone would've been there to grab her, or follow her and the guy who did her in.

Blackie was grim. "Olmo's going to be calling the Bernards, and when he does I want you to stay out of it."

"Do you honestly expect the Bernards to tell you if he contacts them?"

"Yes, I do." He grimaced. "All right, maybe not. I hope they do. I hope with all my black Irish heart they've learned their lesson. But I doubt it." He paused. "You do know I'm going to have to call you in for another talk, don't you?"

"Why? You know everything now."

"Do I?"

I felt a flutter of unease. "What are you after?"

"The truth." His eyes met mine. "I need to know everything you've done and said since yesterday morning."

"Sounds like you're asking for an alibi."

"I can't help what it sounds like."

"You don't think I had anything to do with this, do you?"

He sighed. "All I can say is that you should be prepared to make a formal statement."

First jail, now this. If I hadn't known Blackie better, I would've said he was out to get me. But I did know him, and I knew this wasn't his style. I stepped closer and lowered my voice. "What's going on here? Cause this seems like more than flack from the brass."

"There's been an accusation."

"About what?"

"About this." He motioned toward Sheila. "That maybe you're in on it."

"What?"

"You heard me." He squinted and ruffled his hair. "You've got to admit, it does look suspicious."

"How?"

"Think about it."

"Think about what?"

He inched closer. "At every step, you were there. When the Black Orchid got nabbed, you were there. When the cigar box was delivered, you were there. And now, with this girl . . . you were there."

"They left that box on my doorstep. And she called me."

"That's what you say."

For a moment, we held each other's gaze.

"Who put the poison in your coffee?" I asked.

"Who do you think?"

Only one name came to mind. "Bernard. He's the one. He stepped outside when you came to the door."

"I want to believe you, but . . ."

"You know me. Do you actually think that I'd be involved in something like this?"

"I've got to ask—and you'd better come up with good answers."

I took a step back. "Do I need to bring a lawyer?"

"That's up to you."

All right. So we were back to playing tough. What was it about this case? It had us all at each other's throats. First Sam giving my stories to Selena; then Blackie throwing me in jail—and now accusing me of collusion with murderers and thieves. It made me feel ugly inside. It took an effort not to be bitter.

"You need me to come right now?"

"No, I have to finish up here first. In the meantime, you can go back to your newsroom, write your story, and stay away from the Bernards."

"Lanie! You-hoo! Oh, Lanie!"

The voice cut over the rest, a grating female voice that I knew all too well. I turned to see Selena Troy. She was standing on the southwest corner of the intersection. The cops were holding her back with the other reporters. She was jumping up and down, waving her steno pad and calling out to me.

I turned back to Blackie. "We done here?"

"For now. Just remember to stop by and see me later."

"Tomorrow?"

"Today. In an hour."

Message received. I took one last long hard look at Sheila. I wanted to remember. I wanted to burn this image into my brain. This was the price of well-meant but misplaced compassion. It was a lesson I would never forget. Then I went over to Selena, told her, "The answer is no."

"What d'you mean, no? I haven't asked you anything yet."

"You want me to tell them to let you through. The answer's no."

"But they let you in."

"So?"

She was fuming now. "If you don't make them let me through, I'll tell Sam."

She couldn't be that stupid. I almost felt sorry for her. Almost. "Selena, this may come as a shock to you, but I can't *make* a New York homicide dick do anything. As for telling Sam, go ahead. Tell him you don't know how to work a crime scene. Tell him you don't know how to deal with cops. You'd be doing me a favor."

"Why, you b—"

I turned and walked away. I should have thanked her: she'd given me the one and only bit of levity I was to have that day.

CHAPTER 32

I headed west, toward the newsroom. It was only a block away, but it was a long block, almost the distance of two regular city blocks. I would need the stroll to get my thoughts together, to get my feelings in line.

I felt sick inside, sick with fury. Sheila shouldn't have died that way. I was angry at myself for not having kept closer tabs on her, angry at her for being so damned naïve, angry at the dirty rat who'd killed her.

If only I'd stayed in the room with her. Or talked to Sam . . . or talked to Blackie. If only . . .

A car honked loudly. It was Selena, driving past. She slowed down just long enough to give me an ugly grin, then hit the gas. She sure was in a rush to get back to the newsroom. Of course, it was Wednesday. Maybe she just wanted to make that evening's deadline. But if it was all about beating me, then she needn't have bothered.

I mulled over my predicament. If I walked into the newsroom, then I'd have to talk to Sam, talk to the newspaper's attorney. Getting backup from a mouthpiece, that was probably the smartest thing to do. Why didn't I feel good about it? Because I knew these guys. They wouldn't be out to defend me. Their first interest would be in defending the paper, and if that meant feeding me to the lions, then that's what they'd do.

From what Blackie told me, it would be a matter of *he said, I said*. Maybe not even that. To me, it was obvious that I had nothing to do with this caper, but to others . . . I didn't have proof that the box was left at my doorstep. I didn't have proof that Sheila called me. I didn't even have the letter that prompted her call.

Everything that had led me to suspect that the kidnapping was a fake could lead others to conclude that I was in on it. That maybe I'd even helped come up with the idea so I'd have a big story to cover.

The more I thought about it, the less I liked it. It was the perfect frame, and I'd walked right into it. Dr. Bernard had always resented my involvement. He'd seen his chance to get rid of me and taken it.

Across the street was the police station. I eyed it and turned up my coat collar, my decision made. I would talk to Blackie, with or without the company lawyer. In the meantime, I would keep my mind on the story. I resumed walking.

Olmo would contact the Bernards, and when he did, they would keep quiet. Blackie was dreaming if he thought otherwise. I reached the corner and paused for a car to pass. Sheila's murder would shake them up, but it wouldn't send them to the police. If anything, it would make them more determined than ever to handle this on their own.

As I stepped off the curb, a car pulled in front of me. A smoky window rolled down and a gruff voice said, "Get in."

I froze. Then I realized that it wasn't a gun sticking out of the window, just a hand in a black glove. "Who are you? What do you want?"

I leaned down and saw the face.

"Stax?" I was stunned to see him, especially half a block away from a police station.

He opened the passenger door for me to enter. I took a step back. I was cold and frightened. But I was angry too. So angry I couldn't think straight. How did I know that Olmo wasn't working for Stax? I'd simply taken his word, hadn't I? Common sense said I should run, that I should run and call for help. Instead, I asked, "Did you kill Sheila?"

"Get. In."

My rational side told me to scream. *You're only a few feet from the police station. Scream.* But I couldn't move. "If you had anything to do with . . . I believed you. I kept my word—"

"*Get in!*" Stax hissed between gritted teeth.

I didn't move.

"I've found Olmo," he finally said.

"Olmo?"

He nodded and that did it. I glanced over my shoulder at the police station and down the street to the news office. I imagined Blackie grilling me for something I hadn't done, and Selena typing her version of my story. *I don't think so*. I climbed into the car, slammed the door shut, and sat back as the car shot away.

CHAPTER 33

Up Eighth Avenue. Across 137th Street, 138th. The blocks streaked by. My heart pounded.

Stax stared straight ahead. "We've found the hideout."

"Where is it?"

"You'll see soon enough."

"Fine. How did you know where to find me? Have you been watching me?"

He shrugged. "Watching you, watching them."

"The Bernards?"

He nodded, but his gaze stayed on the road.

"How long have you been watching them?" I asked. "Since the kidnapping?"

"Much longer than that."

"Why?"

"I make it a point to know people—and their families—before I lend them money." He shrugged, as though he was just conducting business as usual.

I didn't buy it. "So you've known Queenie's real identity all along?"

"Why should I answer that?"

"You don't have to. But don't expect me to believe that you were just trying to protect your investment. You were looking for something to use as blackmail."

He gave me a thin smile. "If you ever think about turning to a life of crime, let me know."

"What did you find out?"

He lit himself a cigarette, offered me one. I declined.

"About the Bernards," I said.

He took a long drag. "All right, I can tell you this: they're not straight shooters."

"I could have told you that."

"Well, then, you know everything."

"No, it means you didn't get anything."

Silence prevailed. Streets zipped past. I digested nothing of the receding landscape. I was trying to puzzle out Stax's sentences. I was thinking about Sheila and the terror of what she must've gone through. And I was wondering where Stax Murphy was taking me to. We reached 147th, then 148th. There the driver turned a hard right and drove two-thirds of the way down the block, past rows of brownstones.

"What's here?" I asked.

"I own some property. Olmo has a key."

The car pulled into an empty parking space. Stax and his men got out. I made to exit as well, but Stax stopped me.

"Stay here with my driver."

"But—"

"Don't make me repeat myself."

He closed the door, shutting me inside. He and his men went up to an attractive three-story brownstone. It appeared to be clean and well-kept, with wrought-iron fencing and several stained glass windows.

I watched the windows of the building, hoping to see a movement that would indicate which apartment they'd entered. I watched the clock too. Six long minutes went by. Nothing.

My gaze drifted back down to the front door. No one was going in or out. It was the middle of a cold February day. Anybody who had a job would be there. Anyone who didn't would be staying warm inside. Nobody was doing any running around that they didn't have to, not in that weather. And I thought of Sheila once more, lying on that stone-cold ground.

The front door opened and one of Stax's men emerged. He approached the car and opened the passenger door.

"Mr. Murphy says for you to come upstairs."

The building was as impressive on the inside as it was on the out. But it stank, and it did so in a very particular way. It was a smell that recalled my days of covering crime for the *Harlem Age*.

Stax's henchman led me up a finely carpeted staircase. As with most Harlem town houses, this one was originally designed for a single affluent family, but it now served as a rooming house. Each door had a number, and each was firmly closed.

As we climbed the steps, the air thickened, the stench grew richer. By the second floor, my lungs were starving for air. I realized that I was holding my breath. I closed my eyes and forced myself to inhale. The stink was incredible, but breathing normally was the only way to get past it. After a while the body adjusts.

We hit the third-floor landing and approached a door at the back of the hallway. Stax's man opened it. I stepped inside and the full power of the smell nearly knocked me off my feet. Stax stood gazing out the window, smoking a cigarette. He didn't turn around at the sound of my entrance.

The room was filthy with empty food containers and old newspapers. It stank of Chinese food and dried pizza and that certain something else. There was a dirty white sofa, two battered wooden chairs, and a small kitchen table to the left. There was a mattress on the floor to the right. It had a torn, gray sheet, and a man lay on it. He was dark-haired and darkly dressed: black pants, black shirt, and black jacket.

He was also dead.

"Come in," Stax said.

I felt the henchman's hand against my back. I tentatively walked in toward the dead man, heard the door close behind me.

He was on his side, back to the wall, facing the room. He was gagged, his wrists and ankles bound behind his back. His eyes were open and clouded over, his skin gray. A wide stain of dried blood darkened the mattress under his head and neck. His throat had been slit. A grimy makeshift bandage covered his left hand. His face showed bite marks; rodents had been at him.

Even so, I recognized him. "Olmo."

Stax nodded. "Been dead for days." He threw down the cigarette, ground it out. "Days," he repeated in disgust.

My thoughts raced. Olmo must've died right after the kidnapping. Who killed him? If he was dead, then who sent the notes, made the phone calls? Some third partner? And where was Queenie?

But then I knew. With chilling certainty, the answer came and I knew.

Stax turned to face me. "Well, come on, Miss Price. I didn't bring you here to just stand around. I want to hear what you have to say, to know what you're going to write."

"Olmo's hand. I need to see it."

"His hand?"

I nodded.

Puzzled and suspicious, Stax looked from me to the body. He made a gesture and the henchman went to work.

The bandage was nothing more than a long strip torn from the bed-sheet, but it was stiff with dried blood. The henchman had to pry it off. When he was done, we could all see that the ring finger of Olmo's left hand was missing: it had been cut off at the base.

"But who did this?" Stax gaped. "And why?"

He didn't know about the cigar box. Now I told him. He was furious.

"Whoever did this, I'll kill them." He squatted down next to his nephew's body, touched the injured hand with surprising gentleness. "Why?" he asked the dead man. "Why did you do it? And what conniving bastard did you listen to?"

CHAPTER 34

The answer was right before his eyes, but he didn't know enough to recognize it. Sam and I had wondered whether Olmo had brought in someone to help him, someone to drive the getaway car, for example. But that hadn't been the case at all. Olmo hadn't needed extra help. He'd had all he needed in his main partner, his "victim." And that partner had betrayed him—had cut off his finger, shoved that yellow ring on it, and put it in a cigar box.

We'd all been played for suckers—and Queenie had done the playing.

I hesitated to tell Stax the truth about the kidnapping. It worried me how he'd react, but seeing his grief, his bewilderment, I decided he had a right to know. The look in his eyes turned murderous.

"Why, that conniving son of a bitch!"

"Don't go after him."

"Why not?"

"You kill him and the cops will be convinced you were behind the kidnapping. As far as they're concerned, Queenie's still the victim. They know he thought up the kidnapping, but they think it was Olmo who did the double cross and made it real. They don't know it's still fake and that Queenie's pulling the strings."

He spoke with contempt. "You think I care about the cops? I don't give a damn about them! I'm going to find that son of a bitch and—"

"No, don't! Or at least . . ." I thought fast. "Give me a day. Just twenty-four hours. That's all I ask."

"Why should I? What the hell do you think you can do in a day?"

I worried my lower lip. I didn't have an answer, so I stalled. "Just give it to me and you'll see."

Downstairs, we climbed into the car and sat in preoccupied silence as Stax's men drove us back to 135th Street. I thought about Queenie, about what he wanted. He'd put that cigar box in front of my door. He'd wanted me on this case, had wanted me to know about him and his family. But he'd wanted something else too—the money. It meant as much to him as the revelation about his true identity. Sooner or later, he'd come back looking for it, and I was betting on sooner rather than later. We would have to be ready for him. That's all: we'd have to be good and ready.

It was after five when we pulled up in front of the newspaper building. I was about to climb out when Stax laid a hand on my forearm.

"Remember," he said, "a day and that's all."

It felt like a heavy hand had gripped my heart, squeezed it. I got out and closed the door.

Stax leaned out of his car. "I don't understand," he said. "About Queenie, really, what do you care?"

In the face of his cold anger, I couldn't answer. He smiled grimly and tipped his hat as though I'd just proved his point, then he signaled his man, rolled up his window, and drove away.

I stood there for a moment, blind to my surroundings and sick with dread. *Why indeed?*

I didn't see how Queenie was going to come out of this alive. Did it really matter whether he died with cement shoes in the East River, in a hail of coppers' bullets, or in the electric chair up at Sing Sing?

He'd be dead no matter what.

But the manner of his death, yes, it did matter.

I started toward the newspaper building. Queenie had a right to tell his side of the story and instinct said there was more to that story than just greed. Why was it so important to him that I know about his ties to the Bernards? And why had he chosen this oblique way of telling me? He could've just said something when we were sitting in the Cinnamon Club. Why hadn't he? Was it because the place was too loud, too chaotic?

I paused at the building's entrance. How was I going to present all this to Sam? By now, Blackie must have told him about Dr. Bernard accusing me of being in cahoots with the kidnppers. Then I'd gone and probably made the situation worse by disappearing. Some people might've thought I was running away. For all I knew, someone might've even seen me get into Stax's car.

Now I was back with a wild story about the main kidnapper being dead and Queenie being the one who killed him—full of details about him having slit the man's throat not in self-defense, but as part of some cold-blooded plan that I still didn't fully understand.

I could just hear Sam now. *You know I'm in your corner, but do you realize how this looks? I want to work with you, baby, but where's the body? Where's the proof?* I had no proof, only suspicions. And there would be no body. I was fairly certain that Stax's men had started removing Olmo's remains the moment we left the building. They would make sure it was gone, for good.

A car honked in the distance. I glanced up at the sound of it and saw Sam. He'd already left work; he was down the block, standing there at the corner.

The light changed and he stepped off the curb.

I hurried after him, calling out his name. "Sam!"

He didn't hear me.

"Sam! Wait!" I ran down the street after him.

He was three-quarters of the way across, really only a few steps from his front door, when the laundry truck came out of nowhere. One minute the wide vista of 135th was clear. The next, there was this black truck with the words *Tic-Tac-Toe Laundry* painted in bright orange letters on its side. It came barreling down the street, jerking right and left as though the driver had lost control.

And there was Sam, directly in its path.

He walked with his head bent, his hands stuffed into his pants pockets, his shoulders hunched against the cold. He was deep in thought, but some instinct must have made him look up. Perhaps it was a slight shift in the shadows, or the merest vibrations under his feet. It could've even been my voice; although it seemed to me that it had frozen in my throat.

Whatever alarm went off, he did peer up. For the rest of my life, I will remember his expression. He had maybe half a second to react, just enough time to register that he might be about to die. He could've taken a step forward, toward the sidewalk, in an attempt to save his life. In all probability, it would've been futile, but he could've tried. Instead, he turned back—to look at me.

Our eyes met. In that moment, I saw his love for me and recognized my misgivings for what they truly were: the simple fear of loving him and losing him the way I'd lost Hamp.

For a moment, my heart stopped beating.

In that same instant, the truck struck him down.

CHAPTER 35

The doors to Harlem Hospital's emergency room banged open. A doctor and two nurses ran alongside Sam and shoved the gurney carrying him into an examining room.

They let me hover on the periphery while a team worked on Sam. Then a nurse drew me aside to get his information. When I looked back, I saw them rushing him out of the room. I tried to follow after them, but the nurse held me back.

"Where are they taking him?" I pleaded.

"To surgery."

"But—"

"The best thing you can do to help is to tell us what you know about him. His medical history."

I fell silent. It hit me once again just how little I knew about Sam. They'd evidently mistaken me for his wife. I was being given a chance to help him in a way I couldn't help my husband—but I was at a loss. The irony of it all struck me.

The next three hours were a nightmare.

The impact had thrown Sam into the air and over the truck. He landed on the sidewalk, inches from the jutting points of an iron fence. If he'd struck that, he would've been impaled and surely died. Instead, he hit the ground hard, on his right side.

I reached him within seconds. He was conscious but dazed, his face covered in blood. "Sam! Oh God, Sam!"

He was barely responsive. His breathing was shallow, his body contorted.

"Sam, please . . . please, hold on."

I could feel him slipping away. I looked up, screamed, "Somebody, please! Get help! Please!" I grabbed his hand. "Sam, stay with me. It's Lanie. I'm right here. I'm not going anywhere." I caressed his face and leaned down to whisper in his ear. "I love you. I love you so very much. Don't leave me. *Please!*"

Don Hollyer, the owner and driver of the truck, would later tell police that he'd been distracted because he had been wrestling with his German shepherd, King, over the remains of a ham sandwich. Hollyer was trying to shove the dog away from the sandwich when he struck Sam.

"It was really a very good sandwich," Hollyer would say, "made of Black Forest ham." He told police that he thought he'd hit a large dog until he saw me running toward the twisted body.

The nurse urged me to use the bathroom to clean up. Standing over the sink, I held my trembling hands under the running faucet and watched Sam's blood swirl down the drain. My reflection in the mirror revealed blood smears on my cheeks, and I felt sick with fear and guilt.

I returned to the waiting room, stomach knotted, mind churning. *You distracted him when he was crossing the street. If you hadn't called out to him, if—*

"Lanie!"

I looked up to see Blackie hurrying toward me; George Ramsey was right behind him. I stood up to receive them.

"I came as soon as I heard."

"I don't believe this. Are you all right?"

I assured them that I was. Then Selena Troy and George Greene showed up too, as did other staffers from the newsroom. All had heard different versions of what happened. I told them what I'd seen.

"I distracted him," I said, "calling out to him when he was crossing the street."

"My God, Lanie, you don't think this is your fault?" Blackie shook his head. "Don't do that to yourself."

Ramsey weighed in, his voice gruff: "Where's Sam? What's going on with him?"

"That's just it. I don't know. I've been waiting and nobody's come out to say anything."

A moment later, the door behind us opened and an exhausted-looking doctor walked in. He made straight for me.

"Are you here about Sam Delaney?"

"Yes, how is he? Please tell us something."

He introduced himself as Dr. Maynard. He was in his mid-thirties, had soft brown eyes and a five o'clock shadow.

"He was very lucky," the doctor explained. "He must've turned slightly at the last moment. If he hadn't, we would've lost him."

He turned to see me. And that might've actually saved his life?

Maynard told us that Sam's right leg, below the knee, had been broken in three places. "We had to operate to relieve the pressure caused by the shattered bone, so blood could flow into his lower leg. Otherwise, there was a risk of amputation. His right knee cracked down the middle. We're also working with fractures of his right hip." It sounded horrible.

He's alive, I told myself. *Just be grateful that he's alive.*

"Is he awake?" I asked. "Can I speak with him?"

"No," Maynard's face changed. The change was subtle, but it was there. "Not yet."

"What are you not telling me?"

He didn't answer, but I recognized his expression. I'd been a doctor's wife too long not to.

"Don't treat me like a child," I said. "Tell me exactly what's going on."

So he did.

When he was done, I had only one question: "Where is he?"

CHAPTER 36

Dr. Maynard said that only one of us could go in to see Sam, and then for no more than five minutes. The others agreed to let me visit. Sam was in intensive care and in a small room by himself. The skin around his large frame seemed to have shrunken. His head was thickly bandaged, as was his pelvic area, and his right leg was in traction. His complexion was grayed and waxen. His lips seemed bloodless and his bones jutted out sharply.

Tears slipped unheeded from my eyes. I wanted to say something, anything, but my throat had closed. I took his hand, which was cool and so very limp. Where was the warmth, the strength that was so much a part of him? All thoughts of Junior and Sheila, of the Bernards and their horrible accusations—they all went away. All my emotions were for Sam.

All too soon a nurse appeared to shoo me from the room.

"Wait a minute," I said.

I held Sam's hand against my cheek, kissed it, and laid it gently back at his side. Then I bent to kiss his unresponsive lips before returning to the waiting room. Blackie, Ramsey, and the others were still there. All eyes turned toward me with expectation.

"He's very weak," I told them.

They looked stricken. Selena's makeup was tear-streaked. George Greene's eyes were wide behind his glasses. As for Ramsey and Blackie, they wore expressions I had never seen on them before. It took me a moment to realize that these were expressions of not only pain, but helplessness. They were men of action and decision, and here they were confronted with a situation in which they could do nothing.

Observing their faces, I suddenly remembered. "Blackie, Mr. Ramsey, I have to speak with you . . . alone."

A new edge to the worry appeared in their eyes.

I turned to the others. "It's good that you came. Sam would appreciate it, but he'd also say there's nothing you can do. George," I said, "your baby could arrive any minute. Sam would want you at home with your wife."

He hesitated. "Are you sure?"

"Yes, of course. It's okay."

He gave me an awkward hug, then a nod of acknowledgment to the small gathering, before walking quickly away.

"Lanie," Selena chimed in, "I'm sorry." She appeared genuinely distraught. "I mean it, I apologize for all of it." She glanced at Ramsey, then Blackie, then back at me. "You'll tell Sam I was here?"

I said I would, then she too departed. One by one, the others left.

I sat on one of the benches and gestured for Ramsey and Blackie to join me. I began by describing what happened when I left Blackie at 125th Street, recounting how Stax Murphy picked me up. Both men listened, stone-faced, as I explained how Stax had taken me to Olmo's body. I described how one of Olmo's fingers was cut off and what it meant.

To my surprise, when I finished, Ramsey took my hand and said, "You've done a fine job."

Blackie looked as though he had a lot to add, none of it as complimentary, but didn't know where to begin. I sensed that he was holding his tongue only because of the circumstances involving Sam. When he did speak, it was to advise me to go home and get some rest. "There's nothing you can do here."

Ramsey agreed. Blackie said he would stop by the Bernards and tell them about Olmo.

"It's not really the kind of news that'll bring them comfort," I said.

"No, it won't, but it's a step in the right direction."

"They might not even want Junior found."

"True, but that's not up to them. Their son's a killer, and it's my job to bring him in."

"No matter what he's done, they won't help you."

"Probably not. But I'm going to talk to them anyway."

Chapter 37

I did go home, briefly, to change clothes. The temperature had dropped with the setting sun and snow was falling. Not the fluffy flakes of a winter's dreamtime, but the small pelting kind akin to hail. By morning, there would be ice on the ground.

Standing on my front steps, I glanced over at the Bernard house. Low lights burned in their living room. Blackie had dropped me off and then headed over there.

I let myself in and took a deep breath. What a day. It had begun with Sheila's disappearance and ended with Sam being struck by a truck.

And it wasn't over yet.

I didn't even bother turning on the lights in the frigid house. For the second time in a week, I was covered in blood.

The telephone rang as I reached the stairs. It couldn't be the hospital, could it? Surely nothing could've happened to Sam in the few minutes since I left. I ran into the parlor and grabbed up the phone.

"Ye-es?" Just that short run had left me breathless.

"How's it going, Slim?"

A chill of recognition ran down my spine. "Queenie!" I swallowed. "You—you're—"

"Yes, I'm safe. But you knew that already, didn't you? I'm sorry about your boss," he said smoothly. "I heard about it on the radio. My sympathies."

I said nothing.

He gave a nasty chuckle. "Forget it, Slim. Don't pretend. I know Stax found Olmo, and I know he took you there. So don't fucking pretend you don't—"

"All right, I won't. You're behind this whole thing."

"You got it."

"You killed Olmo."

"Damn straight."

"Why?"

"His part was done. It was a graceful exit."

I felt a surge of anger. "And what about Sheila? A blast to the face. You call that a graceful exit?"

"It was more than the bitch deserved."

"But why? She was helping you—"

"Not me. She was helping *him*."

What? "Him who?"

"Junior."

"Don't play that with me. You're Junior."

"The hell I am! I am *me*, Queenie Lovetree, the Black fuckin' Orchid. And I killed that bitch cause she was telling him to get rid of me."

"Telling who?"

"Are you stupid or something? She told Junior it was time to unload me. Can you believe that shit? *Unload* me? How dare she!"

That's when I understood. Lord help me, I understood. Suddenly dizzy, I felt for the chair and sat down. What had Sheila said?

"He denied everything, said he'd been sleeping in his room the whole night."

"Was he playacting?"

"I thought he was lying. But then I could see he really didn't remember."

He didn't remember. No, of course he didn't.

"Queenie . . . ?"

"Yes?"

He sounded as though he was enjoying this. No doubt, he was. But I didn't know where to begin. All I knew was that I had stepped into someone else's nightmare.

"I don't think he cared about me following him. I think he cared about what I saw."

Was this really the answer? My thoughts were utterly disconnected.

I flashed on my bookshelf: *Dr. Jekyll and Mr. Hyde.* I had read it a year ago. Like most people, I'd assumed it was totally fiction, but now . . .

I found my voice, tried to sound normal. "And he—Junior, I mean—he was listening to her?"

"Yeah. What a stupid motherfucker. He couldn't tie his shoelaces if I didn't tell him, but then he went and got himself another bitch. Thought she was all fine and mighty cause she had a real pussy. She said to get rid of me, and the fool was listening to her. That was the last straw."

I thought fast, trying to remember the details in the book, that fantastical story of split personalities. "So Junior knows about you?"

A hesitation. "Yes and no. He thinks he's being haunted. He's such a superstitious fool."

"He's scared of you." It wasn't a question, but an observation based on a hunch. I could almost feel Queenie's malevolent smile.

"He'd be stupid not to be. Aren't you scared of me?"

"No."

He laughed. "Aw, Lanie. You know something? I like you."

"Is that why you tried to use me?"

"Tried?" Another dark chuckle. "Sweetheart, I didn't fucking try. I did use you and I'm still using you—and whether you're willing to admit it or not, you *like* being used."

I felt another rush of cold anger. "Why would you think that?"

"Because I'm giving you the biggest story of your career."

"Biggest? I don't know about that. The strangest, maybe."

"Damn! You don't give an inch, do you? Well, neither do I." The false gaiety left his voice. "You got my money, Slim?"

"You know I don't."

"But you're going to get it, right?"

I paused. "I don't work for you, Queenie, and I don't trust you."

"It's mutual."

"Soon everyone will know that you kidnapped yourself. Sheila might've provided you with some leverage, but you killed her. You've got nothing to hold over us—"

"The hell I don't. You're going to help me here, cause if you don't, you'll be counting bodies for the next six months."

I tensed. "What are you planning?"

"The Faggots' Ball. I'll make sure it's a real blast."

"You wouldn't—"

"Oh, but I would. If you don't get me my dough, I'll blow the place up. I will bring it down, with everybody and their uncles in it."

There would be thousands of people around. Hundreds might die. But Blackie could salt the crowd with disguised police and—

"You know, Slim, it's like I can hear you thinking. Well, I'm telling you right now: don't even try putting uniforms in there. Just because there's room for cops to hide don't mean there won't be plenty of room for me to hide as well. Don't take that chance. I'm warning you: if I see one friggin' cop, I'll let her rip."

"You're willing to die too?"

He laughed. "You call what I'm doing living? I don't. I'm gonna take that dough and go somewhere where no one's ever heard of Junior Bernard or Queenie Lovetree. I'm gonna start over."

"Junior will have something to say about that."

"No, he won't. Junior's gonna lay down and die. I'm gonna make sure of it."

I felt sick to my stomach.

"You know, those parents of his, they tried to cheat me."

"That was a mistake."

"You don't say."

"You don't understand. Sheila probably grabbed the bag before—"

"Don't lie to me or apologize for them. Tell Daddy Mojo that I want my twenty-five, except it's thirty now. I'll get it if I have to take it out of his hide."

"Queenie, it won't work."

"Then a lot of good folks will die. You want that?"

I grit my teeth. "No."

"Good. So we understand each other."

"All right," I said, and reached for a pen and paper. "Where and how?"

His tone turned businesslike. "The dough should be in municipal bonds. Nice and neat and untraceable. Are you taking notes?"

"Every single word."

As soon as I hung up, I called the Bernards and had them put on Blackie. He swore under his breath when I told him what Queenie wanted—and when and where.

"Do you realize how hard it's going to be to spot Queenie in a crowd like that? Everybody's in full costume. I mean, Lanie, you're killing me. What were you thinking, agreeing to a setup like that?"

"I was thinking I didn't have a choice, and that at this point, a definite chance at getting close to him would be better than a hunt that could go on for days, maybe weeks."

Blackie said he'd come up with a plan and get back to me. He also said he'd talk to the Bernards about the ransom money. He started to debate whether I should be the one to make the drop, but I cut him off.

"Nobody else can do it. Queenie would spot an impostor in a second. Now, I've got to get back to the hospital."

I hung up before he could answer, then changed clothes and headed out again.

Chapter 38

Technically, I wasn't supposed to be in there, but the nurses were kind and overworked, so they allowed me to rest in a chair in Sam's room.

Sleep didn't come easily. I kept reliving the accident again and again, kept hearing the sound of the impact. I finally drifted off to images of Sheila and Olmo, Queenie and Junior, and Queenie's voice. *Aren't you scared of me?*

I woke exhausted in the pale daylight. According to my watch, it was eight o'clock. I'd slept through the shift change. The day nurses, who came on at six, had been kind enough not to disturb me.

My only clear thought was that I had to end this—and end it soon—before any more damage could be done.

Was I saving Junior or hunting Queenie? In the past several hours, it had switched from the former to the latter.

I stretched my stiff limbs and went to take a look at Sam. He seemed paler, but otherwise unchanged.

A nurse came in. She was in her twenties, bright, and full of energy. She smiled. "I hope you had a good rest."

I responded with a nod and sank back in the chair at Sam's bedside. Except for brief breaks to get something to eat or use the facilities, I spent the whole day there. Sometimes I spoke to him, sometimes I read. Mostly, I just sat quietly and held his hand. I was all talked out. The hours sped by. The time was fast approaching when I would have to go home and get ready for the ball—and my appointment with the Black Orchid.

That afternoon, George Greene stopped by. "The publisher's worried. We all are."

"Don't be. Sam's tough. He's coming back to us. You'll tell him that for me, won't you?"

"Of course I will." He stayed only a few minutes.

Blackie dropped by an hour later. "Lanie, you've got to get home, get some rest."

"I am resting, here."

"This is no good." He quickly got to the point: "You got no business doing this thing with Lovetree. It's dangerous."

"I know that. I also know that I have no alternative."

"Why not?"

"Because of her."

"Who?"

Sheila, I wanted to say. But what would be the point? Blackie wouldn't understand. Or maybe he would. Though he'd still say it wasn't my job. And perhaps he was right. Yet somewhere along the line, it had become my job—and I was going to see it through.

"Have you made a plan for tonight?" I asked.

"We talked to the owners of the Casino last night. Also reached the guys who host this thing. They wanted to cancel it. We told them it was too late for that."

"And probably too risky. Even if a cancellation was announced every hour on the hour on all the radio stations in New York, hundreds would still show up. And Queenie might blow the place up out of pure spite. Were you able to talk to the Bernards?"

"Yeah. It took some convincing, but Dr. Bernard agreed to cooperate."

"So you collected all the money?"

"Yes, and we need you to go to the station house, so we can properly tape it to you."

"That wouldn't be wise. Queenie's been a step ahead of us this whole time. I'm sure he's expecting something, and he'll definitely be watching. The last thing we need is for him to see me heading to the station."

"Then we'll do it at your house. I'll send a female officer over."

"In plainclothes."

Blackie gave Sam and me one last worried look, then brushed past Dr. Maynard on his way out. The doctor had been in earlier, but I'd missed him when I was grabbing breakfast. He picked up Sam's chart and studied it, then checked his pulse and examined his pupils. When he was done, I signaled him to follow me to one side and spoke in a hushed tone.

"Yesterday you said that the next twenty-four hours would make all the difference."

"I know, but it's too early to tell what'll happen. I don't believe in false promises. But I do believe in hope."

I was going to hold on to that. Sam would be fine. He had to be. He was going to come back, strong and whole, for himself, for me, for all the people who loved and respected him.

"The nurses said you were here all night, and you've been here all day," Dr. Maynard said. "You need to take a break."

He was right. I couldn't do anything there. But suppose something happened while I was gone?

I turned back to Sam. The rise and fall of his chest was barely detectable. I took his right hand in mine. Without knowing what I was about to say, I bent and whispered in his ear. "You come back, you hear? Come back to me."

His hand remained limp. There was no response, no sign of any recognition that he'd heard me.

"I'll be back tonight," I said, then walked away.

CHAPTER 39

T he Manhattan Casino was a fancy hall at 280 West 155th Street, just east of Eighth Avenue and within walking distance of the Harlem River. Less than twenty years old, the Casino was a popular venue for charity balls, basketball tournaments, and boxing bouts. Many were star-studded occasions. A range of folks—from James Reese Europe, the guy who set France on fire with jazz, to dancers Vernon and Irene Castle, to Broadway music composer J. Rosamond Johnson—all held events there.

But none of those happenings ever attained the notoriety of the Faggots' Ball, which took place every year in late February. Hamilton Lodge No. 710 of the Grand Order of the Odd Fellows, one of Harlem's most venerable social clubs, hosted it. The lodge advertised the party simply as a masquerade ball, a costumed event. It made no reference to "the life." But the ball was known as an all-out bash of gay frivolity. Men donned their finest and most exotic female attire, and enough stars turned out to fill a galaxy.

That night, snow and ice covered the streets under a moonlit blue-black sky, and the air was bitter cold. But it didn't matter. Thousands were swarming the place. People were standing in long lines at the ticket windows. Hundreds of others shivered across the street, behind police lines, and tried to get a good view. Every time a limousine drew up to the canopied entrance, the crowd surged forward.

Singer Nora Holt was just stepping out of her white limo, wearing a silver silk gown, when I arrived. She got a rousing cheer. Others, usually noncelebrities, were less lucky. When they stopped to pose and preen, the remarks were often catty.

"There goes Sherry!"

"Why that's Candy! Girl, can you believe it?"

"And you see what she's wearin'?"

"Lawdy! Some poor chicken's running around with no feathers!"

The Casino had a legal capacity of roughly six thousand. That night, it must've been holding closer to seven. Inside, Hollywood A-listers Tallulah Bankhead, Beatrice Lillie, and Clifton Webb chatted with Astors and Vanderbilts. Bankhead was stunning in white organdy. Barbara Stanwyck was lethal in black and red sateen, and Kay Francis was innocence personified in baby-blue satin with white ruffles.

Of course, high Harlem was there too. I spotted A'Lelia; her constant companion, Mayme White; and man about town Harold Jackman. Langston, Robert, and Wallace were there too.

As usual, John C. Smith's twenty-piece orchestra was providing the music. His musicians put out a vigorous and admirable effort, but they could barely be heard above the excited babble. You could make out the *boom-boom* of the drum, and every now and then the saxophone and cornet players struck a note that soared above the rest, but the singer might as well have sat down; you couldn't hear a word he sang.

Some of the men's costumes were aggressively macho, but suspiciously skimpy. There were muscular, weightlifter types decked out in facial war paint. They wore itsy-bitsy loincloths and illustrious feathered headdresses. They carried hatchets or spears. There were swaggering Roman gladiators, Greek gods, and Spartan warriors all running around half naked.

However, most of the crowd under that sky-blue ceiling and giant crystal chandelier wore costumes of feathers and sequins, of glitter and silk and satin. There were sexy señoritas in black lace fluttering red fans, debutantes in frothy pink chiffon and rhinestones. And then there was one extravagant creature called "La Flame." The fellow attended year after year, wearing the same thing. No one dared mimic his costume, which was simplicity itself: a white satin stovepipe hat, a red-beaded breastplate, and a white sash. They were all bound and determined to outdo one another, to officially become the belle of the ball.

Mardi Gras in Harlem. The partygoers pranced around, hands on hips. Every once in a while, one would catch the eye of an admirer and give a bold *come hither* look. One told her dance partner, "Oh, sugar, you're making it so hard for me to stay a lady!" I overheard another bold one say, "I'm a one-way man now. Which way would you like?" Meanwhile, a third informed a cop who grabbed her by the elbow, "No need to get rough, officer. Everyone will get their chance."

Speaking of cops.

Blackie had refused to tell me more than the bare bones about his plan. Officers disguised as drag queens were apparently going to circulate among the crowd. As soon as they spotted Queenie, they would move against him. The only problem was that Queenie had clearly said that any attempt to arrest him would result in him blowing the place up. Blackie thought Queenie was bluffing. I didn't, and I couldn't understand Blackie's willingness to take the chance. I was sure he had something up his sleeve. As I wandered around, I saw that I was right.

The box seats that ringed the ballroom gave the best vantage point for viewing the huge dance floor. I glanced up at one of the crowded loges; the folks inside seemed normal, but I recognized one guy. He was a cop. And I had the feeling he was armed. Snipers. That would be Blackie's ace in the hole. He'd rigged the box seats with sharpshooters. Worries about the killing of innocent bystanders? To be minimized, of course, through the use of expert marksmen. But to be avoided? No guarantees. A choice between seeing the hall go up in flames with the loss of dozens, even hundreds, and taking out an unlucky one or two was no choice at all.

I turned back to look at the revelers, at the open, laughing smiles, the heads thrown back in gaiety, the jealousy in some eyes and the arrogant amusement in others. These people stood on the precipice between life and death and didn't know it.

It had to stay that way. I had to find Queenie and maneuver him into a position where Blackie's men could take him, quickly and efficiently, before he made any moves.

As I made my way through the crowd, I ran into A'Lelia, and she wanted to know if I intended to come to her party.

"Oh, I'm sorry. I forgot to RSVP," I said.

She waved it away. "Baby, you know I don't stand on formality. I'd love to see you, so come if you want to, and if you can't, you can't."

Mayme was with her, and Wallace and Harold too. Mrs. Newcomb of the Newcomb Debutante Society stopped by to chat. All wanted to share juicy tidbits they hoped I'd use in my column. But I didn't have time. I smiled and gestured, sometimes laughed at a joke or comment, but I never stopped searching that crowd. Every now and then, I thought I saw my quarry. I'd make my excuses and break away. But then, as I got close, I'd see it wasn't Queenie.

The envelopes taped to either side of my rib cage scratched with every move. The bearer bonds made me Queenie's target as much as he was mine. Two hunters seeking one another in a crowded jungle. No doubt Queenie was also scanning the room, much as I had, for Blackie's undercover men.

The ground-floor ladies' room was on the south side of the building. There were four women ahead of me, but the line moved quickly. I slipped inside one of the stalls by the window and locked the door. Then I shrugged out of my top and untaped the envelopes. I lifted the cover of the toilet tank and placed the envelopes inside. They were well-sealed in oilcloth, so there was no way for water to seep in. I replaced the cover, fixed my clothes, and emerged from the stall with a sense of relief. I just had to hope that no one found those envelopes before I could retrieve them.

I rinsed my hands at the sink and checked my face in the mirror. Despite all the makeup, my eyes looked tired. No surprise there.

I headed back to the party. No sooner had I rejoined the crowd than I felt a tap on my shoulder. I turned to find Jack-a-Lee. He'd squeezed his generous form into a peek-a-boo ruby-studded brassiere, a gold silk loincloth, and chartreuse-colored high heels. His see-through chiffon harem skirt was a passionate pink with gold edging. A bejeweled tiara and golden-blond wig completed the outfit.

"Lanie, dahling! It's so good to see you." He grabbed my shoulders and offered me two quick air kisses. Then he stepped back to appraise my outfit: a faux jewel-encrusted oriental crown, beaded sleeves and bodice, and a beaded girdle around my hips, over a filmy skirt.

"Let me guess," he said, "Mata Hari! It's fantastic, dahling. Not as good as mine, of course, but a wonderful try!"

I faked a smile, returned the compliment, and then started to move away—but he caught me by the wrist.

"Now, where are my photographers? I saw you come in. You were alone, no picture-snapper."

"He arrived ahead of time. He's here in the crowd, doing his job."

In truth, I'd forgotten all about my promise to Jack-a-Lee. The newspaper had sent a photographer, however. It always did.

"Do you see him now?" Jack-a-Lee asked.

"He's over there."

"Where?"

"There."

He eased around behind me and I pointed across the room. Ned Johnson was busy taking a photo of Langston and A'Lelia.

"Just go over there," I said. "Tell him I sent you."

"No, dahling. Not good enough. Introduce me. Make sure he gives me the right treatment."

"Please, Jack-a-Lee. Not now. I don't have time to—"

"I'm going to stick by your side till you do."

He meant it.

"All right. Fine."

After introducing him around, I wanted to leave him with Ned and the others, but Jack-a-Lee insisted that we take a couple of group shots. Then Langston and A'Lelia walked off. Ned disappeared before Jack-a-Lee could demand another photo, and I started to turn away too.

"Not yet," he said, and rammed something small and hard against the small of my back. A pistol.

I stiffened. "Jack-a-Lee?"

"Don't make a move unless I tell you to."

"What—?"

"Let's just say I'm helping a friend."

My mouth went dry. "Who?"

"You'll find out soon enough."

"The gun's not necessary."

He put his lips close to my ear. "But it does add a certain *je ne sais quoi*, *n'est-ce pas?*"

We passed under the thick curtain that separated the main ballroom from the side rooms. In less than ten seconds, I was out of sight of Blackie's men. Had they noticed? What were they doing? Maybe nothing. To anyone watching, it would have appeared that I'd simply walked off with a friend: perhaps not a wise thing to do, but certainly not alarming. It could take them awhile to realize what was happening, and I might be dead by then.

Jack-a-Lee opened a door and gestured for me to enter. I stepped into a small, dark room, which smelled of a musky perfume.

"You'll thank me later," Jack-a-Lee said.

"Well, I'll certainly have something to say about it. That's for sure."

He gave me a shove, then stepped back and closed the door.

CHAPTER 40

All noise from the outside became dull and muffled. A shadow shifted in the dark. There was a soft rustling, the sound of breathing. I realized I was being watched.

"Queenie?"

"Right here, baby."

A lamp flickered on to my left. Queenie sat next to it, legs crossed, looking calm, cool, and regal. His mask, a golden full-face affair, hung from a string around his neck. He wore a red and gold satin gown. Rhinestones covered crepe de Chine sleeves. A tiara with dozens of feathers and dotted with rhinestones was perched atop his head.

"You've got the dough?" He waved a feathered fan, revealing the pistol.

"Threatening to bomb this place, that wasn't a good idea."

"Sure it was, or else you wouldn't be here."

He stood, all glittering six-feet-three of him, and walked toward me, the gun held straight and sure, pointed directly at my midriff.

"Turn around, lean against the wall."

I did as told.

He patted me down, his large hands covering every inch. "Where's the dough?"

I turned to face him. "I don't have it."

Despite his considerable makeup and the dusky half-light, I could see his complexion deepen with anger. He slapped me sharply across the face. I staggered, but managed to stay on my feet. He looked as though he wanted to slap me again.

"Lanie, I like you. I like you very much. But make no mistake about it: I will shoot you if you try to screw me over. Now where the hell is my dough?"

"It's outside." I wiped my lip. It stung, but there was no blood. "It's the weirdest thing. I didn't feel like carrying the extra weight."

"You want to know about extra weight?" He grabbed my hand, forced it to his breasts. Made me feel one, then the other. They were hard as rocks. "Grenades," he said. "And dynamite up my sleeve." He was ready to blow the place to kingdom come.

"I don't have the package on me. It was too dangerous."

"Where is it?"

"In the ladies' room."

His lips curled into a grim smile. "I'm tempted to kill you right here." He put his mask back on and shoved me to the door. "Move."

I opened the door and a wall of sound hit me. The music was loud and boisterous, and the crowd was in high spirits. Queenie's gun nudged me forward.

The path to the ladies' room took us back across the dance floor. Blackie's men should've been on high alert by now. They should have noticed my disappearance, sensed that something was wrong. As soon as I stepped on to the dance floor, they would see me. They'd have to. And then it would be over. Blackie's men would take Queenie out and free me from this nightmare.

I started toward the main area, and felt the gun press harder into my side.

"Wrong direction," Queenie whispered.

"But—"

"Don't insult me, Slim. The boxes are filthy with cops."

I tensed. "Then what—"

"Turn left. We'll go around the side." He gave me another jab.

We walked along the perimeter of the dance floor. It was less packed there, and blanketed in shadows. During the short time I had been in the room with Queenie, the crowd seemed to have doubled. I wondered if this was the last time I'd be here.

Blackie's men weren't particularly trying to hide now. Just a glance upward and I saw them, glimpsed the business end of a rifle poking over the edge of the balcony.

Queenie saw them too. He bent and hissed into my right ear: "If they take me, I'll take you—you and every other damn fool in the place. You got me?"

I nodded, knowing it was true.

A little further, we passed a cop. I didn't know him by face, didn't need to. You hang around cops long enough, you learn to recognize them. Same expressions. Same stance. Same way of watching. This one was standing at the edge of the crowd. In costume, like everyone else, but modest. Some kind of western outfit. A good choice. A workman's shirt, some denims, a cowboy hat. To onlookers, the holster and gun made sense. It's like hiding in plain sight. His costume was good, but he didn't seem to know it; he looked embarrassed. That was the tell. You didn't come to the Faggots' Ball if you were the kind who got embarrassed. You stayed home and read about it in the newspaper afterward.

Queenie made him an instant after I did. The cop glanced our way.

"Smile," Queenie whispered.

I tried, but my lips felt numb.

"Come on, now," Queenie said. "Do it like you mean it."

I gave a polite nod. The cop hesitated, then smiled back and tipped his hat. His eyes lingered for a moment before he returned his attention to the crowd.

"Good," Queenie whispered. "You just saved his life. Now, go."

We moved fast after that. My thoughts raced ahead. The ladies' room would be crowded. Queenie might end up killing someone.

"You won't want to go in there," I said.

"Why not?"

"It'll be crowded. You'd better stay outside by the door."

"Oh, so now you're looking out for my interests?"

"No, mine. If somebody does something stupid in there, then you'll do something stupid."

"Like shoot?"

"Yeah, like that."

We reached the door of the ladies' room. "Hold it." Queenie stopped me. "You sure it's in there, Slim?"

I nodded.

"Okay," he said. "Then we're heading in there together. I'm not going to stand out here like a fool, waiting to be recognized. I'll hang by the door while you get the dough."

I pushed open the door to find a knot of women bunched just inside.

"Shit," Queenie muttered.

There were seven or eight women waiting in line ahead of us—Park Avenue types on an adventure trip to Harlem, a club by the looks of them. They were all dressed similarly: white empire waist dresses and little gold tiaras.

"I ain't got all day," Queenie hissed. "Where'd you put it, Slim?"

I motioned toward one of the stalls by the far window. "In the tank, fourth one down, second from the wall."

Queenie whipped out the gun and leveled it at the women. With screams of terror, they backed up against one another and huddled against the wall. Queenie was so close he couldn't miss if he pulled that trigger.

"Now, this is how we're going to play it, ladies: my friend here has to fetch something she foolishly left in the stalls. Nothing will happen as long as you stay quiet. But if you move, if you even make the slightest noise, I'll fix you. Got that?"

Seven heads bobbed in unison.

Queenie turned to me. "Go get it."

As I took a step toward the stall, the door behind Queenie banged open and a woman stepped inside. She glanced at Queenie, registered the gun, and said, "What the hell?!"

"Get over there." Queenie gestured for her to join the other women against the wall.

She cocked an eyebrow at him and put her hands on her hips. "Now, I know you ain't talking to me."

"I said—"

"Now, you obviously don't know me, but I—"

Queenie cocked the trigger.

The woman merely smiled. "You can't be that stupid. You let loose and them cops out there, they gonna be all over you."

Queenie hesitated. He glanced at me, at the frightened pack of women. "What y'all staring at?" He leaned back to me. "What the fuck are you waiting for? Go get it."

I started toward the stall again, but the woman grabbed me by the arm. "Uh-huh," she said. "I gotta go bad, so the next one's for me."

Queenie lifted the gun with a roar, then swung and clipped the woman on the jaw. She staggered backward, but didn't go down. She dabbed at her bloodied lip.

"Why you stupid mother—"

"Make another move, say another word," Queenie warned, "and I'll shoot. And I don't give a good hot damn who comes through that door, cause hell or high water, you'll be dead."

She glanced at me, like we were in this together. We weren't. She was about to get herself killed, and perhaps others with her.

"Don't be stupid," I said. "If you want to die, then that's on you. But once he starts shooting, all hell will break loose, and it won't be just you. It'll be me and maybe others too."

Something changed in her eyes and I knew she was going to back down. I shoved the stall door open and went inside.

Queenie now stood just outside the stall, where he could keep an eye on me and the other women. "If you bring anything out of there—anything but the dough—then I will take you down."

I lifted the toilet tank lid and peered inside. I didn't see the package. My heart stopped. *Where could it be?*

I plunged my hands into the water and felt around frantically. Then my fingers touched something. There! *It's there!*

I snatched the parcel out. It looked untouched. I was so relieved I clutched the dripping mess to my chest. Then I emerged and held out the parcel to Queenie.

"Dry it," he ordered.

I grabbed a towel and hurriedly wiped it down.

"Now open it," he said.

I unfolded the layers of oilcloth to expose a dry envelope. I showed Queenie the bearer bonds.

"Very good." He snatched the envelope out of my hands and shoved it into his bosom between the grenades. "Okay, now you go out first."

I moved past him, deeply aware of the gun trained on my back. The other women stared hard, their mouths parted in fear. Even the loud-mouthed one seemed to have finally understood what was at stake.

Then I was at the door.

"Hold it," Queenie said behind me. "We're going to take it slow, just like we did when we came. No sudden moves. No secret hand signals or stupid shit like that. You got me?"

I barely managed a nod.

It was not enough for Queenie. "What was that, Slim? I didn't hear you."

"Y-yes," I stammered. "I understand."

"Good." He gave me a little push.

We stepped into a corridor off the main room and started to retrace our steps. The party was in full swing. It seemed as though we had been in that bathroom for hours, as the party was wilder, the crowd louder, the laughter raunchier.

I had to get Queenie out of there, away from all these people. I picked up the pace, pushing through the crowd. I glanced over my shoulder, saw Queenie an arm's length away.

"Which way?" I mouthed.

He motioned toward the right.

Up ahead, where we had entered, a cop was stationed on the corner.

We almost made it.

My gaze touched the cop, merely brushed him, but he felt it. He turned. Our eyes met, and I suppose he saw something there, because he shifted to the left, to Queenie, and he definitely saw something there.

He was fast, but not fast enough. It was over in seconds. One shot and a man was down.

There was a sudden hush, then a terrified scream. Queenie reached for his breast. Pulled out a grenade. With his teeth, he yanked out the pin.

"No!" I screamed, and lunged toward him.

Queenie batted me aside and lobbed the grenade. He threw it high. Then he yanked me by the arm and shoved me forward. "Go right and keep to the side."

Behind us, the blast was deafening. By then, we'd turned the corner. We were in the corridor. More screams, big chunks of plaster raining down, and smoke. So much thick smoke. And a rain of warm red drops and soft pink matter.

Queenie pointed forward. "Up there. A stairway. We're taking it to the roof." He knew exactly where he was going.

I scrambled up the stairs, with Queenie pushing me from behind. I had to hold my long skirt to keep from tripping. In no time, we were one flight below the roof. Moonlight filtered through the dingy skylight overhead. There was a commotion downstairs. Blackie's men. They'd gotten through.

"Hurry up!" Queenie gave me another shove.

We moved up the last flight of steps double-time, but the cops clattering behind us came into view. One fired off a shot that passed just under Queenie's nose. He produced a second grenade, pulled the pin, and tossed it down at them. I twisted away and dashed up the stairs. The grenade exploded below. People screamed, the building shook, and Queenie laughed. Within seconds, he had caught up to me.

"We're in this together, Slim."

The door to the roof was locked. He shot off the lock and yanked open the door. The frigid cold was a shock. I was half-naked and in sandals. Queenie dragged me to the edge of the roof and peered down.

The street below was brightly lit and swarming with cops, most of them watching the Casino's main entrance. Blackie had blocked off both ends of the street, from Eighth Avenue to the river. Traffic was snarled with angry drivers who simply wanted to get through.

"There's no way out," I said, trembling. "Please, Queenie, this is madness."

"Shut up!"

He glanced left, right, then saw something that made him smile. "Over there."

The roof to the Casino adjoined that of another building, and that adjoined another. We clambered from rooftop to rooftop, building to building, until we reached the last structure overlooking the river. The street below had been barricaded, but only one patrolman stood guard, and he was directing traffic.

"Here," Queenie said. "We go down here."

I glanced at the fire escape. It looked none too safe.

"No," he said. "We go right through the building. Hidden from prying eyes."

He found a loose brick, used it to bash off the padlock securing the door to the inside, and hustled me down a poorly lit stairway.

The place was a warehouse, closed for the night. Queenie pried open a window and made me climb through. We were in an alley between buildings. The cop directing traffic was more than half a block away and hadn't noticed a thing. Queenie stepped in front of a car paused for the light, put his gun in the driver's face, and told him to get out. Then he ordered me into the driver's seat. He piled in beside me and said, "Drive!"

"Where to?"

His answer stunned me.

CHAPTER 41

Ten minutes later we pulled into the dark alleyway that ran between 139th and 140th Streets. I navigated past the other parked cars and drew to a stop behind the Bernards' house.

Queenie let us in through the back door and guided me up the small stairway that led to the ground floor. The first thing I noticed was the smell. It was a mixture of blood and human waste.

When we rounded the landing, I glanced into the front parlor. It was immaculate and undisturbed. So where was the odor coming from? But then a cold breeze swept through an upstairs window and down the stairs, and I knew.

None of this is real, I told myself. *It can't be.*

But it was. The situation was real and dangerous and my chances of survival were dwindling with every step.

Think. Stay calm and think.

Could I lock myself in a room? Send a signal to someone in the street? Find a telephone? Maybe even start a fire?

I felt a deepening sense of dread. If I did somehow survive, then I'd be climbing these steps in nightmares for months to come.

Queenie prodded me with the gun. "Get going."

At the parlor level, I paused. "It's so quiet in here."

"Looking for Junior's mommy and daddy? They're upstairs, waiting for you to join them."

I saw the blood when we reached the second-floor landing. Droplets marked a trail leading from front to back. Queenie nudged me down the hall toward the front bedroom. I made it as far as the door. Even the gun at my back couldn't make me go further.

Alfred and Phyllis Bernard were in there all right. Each had been trussed to a dining room chair, their wrists bound behind them. Both were nude and drenched in blood, which also spattered the walls and the ceiling, dotting the floor leading to where I stood.

"Go on. Get inside. I want you to take a good look."

Queenie gave me another shove. I came up short before Phyllis Bernard. Overkill did not begin to describe it.

Her head was thrown back, her knees tied together. Her eye sockets were gaping blood-filled holes. Her eyeballs hung on her cheeks, barely attached by strands of tissue. He'd finished her off by slashing her throat.

He'd emasculated Dr. Bernard, stuffed the genitals into the doctor's mouth. Bernard's eyes were intact but grayed over. From the way they bulged, he appeared to have been garroted. There was a silk tie around his neck. It had been knotted into a bow tie and cinched so tight that it cut into his flesh.

"What do you think?" Queenie asked.

He stood at my side, surveying his handiwork. I didn't answer.

A large gilded mirror hung on the wall above the fireplace. Scrawled on it was a message in red lipstick: *To Phyllis, you blind bitch. May your eyeballs RIP. To Daddy Mojo: For all the years you made me suck, now it's your turn. Kick it, baby.*

So much hatred. So much fury. Why?

The most chilling line came last: *Hi Lanie, I'll be seeing you.*

"I had planned to be long gone when you found this," Queenie said, "but obviously my plans had to change."

Trembling, I backed away. He grabbed hold of me, but I pulled loose.

"I'm going to be sick," I gasped, and he stepped aside.

I hurried down the hall to the bathroom and came to a stop. Quick impressions of a bloody butcher knife in the sink, watery pink stains in the tub, pink splatters on the walls. I lurched toward the sink and snatched up the knife, but Queenie was right behind me. He grabbed my arm and bent it back, then wrenched the knife away. He studied it for a moment, faintly smiling, as though examining a favorite memento. Then he regarded me and without a word punched me in the gut. That was it. My stomach heaved. I dropped to my knees, leaned over the toilet, and let go.

Queenie stood in the doorway, watching with disdain. "Tough crime reporter, huh? I thought you would handle it better than this."

I ignored him, gasping and puking my guts out. Two wretched minutes later, I leaned against the wall, feeling dizzy and gripping the chain to flush the toilet. Anger replaced sickness. "You gutted those people. You slaughtered them."

"I gave them one last grand old time." He hauled me to my feet.

I swatted his hand away. "Is that why you brought me here, to give me a grand old time too?"

"Mm-hmm. But not the way you think. We're business partners. I told you: I'm gonna give you what I've given no other, a chance to write my story, to see inside my head. So you can drop the self-righteousness, Slim. You're gonna earn fame and fortune off of me, and you know it. Now, come on upstairs. We've got to change."

"The police must be on their way. They'll be looking for us."

"This is the last place they'd think to come. You didn't even expect me to bring you here, and you're a hell of a lot smarter than those Keystone Cops." He turned on the faucet. "Rinse out your mouth. I can't stand sour breath."

CHAPTER 42

He forced me up the stairs to the third floor. There were two bedrooms to the rear, roughly the same size. Queenie entered one that functioned as a walk-in closet. Racks of women's clothes everywhere. Large women's clothes—big enough to fit a man. And a closet with shelves of oversized women's shoes and a drawer full of lacy man-sized undies. On the far wall was a vanity with a mirror and a spread of expensive makeup, hairbrushes, and wigs.

"This was my little hideaway," Queenie said, completing the tour. "I've got some fine stuff here. Look at this." He rifled through the racks.

The outfits appeared to come from the shops of some of the world's finest designers. Dresses, furs, feather boas. Glittering, sequined, red, silver, and gold.

He pushed aside a glittering burgundy gown to reveal a smart chestnut tweed traveling suit. His eyes lit up and he smiled. "Perfect!" He glanced at me, at my dirty face, torn costume, and disheveled hair. "Go clean yourself up. Use the bathroom down the hall." He saw an idea enter my eyes and it made him laugh. "You're not that stupid, are you? But if you do try to make a break for it, you'll be dead quicker than you can blink. Got me?"

I got it. I started down the hall.

"Hold on." He went to the adjacent bedroom. He hummed to himself, happily, and returned with a second outfit, a well-cut charcoal wool suit. He held it up for me to see. "This was Sheila's. Her size looks about right."

"You don't actually expect me to wear that."

"Why not? She can't use it anymore."

"No." I backed away.

He forced the suit against my chest and pressed the gun to my temple. "You don't seem to understand. You can't travel with me the way you're dressed. People would notice, ask questions. So take the damn dress, or I'll drop you here and now."

I took it. His eyes felt like hot coals on my back as I headed down the hall. I thought of Sam lying in his hospital bed. I thought about getting back to him. About how I wanted that more than anything else in the world.

I thought about Sheila, about how she'd loved Junior and been so desperate to save him. Then I thought about how the last thing she saw was a gun pressed against her forehead—her husband's face behind it.

Hunting Queenie or saving Junior?

At any given time, which was I doing? Was it possible to do both? At the moment, I was doing neither. I was simply trying to stay alive.

After I returned wearing Sheila's clothes, I found that Queenie had also changed outfits. He'd donned a fresh wig and a big, floppy hat that hid most of his face. He looked sharp. He looked ready.

"You look like shit," he said. He had me sit at the vanity, then retouched my makeup. As he bent over me, deftly applying eyeliner and mascara, he said, "You really do have beautiful eyes, you know. You should build them up more."

I said nothing, just tried to make myself invisible. He hadn't washed up and stank of sweat, dust, cordite, and a very generous douse of Chanel No. 5.

Minutes later, he was done. "Open your eyes, girl."

He'd heavily applied kohl to my eyes. They appeared larger and darker and more mysterious. My lips were lush and ripe, like cherries. I felt like a stranger.

"You like it, don't you?" he said. "This is how you should do your makeup every day."

Was I really sitting in a house with a stone-cold killer, wearing his dead wife's clothes, doing makeup and swapping beauty tips, with the slaughtered remains of his parents one floor below?

He fussed over my hair and outfit and made me try on various pairs of Sheila's shoes. All the time I watched him, attempting to understand.

"Do you see yourself as a real woman?" I asked. My own question surprised me. From the look on Queenie's face, it surprised him too, but apparently for different reasons. To him, the answer was obvious.

"Hell yeah! I've got the parts, sister." At the look on my face, he smiled. "Didn't expect that, did you? But yes, I've got it *all*."

I was stunned. "You have what?"

"You heard me. When it comes to that, I have more riches than man or woman could dream of."

"But how is that possible?"

"You want me to show you?" He took a step back, made to raise his skirt. I shook my head, alarmed. "No—no!"

"Why not? It's nothing to be ashamed of."

"I just . . . I've heard of it, but I never thought . . ."

"Never thought it could be real? Well, it is. I'm one in a million."

"Is this why Mrs. Bernard dressed you up as a girl when you were little? Is this why she called you Janie?"

"Oh, so you heard about that."

Things were beginning to make sense now. I had not been able to figure out why Mrs. Bernard dressed her boy up as a girl. But if he were indeed as much a she as a he, then . . .

But that still didn't explain how Junior ended up with two distinct personalities, nor did it explain Queenie's rabid hatred of the Bernards.

Obviously, something had gone very wrong.

"Hey, don't feel sorry for me," Queenie said, studying my face. "Cause I have had my fun and then some. Being double-sexed is not the problem."

"Then what is?"

"It's not the body, it's who I have to share it with. *His* body. *His* parents." He motioned toward the stairway. "Those sacks of shit downstairs? They weren't my mama and daddy—they were *his* parents."

Okay, but if he rejected the Bernards as his biological parents, then how did he rationalize his existence? Or did reason count for nothing with him?

He stopped brushing my hair and beamed down at me. "I'm so proud."

"Of what?"

"Of the fact that you're interested in my etiology."

I gave him a look.

He laughed. "Did you hear that? I used a college-boy word. Etiology. You know what it means?"

"Means origins." To be more specific, it means the origins of a disease or disorder. But I wasn't about to tell Queenie that.

"Yeah, of course you'd know the meaning," he said. "You're a smart lady, real knowledgeable. Wonder how I knew to use it?"

"Being stuck in Junior's head like that, I guess it has certain advantages."

"Yeah, it does, don't it? One of them being that I know what he's thinking—"

"But he doesn't know what you're thinking."

"Exactly." He started brushing my hair again. "That dumbass thought he could trick me out with this kidnapping scheme. Thought he could pull it off without me. That all he had to do was show some gumption and I'd disappear." He snapped his fingers. "Just like that."

"So you took over."

"Mm-hmm."

I didn't believe him. I knew next to nothing about Queenie's special brand of sickness, but I did know that he was a liar. I couldn't trust anything he said, not about himself or his power over Junior, and certainly not about his plans to let me live.

Queenie set the brush aside and regarded my hairstyle with satisfaction. "Let's just say I gave Junior's plan some direction, and now I'm giving you yours."

CHAPTER 43

W e slipped back out into the night, carrying food and water in a large carpetbag. It felt as though we'd been in the house for an eternity, but according to my watch, less than fifteen minutes had gone by.

I had kept hoping that Blackie and his men would arrive. But why should they? He would have expected Queenie to drive straight out of town, or to go underground in some out-of-the-way place. Queenie's decision to head back to Strivers' only seemed obvious to me now because that's where I'd been taken.

My other hope had been that Mrs. Cardigan would see something suspicious and call the police. But Queenie had made sure we came in through the back way, and it was highly unlikely that Mrs. Cardigan or any other neighbor would've been looking out there at that time of night. Even if they had, what would they have seen? There were no lights in the alleyway, and Queenie had made me navigate without headlights. His decision to return to Strivers' was arrogant and risky, but apparently it was smart too. He now instructed me to head uptown to 145th Street.

"You know who I'm thinking about?" he asked as I drove.

"No, who?"

"Luther Boddy."

Well, that explained the hat. Boddy was a twenty-two-year-old boot-black and ex-con. He was a police favorite, of sorts. The coppers used to like to pick him up for "routine questioning." They'd beat him with a lead pipe covered in a rubber hose. Beat him so bad, he'd have to stay in bed for days to recover.

One day in January of '22, two detectives approached him for questioning. A patrolman had been shot a few days before. The detectives picked Boddy up at a school just a block from the West 135th Street station and across the street from the *Chronicle*. They started to walk him over and he panicked. Pulled a pistol from his sleeve and shot them both. As he'd later testify, he simply wasn't going to let himself be beaten again.

The killings unleashed one of the largest, most sensational manhunts in New York City's history. Within hours, hundreds of heavily armed cops hit the streets, scouring Harlem. Their orders were to bring him in. Many said they were ready to kill him on sight.

Boddy moved fast. He got out of Harlem. The next sighting was in Hell's Kitchen. By the time the cops got word of it, he was gone. He found shelter for a day and a night at his mother's house in New Jersey. His own brother ratted him out. But by then, Boddy was in the wind. He'd dressed himself in women's clothes—large, floppy hat included—and set out for Pennsylvania.

Forty thousand cops were after him. Even so, he made it all the way to Philadelphia. He did it partly on foot and partly by commandeering a taxi cab. He didn't do it in style, but he did it. Philly, however, was as far as he got.

"They caught him," I said.

"Yes, they did," Queenie said softly. For a moment, he was still. Then he added, "But they're not getting me."

Despite the renewed determination in his voice, Queenie's reference to Luther Boddy was telling. Boddy had killed two cops. Queenie had killed at least one, probably more with those grenades. Then there were the club patrons and Olmo and Sheila. If the NYPD had sent hundreds, then thousands, of cops after Boddy, how many would they send after Queenie?

By the time Boddy had been caught, convicted, and electrocuted, he'd become a folk hero, a martyr to police brutality. Some thirty thousand people came to view his remains at a funeral home in Harlem. Thousands more lined the streets to watch his hearse move slowly down Seventh Avenue.

Did Queenie think that people would feel the same way about him? It was highly unlikely, but even if for some reason they did, would it matter?

Folk hero status didn't save Boddy. Some might say it even hurt him. The powers that be didn't want people admiring a cop killer, so they put an end to him, quick.

Queenie had picked up another handgun in the house. He had me drive to a used-car lot on East 145th. No one seemed to be on duty.

"No guard?" I asked.

"Why do you think I chose this one?"

I was soon back behind the wheel, this time of a Model T Ford. The keys had been waiting in the car.

"You bribed the guard?"

"Hell no." Queenie was insulted. "I bribed the owner."

All right. "Where are we headed?"

"Canada."

If he'd said Mars, I wouldn't have been more surprised.

He gave me dull smile. "What? You don't like Canada?"

"Honestly, I never thought about it."

"Well, it's about time you did, cause that's where we're headed. To St. Catherines, in Ontario."

"May I ask why?"

"It's where Harriet chose to settle down."

I thought better of asking who Harriet was.

I headed west on 145th before turning north on Broadway. He kept the gun in his lap, invisible to the casual eye, but clearly trained on my midsection.

"I hope you have the safety on," I said.

For some reason, he thought that was funny. "Well, I don't want to lose you, Slim, not before my story's told. On the other hand, I'd urge you to avoid any bumps in the road, or sudden shifts in direction, if you know what I mean."

He sank lower in the seat and we continued in silence, sweeping up Broadway. The lights of stores on both sides flowed past. At 181st Street, I turned left to head over to the Washington Heights Bridge.

"Whoa! Slow down a minute," Queenie said. The entrance to the bridge was a scene of flashing red lights. "Cops all over the place," he muttered with disgust. "Cut the headlights and back up. Do it real slow."

I retreated to Broadway, then swung the car around to face north again. The whole time, my heart was in my throat. If the cops saw us and recognized Queenie, one of them might open fire.

But none of them seemed to have noticed anything. They were too busy searching the cars that were already at the bridge. Furthermore, at this distance, under the cover of night, a black car with no headlights was virtually invisible.

"What next?" I asked.

"Let me think, just keep driving."

I headed up Broadway. At this rate, we would soon reach the northern tip of the island. "Manhattan's not that long," I said, "and there aren't too many ways to get off it."

"Shut up."

"They're going to have people at every bridge, every tunnel."

"Shut up, I said, and let me think."

I piped down. One way or another, this whole thing would end soon. Part of me wanted it over; but another part wanted more time with the Black Orchid, quiet time, when I could get his story, when I could maybe even reach Junior, actually *meet* him. Theoretically, I could do all that once Queenie was captured. Only I didn't feel that he would ever let himself be caged. Something told me he'd rather die than be taken prisoner, and that one way or another, this would be my last chance to learn his secrets.

Then my thoughts turned to Sam. Maybe he was awake by now. I hoped with all my heart that he was awake, that he would be okay. I wanted to talk to him, hold him, and be held by him.

But how? Did I actually believe that the Black Orchid would set me free? He wanted immortality and he thought I could give it to him; it was his reason for keeping me alive. But he was moody and paranoid. He could change his mind at the toss of a dime. Maybe, eventually, he'd fall asleep. That would be my chance. I'd outlast him. He'd fall asleep and I'd be gone.

Broadway turned into Route 9, and we eventually crossed into the Bronx.

"This is good," Queenie said. "Real good." He frowned and sat up suddenly. "What were you doing taking me over to that bridge, anyway? We didn't need to go over that bridge. Just drive north and we'll hit Canada."

"But if you want to get to St. Catherines, you head west first."

"Really?" He chewed that over, then shook his head. "I don't think so. You're trying to screw me, aren't you, Slim? Everybody knows that Canada's north. It's north, damnit! So, you just take this heap up, keep on driving till we get there."

A three-quarter moon hung in the sky. As we put more distance behind us, Queenie became festive, humming to himself and sometimes breaking out in song. At one point, he twisted round to watch Manhattan's receding skyline, then turned back, pumped one fist in the air, and let out a shout. "Look out, Canada! Here I come!"

I threw him a curious glance. "Why Canada?"

He looked at me as though I were a simpleton. "I told you, Canada's where Harriet went."

"Harriet who?"

"Harriet Tubman! Who else?" He smiled and slapped his thigh. "Yeah, if it's good enough for Harriet, then it's good enough for me."

Stunned, I remained silent.

"I know what you're thinking," he said.

"What's that?"

"That Harriet and I don't have a damn thing in common, other than the color of our skin."

I cleared my throat. "The thought crossed my mind."

"Well, you're wrong. Harriet and I are very much alike. Harriet, you see, was born into slavery. I was also born under the whip, only my masters were black. And because they could call themselves my parents, no one cared or noticed what they did to me."

The tone was petulant, the comparison a stretch, but it was interesting. "Go on."

"She too fought for her freedom. She struggled to find that place where she could be herself, with no one to lord it over her. That's what I'm doing, seeking my own way."

How many times had he practiced that little speech?

"But Queenie," I cut in, "Harriet Tubman risked her life to save people. She led slaves to freedom. She never killed anyone."

"But she threatened to. That bitch was fierce. She told those runaway motherfuckers that if one of them tried to turn back, she'd kill him dead."

"That was to guarantee everyone's safety."

"It doesn't matter why she said it; it just matters that she did. Harriet was a determined woman, just like me. She was ready to do what had to be done. If that meant putting somebody down, then so be it."

Nobody ever accused Queenie of being subtle. I took his last words as the threat they were meant to be, and went back to driving. We had a long road ahead of us. The drive to Canada meant passing through Connecticut, Massachusetts, Vermont, New Hampshire, and beyond. We'd be nowhere near St. Catherines if we got that far north. But with each passing mile, the chances of Queenie being captured decreased. He was sure of that, and so was I.

For now, we were still in New York State. A lot could happen along the way. Cops were known to flag down black people, just as a matter of principle. And I knew that Queenie would shoot first and ask questions later. Then the chase would be on. The problem was that cops chasing after him were just as likely to shoot me. For a moment, I wasn't sure who might pose the greater danger—my kidnapper or potential rescuers.

The road, normally slow with heavy traffic, was empty that night, treacherous with ice. But I was thankful for it. Between the gun and the ice, I had enough fear to beat back exhaustion and stay focused.

Next to me, Queenie lit himself a cigarette and patted his chest where he'd hidden the bearer bonds. They would make a nice nest egg for his envisioned new start. I had to give him credit: he'd put a lot of thought into this scheme.

"Meeting me at that premiere, even that was part of the plan, right?"

He chuckled. "Sure was."

"And the package in front of my door?"

"Slim, you made the perfect little helper. You were a neighbor, and you had a job that scared Junior's parents to death. They hated scandal. I knew you'd keep up the pressure. They'd want to pay up and get this whole nasty little episode behind them."

From the very beginning, he had made me his accomplice. The whole thing, including killing Charlie Spooner and the Harvard kid and the others at the Cinnamon Club, it had all been done, in part, to impress me. The wheels had gone into motion the minute I called Queenie and told him I'd be stopping by.

"How could you be so sure that I wouldn't take that box to the police?"

"It was a gamble, but I figured you'd be a pretty safe bet. You're a reporter *and* a bleeding heart. You'd want the story. Better still, you'd want to help. And I called it right, didn't I? You fell right in like a good little soldier."

"But didn't you realize that once I started asking questions, I wouldn't give up—I'd want answers?"

"The way I was planning it, by the time you found them, I'd be long gone." He sounded so smug.

"And killing all those people at the club, that was your plan too? Did you tell Olmo to do that?"

"I told him to make it look real."

"And he did."

"Damn straight."

The knot in my gut tightened. *Take it easy and think. You need to think and find answers.*

"Why are you looking at me like that?" he asked.

"Oh, I was just thinking."

"About what?"

"About how you know so much about hair and makeup and all."

"Oh, yes. I have a very fine feeling for all that." For a moment, he looked truly happy. Then he put his hand to his forehead, leaned on the armrest. "But people think I'm just a man in drag. They don't realize that I *am* a woman. I just suffered some bad luck is all. I wasn't just born into such a body. I have to share that damn body with a man—and a man who doesn't have a clue. He really doesn't know his ass from his elbow." He drew a deep breath. "Then again, that's why I'm here. Because he needed me. I guess I should be grateful." His eyes roved over me with minute appraisal, returned to my face. "You got a man?"

I kept my eyes on the road and said nothing. I wasn't about to talk about my relationship with Sam.

"You ain't got no man." He sniffed me, actually leaned over and sniffed. His face was less than two inches from mine. "You know how I can tell?"

I remained silent.

He sneered. "Cause you ain't got no man-smell on you. You know, you can tell when a person's been getting it, regular-like. Their whole way changes, their movements, their looks, their *aroma*. You got the aroma of a dried-up carrot."

"Well, thanks."

"Anytime." He chuckled and took another draw on his cigarette.

We were quiet for a while, caught up in our own thoughts. Queenie stared out the window. There was nothing visible out there; darkness had swallowed up just about every detail. But he now seemed worried and scared. Scared killers make stupid decisions, the kind that can get both them and their hostages killed.

He was clearly preoccupied; the gun was resting in his lap. I ran through my options: I could try running the car into something and hope for the best. Or I could keep on driving, hope to see a cop car, hope to get their attention. Or I could wait for him to fall asleep, then pull over and try to make a run for it. I dismissed all three options in quick succession. They each had the same problem, an unacceptable likelihood that we'd both be killed or seriously injured.

For now, I'd drive and wait for the right opportunity. When it presented itself, I would know what to do. At least, I hoped I would. In the meantime, I would get him talking. Try to draw him out, learn more about what made the Black Orchid tick.

Chapter 44

"What's your earliest memory?" I asked.

He turned to me and flashed his pearl-white teeth. "You sure did miss your calling. You should've been a doctor. I'm gonna call you Doc Lanie from now on." He chuckled. "My first memory? That's easy. It's Daddy Bernard stuffing himself down my throat. It's his hand on my head, telling me to take it in a little more, just a little bit more, and suck it harder, *harder*, HARDER!"

He saw my expression and laughed. "Oh, you don't like that memory? A little too-too for you? Well, let me see what else I can come up with."

I forced myself to take a deep breath. I was sickened but I can't say I was surprised. I'd seen enough of human nature to know that adult killers had often been child victims. "How old were you?"

He raised an eyebrow. "Well, for me, I guess I was a newborn, wasn't I? But as for this old body, it was the tender age of five. Maybe earlier. By the time I was five, six, at the latest, Daddy Bernard was busy teaching me the fine art of giving blowjobs."

Despite my anger toward Queenie, I also felt an incredible sadness. What he'd gone through—if he was telling me the truth, and I found that I believed him now—no child should suffer. He'd gained knowledge that no child should have. I thought about what Mrs. Cardigan had told me, that the child seemed "knowing" and had a smart mouth, that the Bernards sometimes even seemed afraid of their offspring. *No wonder*, I thought now. They were probably terrified that little "Janie" would give them away.

"Oh yeah, I got another memory for you," Queenie said. "Daddy Bernard . . . he celebrated my seventh birthday by giving me my first lesson in bum fucking. From then on, he took and I gave. Junior would lay in bed, just dreading the sound of his daddy's footsteps. He'd count them, *One, two, three.* Knew exactly how many it took Daddy Bernard to get to his door. And by the time old Daddy turned that doorknob, Junior would be gone. It was me who took it. Never Junior. Just me."

I thought of Dr. Bernard's mutilated remains, and the note: *For all the years you made me suck . . .* Then I thought of Phyllis Bernard, of her gouged-out eyes.

"But you also blame your mother, don't you? You also think you're here because of her."

Queenie exploded. "Stop calling her that! I told you that bitch wasn't my mother. I'm my own damn mother! And I don't know why the fuck I'm here. Do you know why *you're* here? Don't nobody know, do they? We're all just here, and there ain't no turning back. Once you're here, you're here. You just keep on keeping on."

Maybe I should've stopped there, but I couldn't. "What did she say when . . . you know, he was hurting you?"

"Say? She didn't say anything. She was deaf, dumb, and fucking blind. All that bitch ever did was tell me not to mess up my clothes. She dressed me up during the day and he undressed me at night."

"You mean she was there when he . . ."

"Hell no! That would've damaged her delicate sensibilities. You know, the two of them hadn't done it in years. He must've raped her to get Junior. All she cared about was pretty things and pretty people, and all she wanted was a pretty baby girl. When she found out she didn't get one, she made one."

"What do you mean? I thought you said . . ." I hesitated, cleared my throat, uncomfortable with the words. "I thought you said you have both, you know, parts."

"I do. They had a choice: raise a girl child or a boy child. A girl is what she wanted, so they went with it. Funny when you think about it. I was the one she really wanted, not Junior, but somehow I'm the outsider, the freak."

"Almost sounds like you were jealous of him."

He shot up in his seat. "Hell no! I wouldn't have wanted them as parents. Nasty hypocrites, the both of them." He paused, then added morosely, "But I got to give it to her. The bitch had taste." His expression turned wistful. "Just my luck. By the time we turned thirteen, she'd lost interest in dressing us up. That was a damn shame."

"Why?"

"Because by then I was really into it. I mean, shit, it was the only upside to the whole thing. But my voice was dropping; I was growing a little hairy in all the wrong places; and, well, it was just getting too damn complicated."

So, with puberty, Junior's body had suddenly decided it was masculine after all. That would explain why the Bernards yanked the child from public view.

"Did you and Junior always live with them?"

"Yup. They thought about sending us away. But where and how in the world could they keep me quiet? Suppose I came out, talked to somebody? Better not take the chance. So, they kept us in the house. That damn house in Brooklyn. For five years they kept us locked in there. Told everybody they'd sent their little girl down South to live with relatives. People are so stupid; they believed them. We used to stand at the windows just wishing that for once someone would look up and see us."

"What about relatives? What happened when they came by?"

"Hardly ever happened." He shook his head. "Few times it did, Mrs. B told them I was out of town, visiting Daddy Bernard's kin. When his kin came to town, they said I was visiting her kin. But hardly anybody ever came, and nobody asked twice."

"Okay, then, what about your studies? How'd you get your schooling?"

"Phyllis taught us at home. Daddy Mojo, he only stopped by when he needed something. He'd come in the room practically holding it in his hand. Then Junior would disappear, and I'd take care of business."

I glanced at him, knowing I couldn't begin to imagine what Queenie had gone through. And knowing that it was Queenie who'd taken over when the going got rough; he was the one who weathered the storms that had cracked Junior's mind. I could see him as the child he'd once been—hurt, angry, and terrified—one who by age seven had endured more abuse than most face in a lifetime.

"You think he bothered other children?" I asked.

He gave a grunt. "He brought one of them home once. Some kid he'd found on skid row. The kid was starving, didn't have a place. You could tell he didn't want to be doing it. But he did."

I frowned. "How do you know?"

"How do you think?" He looked at me incredulously. "First, Daddy Mojo watched while this kid did me. Then he did me too."

"Dear God," I whispered.

"God didn't have nothing to do with it. I'd just about bust out laughing when the reverend came over. Man, I used to wonder what he would've said if he'd known who he was breaking bread with."

"And you never said anything?" I felt naïve the moment the words left my mouth.

"How could we? I told you they kept us locked up. But even if they hadn't—shit, you sound like you blame us."

"No, I—I'm just trying to understand."

"You—" He laughed bitterly. "All right. You want to know if we ever said something? Well, I did, once. Must've been seven or eight. I tried to talk to the Sunday school teacher. What do you think she did?"

From his expression, the answer was obvious. "Nothing."

"Oh no, she did something, all right. Hushed me up. How dare I tell such nasty lies about my fine upstanding daddy! Said she'd wash my mouth out with soap if I did it again. The thing is, she knew I was telling the truth. I could see it in her eyes. But she had a thing for Daddy B."

"You could tell that? At your age, you could see that?"

"Honey, at that age, I could tell that and a whole lot more. Later, when we got older, and I was much stronger, they made sure we weren't heard, much less seen. They didn't just keep us locked in that house. They kept us locked in our room. When visitors came, we didn't dare leave it, not even to go to the bathroom. That woman used to bring in a chamber pot and carry our meals upstairs on a tray. As for the rest . . ." He took a deep breath. "You'd never understand, Slim. Nice, so-called normal people like you never do."

CHAPTER 45

We lapsed back into silence. I recalled that last talk with Sheila, realizing how much about her marriage she had still kept hidden, and I mulled over what Queenie had just shared. An ugly story. Sordid. Painful. The Bernards had destroyed a child's mind. They had created a monster, and he had destroyed them. I wondered about that child, about what he must have gone through, what he must have contemplated during those long years of torture and imprisonment.

"Did you ever think about running away?"

"Sure I did. Damn near every minute, day and night. For years. But when it came down to it, I was just too damn comfortable. And I was getting stronger while Junior was getting weaker—and so were the Bernards. I figured that all I'd have to do was wait. They'd kick the bucket and I'd get everything. But they sure showed me."

"What did they do?"

"Something I wouldn't have expected in a million years: they sent Junior off to college. That shocked the socks off of me. When I woke up in that dorm room, honey, I was fit to be tied."

I was stunned too, but not just because the Bernards had relented and given Junior his freedom. What puzzled me even more was Queenie's surprise. Why hadn't he known of Junior's plans to go to college and the process he'd gone through to get there? There must've been discussions, maybe even arguments, definitely negotiations, promises made. Then there would have been the whole application process, the testing, the interviewing. Finally, the acceptance and the packing, followed by the actual trip and arrival. How could Junior have accomplished all of that without Queenie being aware of it? Maybe Junior was stronger than Queenie realized or wanted to admit.

"But what really screwed things up," he continued, "was when he met that Sheila bitch."

At the mention of Sheila, my nascent sympathy for Queenie vanished. "He loved her."

"He didn't need to love her. He had me."

"So you were jealous."

"No—"

"And you meant to kill her from the very beginning."

"Put it like this: I knew I had to get rid of the bitch. Junior's stupid kidnapping plan gave me the chance."

I peered at him. "She loved you, you know. You destroyed the one person who was totally on your side."

"She loved *him*. She should've known better than to mess with me. I always knew what that whiny-ass husband of hers was up to. But he never knew a damn thing about me."

That was a lie. Queenie had just admitted that he didn't know everything that Junior knew. He hadn't known about the plan to go to college. And the bitterness in his voice. It was the voice of someone who felt neglected and ignored, who felt his work had gone unappreciated. So he reveled in his supremacy over Junior, but resented it too.

"Just when did you step in with the kidnapping?"

"I knew about it from the get-go, just as soon as it popped into his head. I let him play with it and I made my own plans. It was easy once Stax sent Olmo after me."

"A bad mistake, huh?"

"Bad for him, good for me."

I was really beginning to understand now. It was Olmo who'd enabled Queenie to go through with his plan. "Olmo made all the difference, didn't he?"

"Honey, I laid the kind of loving on him that a man don't forget. He didn't know what hit him. By the time I finished with him, he was in my hip pocket."

"But Sheila said Junior mentioned Olmo to her. How could he have known him, when it was you who—"

"When it was me who met him?" He laughed. "I simply told Olmo what the deal was, told him how to approach Junior. At first, Junior didn't know what Olmo was about. But Olmo played it right. Pretty soon Junior was spilling his guts, begging Olmo to help him."

Incredible. Queenie had actually used his lover to trick himself—his alternate, original personality—into a double-cross. Then he'd double-crossed the wife and the lover. And what had he said?

"Junior's gonna lay down and die. I'm gonna make sure of it."

So now he intended to double-cross himself too.

CHAPTER 46

For a while, Queenie was voluble, talking about his plans, his dreams. I soaked up every word. I formed phrases to use in the piece I would write, and tried not to worry about whether I'd live to write it.

Queenie remained introspective. "Know who I'm thinking about?"

It was a rhetorical question. "No."

"Olmo."

I glanced over and darned if I didn't see a wetness gleaming in his eye.

He felt me staring at him, raised a hand to his face, and turned it away. He cleared his throat. "You got a man?"

That same question again: I had the same response.

"You don't have to answer. I know you do despite what I said before. Pretty woman like you . . . It's your boss, ain't it?"

No comment.

He continued: "What happened with that accident, it's a shame. You want to be back there with him, don't you?" When I didn't answer, he said, "Stupid question," then sighed. "Well, I don't blame you, Slim. I don't blame you at all. And when you get back, *if* you get back, do something for me."

"What?"

"Hold on to him. Never let him go. If he's the kind of man I think he is, the kind who sees you for what you are, who you are, and still wants you, then never let him go."

I was stunned and could only nod my head. Queenie faded back into silence. When I glanced over at him just after three a.m., I heard the soft drone of a light snore.

I thought about driving off the road, jumping out, and leaving him. But there was a good chance that any change in the speed of the car would wake him. He'd be after me in a second. True, visibility was bad—it was pitch black outside—so he'd have a hard time shooting me, but that velvet darkness also meant I'd have a hard time seeing where I was going.

We were in the middle of nowhere. Where would I go?

I soon realized I couldn't keep on driving like this. He was asleep and I'd caught myself dozing off. I had to pull over and rest.

I searched for signs of a place where we could spend the night. Finally, just after midnight, a billboard caught my attention. *Bricks Family-Owned Hotel.* By then, I wasn't even sure where we were, but we must've been north of Tarrytown.

I slowed and turned off the road. Queenie woke up instantly, jittery and paranoid. He pointed the gun at me, ready to pull the trigger. "Where are we? What the hell are you doing? Stop before—"

"Calm down. I'm just pulling up to a hotel, that's all."

"I'm not tired," he said, in all seriousness.

"Well, I am."

I made to get out of the car and he gripped me by the elbow. "Get back here."

I yanked my arm away, too exhausted to be scared. "You can keep on driving if you want to, but I'm going to find me a bed."

"I can't drive," he said.

"Of course you can't. You're too tired."

"No, I mean I can't drive. I don't know how."

I was surprised. "You mean Junior never learned to drive?"

He shook his head. "No, he did, but . . ."

"If he knows, then you should know."

"It doesn't always work that way."

"So you two don't share the same skills?"

"Not always. Take shooting, for example. Junior's scared of guns. Wouldn't go near one if you paid him. Me, I love 'em. And I'm a crack shot too. Whatever I aim at, I hit." He gave an evil little smile.

I was growing tired of his threats. "Would you really shoot me when we've still got so far to go?"

"No, but I'd shoot one of *them*." He motioned toward the little house. "Whoever's in there. You step out of line, they pay for it."

He'd pushed the right button. I looked toward the house with longing, then sank back in the car. We were soon on the road again. A half hour later, Queenie's head was sagging once more.

CHAPTER 47

It was frigid in the car. The cold and the exhaustion were getting to me. I was shivering and my eyelids were heavy. One minute I was again considering whether to drive off the road and attempt a getaway; the next, I *was* driving off it.

Somewhere in between I'd fallen asleep.

I awoke with a jolt, just as the car busted through a wooden railing. I held on tight to the steering wheel and the car bumped and rocked its way down an embankment. Wavy stalks of tall, dead grass and low-lying tree branches smacked the windshield. Rocks clattered against the sides of the car. On reflex, I hit the brakes, but the car was flying downhill with momentum. It banged and bucked at least another ten yards before slamming into a tree and rocking to a nauseating halt.

The impact sent us both lurching forward. I banged my chest against the steering wheel; Queenie's head met the windshield with a resounding thump and he sagged against the passenger door. Dazed and in pain, I put a hand to my ribs. It hurt to breathe. I'd never damaged any ribs before, so I didn't know if the sharp pain that accompanied every breath meant a bruised rib or a broken one, but I knew it meant trouble.

I felt around for my purse, dug out a lighter, and flicked it open. Queenie's face was slick with blood in the wavering light. He was deathly still, but when I felt the side of his throat, I found a pulse, a strong one. He was alive, but oblivious.

Now was the time make a run for it. I was unsure where we were and I hadn't seen any cars in the last hour and a half, but it didn't matter. It was almost dawn now. There would more traffic as the sun rose.

Queenie stirred. He moaned and twitched as though having a night-mare. "Sheila?" he whispered. "Sheila, baby, are you there?"

A shudder rippled through him from head to toe and he blinked open his eyes. He put a hand to his forehead, then turned it to shade his eyes from the flame of my lighter. Confusion and fear filled his face. He looked stunned when he saw that his hand had come away bloody.

"What in the world . . . ?"

His eyes darted to the busted windshield, to the darkness outside, and then came back to rest on me. "Who are you? What—where are we?" His voice was as mellow as always, but deeper and definitely more masculine. And now I saw something else: Queenie's golden eyes had turned a choco-late brown, and they reflected a deepening sense of panic.

"Junior?"

He studied me in bewilderment. "I know you. You look familiar." A deeper frown, more puzzlement. "You live on my block, don't you?"

Hunt Queenie. Save Junior . . . Which is it now?

I reached out a hand to help him. "Here, sit up."

He pushed himself away from the door and sat upright with a wince. In doing so, he looked down at himself and saw what he was wearing. He put a hand to his head and felt the wig and hat, which had been knocked askew. "What am I doing dressed like this?" A look of understanding crept over his pretty features, and of horror. "Did *she* bring me here?"

There was no mistaking who he was talking about.

"We're on the run. The cops are after us."

His eyes widened. "What for?"

I gave him a brief summary of what happened at the ball.

He shook his head. "But that can't be—I'd never. And the ball isn't for another week or so."

I gave him the date. "It was last night and you hurt a mess of people, including cops, trying to get out of there." Before he could ask why he'd done it, I told him.

"You mean we actually went ahead with the kidnapping?"

"Yup."

"No, it can't be. Why, I—" He stared at me. "But what do *you* have to do with this?"

"It's a long story and we don't have time. Just trust me. We've got to get out of here. You're in great danger. We both are."

"From who?"

How could I explain that the greatest danger to him was himself?

"Where's Sheila?" he asked.

I paused. "She's dead."

"No! Why are you doing this? Why would you lie to me like this?"

"She's gone . . . She was killed."

He froze. His breathing became shallow and his eyes filled with dread. He didn't want to know, but he had to ask: "How? Not because of . . . ?" He read the answer in my face and closed his eyes. "I don't believe this. It can't be. It just . . . can't be."

"Junior, let's go."

"Go where? I'm not going anywhere until you tell me everything."

So I told him about Sheila and Olmo. Finally, I told him about his parents.

"I did that?" he whispered.

"No, Queenie did."

"And I—*she*—forced you to come along?"

I nodded.

He looked out into the blackness of night. "And you say the cops are after us?"

"No doubt about it."

A long silence followed as tears slid down his face, leaving tracks in Queenie's elaborate makeup. Finally, he turned away, his hands covering his face, his body convulsing in wrenching sobs.

I let the lighter go out. Maybe the dark would comfort him, help him see more clearly.

"Junior," I said softly, "it would be better if you turned yourself in. That's our best chance of surviving."

"Survive? What for? Even if I could convince them it wasn't me, even if I could make them see and they let me go, I couldn't go back to that house. Not now. Not after what's happened. But they're not going to let me go. I can't go to jail, either. I'm not saying I don't deserve to. It's just . . . I wouldn't survive two days in there. I'm not going down like that. Not me."

"Junior, please—"

"No! I admit I wanted the money. I deserved it. I'd earned it. All those years . . . with them."

"I know what they did to you. It was evil." To his questioning look, I added, "Queenie told me."

"Queenie." His voice was hard and flat. He sized me up. "I can see where she'd talk to you. She would like someone like you. She'd figure she could use you."

"What's the last thing you remember?"

"Wednesday night. Having dinner with Sheila." He screwed up his face in agony. "I'm crazy, aren't I? I was always worried, but I never did anything bad before. I never killed anyone."

How would he know? He could have, but just not remembered. "It was Queenie who killed them."

"But I *am* Queenie." He tapped himself on the chest. "I did this, and no one else."

"Turn yourself in. You can get help."

He laughed bitterly. "I'm a cop killer. They're not going to help me, except to the electric chair."

He was probably right.

"I'm not going to do it," he said. "I'm not going to let them lead me like a damn dog to no electric chair."

In that, I heard echoes of Queenie.

"All of my life, people have been telling me what to do. Well, I'm not taking it anymore." He raised his chin. A single tear spilled from his eyes and his voice dropped so that it was low and raw. "You don't know me, you hear? You think you know a little something. You talked to Queenie and you probably talked to Sheila too. Or they talked and you listened. But that doesn't mean you know me."

"I listened when they talked."

"I'm sure you did. Cause you wanted something. A big story you could put in the paper."

"I wanted to understand. And I still do."

"Well, understand this."

Before I could do anything, he grabbed the gun in his lap, shoved it under his chin, and pulled the trigger.

CHAPTER 48

The gun clicked empty. At the sound, Junior's face sagged in surprise. He stared at the gun in disbelief. "Damn, damn, damn! I can't even kill myself right."

I closed my hand over the gun and took it away from him. He didn't resist. He was limp.

"Talk to me," I said. "Tell me your side of it."

"Why?"

"Because it matters."

He slumped back, turned his face away. I gave him time. After a while, he started talking. He story came in bits and pieces.

To summarize: His family had been living in a small house in Brooklyn before they moved to Strivers' Row. That was in 1923, when Junior was eighteen years old. They sent him down to Howard University in D.C., right before they moved.

The move to Strivers' meant a new beginning. By then, his sexual identity as predominantly male was unmistakable, and it was getting harder to keep him in line. He was big enough to knock Dr. Bernard flat on his butt, if he ever took a mind to. Junior would never do that, of course. Not him. The boy was totally compliant, but his alter ego wasn't. That *thing* that seemed to take him over every now and then, they couldn't trust it. Its appearance was what prompted them to start locking him up in the first place.

So they forged a new birth certificate and somehow came up with fake school records. They let him go, because at that point it was easier than holding on to him. Once Junior was gone, he stayed away. For four glorious years, he enjoyed his freedom.

"During the summer, I'd find work in D.C., stay with friends . . . I was happy. As a matter of fact, I'd say it was the happiest time of my life."

He had friends; he was admired. No one knew about his dirty secret, about the rapes and the blackouts that had plagued him for as long as he could remember. And Queenie stayed silent.

Then, in his senior year, Junior did something his parents never expected: he took a wife. Her name was Sheila Holt, and he was deeply in love with her. He wanted to do everything for Sheila.

"I felt real when she looked at me, not like somebody's creation, somebody's nightmare. I felt loved. I felt confident. I felt proud."

What about making love? I asked him. What about women in general, and Sheila in particular?

A shadow crossed his face and the soft glow of remembered happiness faded. "I don't want to talk about that. All I can say is that she was patient. The others weren't, but she was patient, real patient, and giving. And that's one of the reasons I loved her."

He'd been peering down in his thoughtfulness, but now he raised his eyes to me.

"I really thought she'd save me, you know? I thought I couldn't live—I couldn't survive—without her."

Then graduation came, and with it the requirement to enter a rather harsh and unsympathetic world. Junior's newfound love made him happy. It gave him strength and inspiration. But he still couldn't summon the courage to strike out on his own. Furthermore, Sheila didn't want him to. She wanted to move to New York. She wanted to live in a fine town house on the legendary Strivers' Row, and he didn't want to disappoint her. He knew she'd married him for love, but he also knew that she'd married him for status. To deny her made no sense, none that he could convince her of, not without telling her the truth, not without sharing his family's dirty little secret.

So it was decided: they would go back to Harlem. He'd told her nothing of his family history. That was over now, anyway. Sheila would bring love and happiness into their home.

Junior was surprised to find that his parents were thrilled at the news of his marriage. Yes, come home, they said, by all means. Once he and Sheila were there, he saw why his parents were so happy to have her. They had a problem, you see: someone who knew them from the old neighborhood had moved to the block, and for all they knew she might spread the word about them having a beautiful baby girl who had "mysteriously" disappeared. Mrs. Gladys Cardigan, they said, was worth watching. And the thing was, she actually lived *right next door.* How terrible and unbelievable was that? Mrs. Cardigan would raise questions if they suddenly presented a son. So Sheila would be the daughter they never had, and Junior would be their son-in-law.

Junior was astounded and hurt, but he buried the pain and tried to argue the practical. How was he supposed to explain it to Sheila? That, they said, was his business. He'd just better make sure she went along with it.

Junior was confounded. He thought and thought, but couldn't come up with anything to say to her. He decided, in effect, to let his parents take care of it. It was their lie; let them shoulder it. He was amazed and irritated to see that when they introduced Sheila as their daughter, she merely took it as a sign of affection. She never noticed when they simply introduced him as Junior, or didn't mention his name at all, just calling him "her husband."

Everything went fine for about a month. Then Sheila received a social invitation in the mail. It wasn't addressed to Mrs. Junior Bernard, but to Mrs. Junior Holt. She was a bit put off, more than a bit, actually. Having the right to bear Junior's family name was an important part of her identity. He shrugged it off as some secretary's error and tried to get her to do the same.

"All right, fine," she said, "but I'll call that secretary and get it straightened out."

"Why bother? It's not a function you want to attend, anyway."

She thought about it. He was right, she didn't really want to go to this particular event or encourage invitations from the folks behind it. Better to ignore the whole thing.

Ignore it she did—until she received two letters addressed to Mrs. Junior Holt the following week.

This time she was going to do something about it. Of course, Junior tried to dissuade her, but his efforts backfired. Her suspicions were aroused, and her concern about supposed secretarial errors switched to concern about matters closer to home. She was adamant: *Tell me what is going on!*

He explained that it was part of an agreement he'd made with his parents: they were to act as though she was the daughter and he the in-law. No, he couldn't say why, but he hoped she would comply. Those were the conditions under which his parents had taken him back into the house.

"Does that mean they threw you out before? Why? What could you have possibly done to deserve that?"

He started to deny having done anything. Then he realized that an admission to having committed some horrid, nearly unforgivable, unmentionable sin might be just the thing. Unfortunately, he was a terrible liar, guilt-ridden and wholly unimaginative. He couldn't think of anything on the spot, so he promised to tell her everything—not then, but one day. When she still pressed for details, he stammered out some vague story about having stolen things when he was small and the family being so embarrassed that they'd—

"What? Sent you away and denied ever having had you?"

"Something like that."

"Why, that's the most ridiculous thing I've ever heard. I have half a mind to go downstairs and—"

"No! Please, don't. Let it be."

She looked at him with such pity that his heart broke. She wrapped her arms around him and held him. "I'm so sorry, baby. So sorry. I can't imagine what—"

"Shh," he silenced her with a kiss and led her to bed.

Junior said he felt an odd mixture of pride and disgust. He'd lied to his Sheila. And something deep inside him sensed that this was the end of their idyllic relationship, or even worse, the beginning of his descent into a private hell.

He was sure by now that Queenie had returned. He feared that this part of him was growing stronger every day, because he himself felt weaker. He was missing blocks of time and sleeping all day, exhausted for no apparent reason.

Then came the day when Sheila confronted him about the Cinnamon Club, and he knew.

It had been a grave mistake to return to his parents' house. He would've been better off starving somewhere else, anywhere else, than living like a prince here, shackled by memories that weren't simply phantoms of the past, but very real manifestations of the present.

He had a horrible, abiding sense that he was running out of time, that he was about to drown, that he had to do something fast to save himself—and save Sheila—or it would be too late.

The first pale rays of daylight were stretching across the sky when Junior finished telling his story. He seemed exhausted, utterly spent. I again mentioned the possibility of surrendering, and this time he responded with silence. He sat there gazing out at the snow-covered landscape through the broken windshield.

"I'd like to sleep now," he said finally. Then, without another word, he leaned against the door, hunkered down, and closed his eyes. Within minutes, his chest indicated the slow, even, rhythmic exhalations of the deep sleeper.

Once again, I faced the issue of whether to run. If Junior woke, he wouldn't go after me. He was as gentle as Queenie was murderous. But he was also very vulnerable. In fact, his spirit seemed broken.

The gun felt heavy in my lap. I checked it and found that it had one bullet left, one that could've killed him. But instead of going off, the gun had simply jammed. I didn't believe in signs, but this was hard to ignore. I removed the bullet and dumped it into my purse. As for the gun . . . I should've tossed it out the window, but I was so tired, beyond even the simplest of decisions. My gaze returned to Junior's tear-stained and bloodied face.

It was strange to finally meet Junior, after hearing so much about him. I could see why Sheila loved him. He must have appeared to be everything she'd dared dream of: attractive, intelligent, well-spoken, the son of a socially prominent pair, but neither arrogant nor insensitive. And he genuinely loved her and would never have hurt her. Of that, I was convinced.

But would the courts?

Would a judge and jury believe that his mind was split, his body host to a second personality, one with diametrically different attitudes, ambitions, and hostilities? Would they believe it wasn't Junior, but his "other" who was to blame for the murder and mayhem?

Not likely.

Was I really choosing to stick by his side? Like Sheila, I'd begun to feel protective toward him. And those feelings certainly didn't get her far.

I closed my aching eyes. The throbbing in my rib cage was dull but present. I let my head fall back on the headrest and then I too was gone.

My sleep was anything but restful. There were dreams, nightmares, of chasing sirens, blood-spattered walls. There were voices of the people Queenie and Olmo had killed. Last, but not least, was Sam's voice.

What are you doing, Lanie? Where are you? I need you. Come back to me.

CHAPTER 49

It was two in the afternoon when we stirred. I felt fingertips touch my lap, felt something being dragged away, and then a rough hand shake my shoulder.

My eyes opened to stare down the barrel of the .38 I'd taken from Junior. The gun was empty, but he didn't know that. Queenie didn't, that is. Junior's dark eyes were once again light, flecked with a hard gold and brimming with anger.

"What the fuck is going on?" he demanded. Even the voice had changed. His eyes darted around, taking in the broken glass, the unfamiliar landscape. "Where the hell are we?"

"I don't know. We had an accident. I fell asleep and the car went off the road."

Queenie touched his forehead and grimaced. He had a bad swelling where his head had met the windshield. He regarded me with suspicion. "You do it on purpose?"

"No," I said. "Obviously not."

"What were you doing with my gun? You try to run away?"

"If that's what I'd wanted to do, then I would've already made tracks. You were in no condition to stop me."

I should've guessed that this would happen, or at least that there was a good chance that upon waking Junior would be gone and Queenie back in his place. After all, Junior was the weaker personality. He'd only been able to come out because of the head injury. And then to be confronted with the terrible news of what his alter ego had been up to—it was inevitable that he would try to escape, as he always had, whether consciously or unconsciously, by turning inward. And that meant an invitation for the Black Orchid to step out to once more take control and deal with a difficult and terrifying situation.

I should have known.

Deep down, I had. I had known that Junior was still in danger, more danger than ever, from himself.

Just as Sheila had.

And like Sheila, I had this stubborn desire to save Junior. He had put himself in this mess, yes, but only due to what his parents had done to him. As for Queenie, despite what I had seen in that house—or maybe because of it, and because of what he had told me—I felt not only horror, but sympathy too.

Queenie was a murderer. He was also a victim. It was Queenie who'd had to endure the brutal rapes, week after week, month after month, year after year, while Junior hid. It was Queenie who'd had to serve as a sacrificial lamb, over and over again. His sole raison d'être had been to suffer. He had been forced to be the warrior when in fact he was still only a child. That child had seethed with rage at the abuse he'd suffered. Was it any surprise that he'd grown into an adult, a monster by many people's definition, driven by fury and a desperate desire to break free?

I wasn't apologizing for him. Nor did I find his heinous actions just. But I did find them understandable.

Did I really think I could talk Queenie into surrendering? I didn't know. There was a slim chance, perhaps, that I could. If the police caught up with us, there was an even slimmer chance that I could talk them into letting Queenie live, instead blowing holes in him—that is, if they gave me a chance to talk, if they didn't "accidentally" blow holes in me as well.

All this went through my mind. Thoughts battled. I couldn't abandon Junior—or Queenie. Then I told both sides to be quiet. I knew what I had to do.

"What now?" Queenie asked, still dazed and openly worried.

"Well, I don't know about you," I said, "but I'm hungry."

* * *

We ate the last of our food. There was just enough to take the edge off my hunger, but Queenie was still bad-tempered and ravenous. We got out and examined the damage to the car. The front was smashed up pretty badly. In fact, it had crumpled like an accordion. There was no point in even trying to get it started. We took in the surrounding countryside: not a house within sight.

"Do you know where the hell we are?" Queenie asked again.

"Somewhere north of Tarrytown, I think."

"Where the hell is that?"

I didn't answer, just started walking.

Queenie followed. "Where are you headed?"

"Back to the road."

Queenie yanked me back. "No road. We'll stand out. In the car, no one noticed us. But like this . . . no way." He gestured over toward the trees. "We'll stay undercover. Find a house, maybe."

"And then what? Kill everyone in it?"

His eyes were cold. "Be nice, Slim. Be nice."

We had left our fur coats at the Casino, so Queenie had found substitutes at the house. The coats were warm, but not meant for long exposure to freezing temperatures. The same was true of our shoes. We were both wearing lightweight Mary Janes, suitable for the car, but inappropriate for trudging through ankle-deep snow.

After twenty minutes, we were freezing. Queenie's vision was blurred, perhaps due to the head injury he suffered in the accident. Every now and then I had to close my eyes against the pain in my ribs.

We had just rounded a copse of trees when we saw a trail of smoke rising from a not-so-distant house.

"Yes!" Queenie said in an intense whisper. He grabbed me by the hand and pulled me along, full of renewed energy.

It was a small farm consisting of two buildings: the main house and a barn. There was a fenced-in area, but no sign of livestock.

"You go up to the door," Queenie said, pointing to the house.

"And do what?"

"Knock. Get them to open it up for you. Then I'll come in behind you."

For a long moment, I just stared at him. Then I said, "No." My voice echoed in the stillness. That one word rang as loud as a pistol shot.

Instantly, he brought the gun up and pointed it at my face. "I'm getting tired of you sassing me. Now, do as I say or—"

I shook my head with grim determination. The pain in my side was increasing. "I'm not going to help you kill more people. You want to go in there, then go ahead. But you'll get no help from me."

He pulled the trigger. My heart thumped. The gun clicked. He pulled the trigger again. And again and again. He looked at it with confusion and then at me in rage.

"You took my motherfuckin' bullets. Bitch!" He reared back and smacked me with the butt of the gun.

The blow connected with my jaw and pain exploded in my head. It radiated outward from the point of contact like fractures in glass. I stumbled backward and landed on my side. The jolt to my ribs unleashed another bolt of agony. In two seconds he was over me, ready to deal another blow.

"You want me to kill you, don't you? Because that would wreck my plan. Well, I'm not going to do it. Not yet. Now where the hell are my bullets?"

"You didn't have any left."

He ripped the purse out of my hand, tore it open, and came up with the sole bullet. Disgusted, he rammed it into the gun barrel and then squatted down next to me with his lower lip curled angrily.

"I swear, if you trick me or defy me again, I'll . . ." He was so angry, he could barely get the words out. "Let's just say there are lots of ways to achieve immortality. A reporter isn't the only one."

It took all my strength not to show fear of that gun or grimace at the mind-numbing pain in my side. After several seconds, some of his thunderous rage faded.

"Tell me you understand," he said in a gentler voice.

I closed my eyes against the pain.

"Tell me," he repeated.

I looked at him, saw the sadness in his eyes, and gave a jerk of a nod. He put out a hand and helped me to my feet. That's when we heard it, a sound that made us both stiffen and freeze, the sound of a rifle being ratcheted behind us. We slowly turned.

A man who appeared to be in his sixties, wearing a green hunter's cap, a ripped plaid red-and-green hunting jacket, and a tattered oatmeal-colored knit scarf, stood ten feet away. He had a rifle pointed directly at us.

"Hands up, the both of you."

He had clear blue eyes in a face of wrinkles and a full gray beard. Granite-gray tufts of thin curly hair stuck out from under the sides of his cap.

Queenie slowly raised his hands. After a moment, I followed suit.

"Drop the gun," the farmer told Queenie.

He dropped it.

"And step away from it."

Queenie did as instructed.

"Now, who are you?" the farmer asked, squinting at Queenie.

"My name's Alice," Queenie said. "My friend here—" He gestured toward me, but the farmer cut him off.

"Your friend? If you're friends, then why'd you have a gun on her?" He didn't wait for an answer. "Tell you what, why don't we go inside and sort it out there?"

"Look," Queenie said, "this is all a misunderstanding. We had an accident with the car—"

"Where?"

"Oh, about a half mile back."

The farmer glanced at me and I nodded. Then he snapped his head in the direction of the barn. "Over there," he said. "Come on. Let's go."

Queenie licked his lips, his eyes darting between the barn and the rifle. "What do you want us in there for?"

The farmer hitched the gun a bit higher. "No reason not to tell ya. I heard a report on the radio. Something about two niggra women, one tall, one small, 'cept one of 'em wasn't a woman at all. Was some kinda pervert, dressin' in women's clothing. Report said he killed a coupla cops. Got good reward money out for him." The farmer arched an eyebrow. "Got any more questions?"

Queenie's face hardened.

"I said *move!*" the farmer barked.

I started trudging toward the outer building. Blinding pain radiated from my side at every step. Queenie dragged behind.

"If you don't get a move on," the farmer said, "I'll shoot you down. That reward money said dead or alive."

I glanced back to see Queenie tighten his lips. He was angry, but he picked up his pace. As a matter of fact, he passed me and got to the barn first.

The doors were unlocked. Queenie stepped inside, and I followed. In the gloom, I could make out a Studebaker. Ten seconds later, the farmer entered. Queenie knocked me backward into him. The old man went down hard on his back and I landed on top of him. Queenie grabbed the rifle and stood over us.

"Now, you take orders from me, old man. Get over here."

He stepped back and the farmer and I got to our feet, then Queenie motioned to the car.

"That work?"

The farmer nodded. His cap had been knocked off and his hair looked wild. His weathered face was drawn. He was scared but he wasn't cowed.

"Give me the keys," Queenie said.

The farmer reached for his jacket pocket, then stopped. "I ain't got 'em on me. Just remembered. Left 'em on the kitchen table."

"You sure 'bout that now?"

The farmer hesitated. I prayed he was telling the truth. He swallowed, then looked at Queenie and gave a slow nod.

Queenie jammed the rifle up against the farmer's temple and the old man winced. "Search him," Queenie told me.

I didn't move. The farmer stared at me, pleading. Once again, Queenie was making me an accomplice.

"No," I said. "If you want to check his pockets, then you do it. I'm not going to help you with this."

I'd thought I couldn't feel fear anymore, but I was suddenly trembling. I think it was because of the farmer. Having him there, another potential victim, made all the difference.

Queenie spoke clearly and succinctly: "If you don't put your hand in his damn pocket and check for those keys, I'll blow his fucking head off. Then I'll check for myself."

The farmer was terrified, that was plain. Whatever stubbornness had led him to deny having the keys, whatever feistiness had led him to think he could outmaneuver Queenie, it was all gone.

In that freezing barn, with the wind whipping inside the open door, I could feel myself break out into a cold sweat. I was thinking desperately, try-ing to figure out how to save myself and the old man, but I didn't see what I could do.

"Go on," Queenie said.

I edged forward, reached for the farmer's thick jacket pocket. "I'm sorry," I whispered to him. I stuck my hand inside and pulled out a thin bunch of keys, one of which was clearly for the car.

"You lied to me, old man. You dared lie to me!" Queenie shouted.

The farmer flinched. He was too scared to answer.

"Anybody else in that pretty house of yours, Farmer John?"

A terrified shake of the head was all the old man could manage.

"Why should I believe you? Why should I believe a word you say?"

"Please," the farmer begged. "You got what you wanted. Please, just go. I won't say nothing. I promise."

"Liar, liar, pants on fire." Queenie took a step back and aimed the rifle.

"No!" I moved between them and threw my hands up. "Please don't do this. I won't let you."

Queenie looked at me as though I was crazy. "You won't *what?*"

"You want him to live so he can tell everybody how you spared his life."
I turned to the farmer. "Right? You'll talk about how you met the Black
Orchid and how polite he was. You'll say how he took your car, but only did
it only cause he had to, and that he could've killed you, but didn't, right?
That's what you'll say?"

I begged with my eyes. *Please agree.* He looked down the barrel of the
rifle and gave a short, shaky nod.

"Tell him what you'll say." I moved so he could look Queenie in the eye.

"I'll s-say you were n-nice an-and p-polite and—"

"All right, all right, I get it." Queenie lowered the rifle to his hip. "Lanie
P., you ain't nothing but a con artist." He grinned at me. "I have got to admire your guts." Then he shifted to the old man. For a moment, he studied
him, that same smile playing on his lips. "I just wish you hadn't lied to me."

The old man stuttered. "B-but I w-won't do it again—"

"I know," Queenie said. "I know you won't." He tilted the rifle and fired
from the hip.

I screamed at the explosive sound and felt the heat as the bullet sped
past. It hit the old man square above his left eyebrow. I saw him jerk at the
impact. I saw his look of despair and pain. Then the upper third of his face
disappeared in a cloud of blood and brain matter. He dropped like an empty
sack, his blue eyes bulging, his skull shattered and spilling blood across the
packed dirt floor.

Queenie pushed me aside, walked up to the body, and stared down at it.
"Fool me once, shame on you. Fool me twice . . ." He dug his toe under the
old man's cheek, lifting the head. "Shame on me."

"Why'd you do that?" I cried. "You didn't have to do that!"

"He would've told."

"So what? We would've been miles away by then."

He gripped me by the shoulders. "Like I said, I'll do everything necessary—"

I wrenched away. "You're crazy! You know that? Crazy! Worse than a
rabid dog."

"Shut up! Just shut up! And get in the car!"

"No!"

His lips twisted into a snarl. "Not again. Please, Slim. Don't make me—"

"I said no. I'm not going anywhere with you." I was not being brave, I was exhausted. The farmer's death had shocked me, had snapped some fine filament of trust I thought I'd built with Queenie. It had shattered my last illusions about any influence I had over him.

"I genuinely liked you," I said. "And I wanted to help you. Despite all you did, I actually thought I could save you. But nobody can." I shook my head. "I must've been out of my mind."

He opened his mouth to say something, but nothing came out. Instead, he fell back a step. He raised one hand to his forehead and blinked. A look of confusion crossed his face. He blinked again and shuddered, like a dog shaking off water. For a moment, he seemed to be choking. He heaved down, gasping for air. Then the spasm was over. He fixed his eyes on me and said, "Get in the car."

"No."

He grabbed me by the arm and dragged me to it. I tried to throw away the farmer's keys, but Queenie forced my hand down. I kicked and clawed, but he was stronger. He yanked open the driver's-side door and shoved me inside. Keeping the rifle trained on me, he went around and clambered in the other side.

"Now, it's Canada," he said with gritted teeth. "Canada or bust!"

CHAPTER 50

The Studebaker was several years old, but its wheels had a better grip than the Ford had. The dirt road leading from the barn to the main road circled past the house. As I maneuvered my way, the car rocking from side to side on the uneven surface, I peered over toward the house. A curtain twitched at an upstairs window.

I shot a look over at Queenie, wondering if he'd seen it. He sat forward, leaning on the butt end of the rifle. He was tense, his eyes moving left and right like searchlights. Still, he did appear to have noticed the slight movement.

"Hope you're satisfied," I said, more to distract him than anything else.

He glanced at me, but kept his silence. I felt reassured. If he'd seen anything, he would've reacted.

"You know what I'm thinking?" he said. "I'm thinking that Farmer John probably wasn't living there all by himself—not in a big house like that."

I said nothing. Maybe he *had* seen something. Maybe he hadn't needed to. Logic was telling him what a chance glance had told me—that there was somebody left to sound an alarm.

"I'm thinking," Queenie continued, "that maybe we should go back and clean house."

Imperceptibly, I pushed down harder on the gas pedal and the car picked up a notch. Queenie didn't seem to notice. He'd shifted and was staring back at the house.

"Turn around," he said.

I acted as though I hadn't heard him and pressed even harder on the gas pedal. The increase in speed was obvious now.

Queenie swung around. "What the hell are you doing?"

"Getting us out of here. That's what you wanted, right?"

"I told you to—"

"Turning around, it's not going to work, not on this road. Furthermore, if there's anybody back there—and that's a big if—they've called the cops already, don't you think? We go back there now, we'll be sitting ducks."

He narrowed his eyes. "Funny how you can go from not giving a damn about me one minute to being my best friend the next."

I just kept my eyes on the road. After a few seconds, Queenie settled down, faced forward. I let out a slow breath.

"Signs up ahead," I said. "We'll be on the main road in a few."

Queenie tensed. "There could be cops. Do it right, Slim. Do it right."

For the next five or six minutes, we rode together in tight silence. There were no cops. I relaxed a little. Then we hit a road where the snow had melted and the driving got better. I relaxed a little more.

Another ten minutes went by.

Soon the road turned upward to a steady slope. Steeper and steeper it went. It narrowed and bent at unexpected angles. I was not a confident driver under the best circumstances. This was the worst: a narrow, twisting road with a drop-off on one side to a cold, rushing river below. The higher we climbed, the worse conditions became. Patches of ice on the road and a gun at my side: nervous was an understatement. Our speed slowed to a crawl.

"Pick it up," Queenie said, staring up at the rearview mirror.

I shook my head. "I can't. There's ice and—"

Queenie twisted in his seat to look backward. "Pick up the fuckin' speed. Now!"

"Why? What—?"

Now I glanced up at the mirror. A police car. Around five car lengths back. It had crept up on us. I was sure that thirty seconds earlier it hadn't been there. Was it after us, or did it just happen to be behind us? I almost hoped it was the latter. A chase on this road would kill us all.

"Move!"

Queenie jerked back around. He slammed his foot down on top of mine, forcing the accelerator to the floor. The Studebaker hitched forward, gathering speed. Behind us, the police siren suddenly split the air. No doubt about it, they were after us now. We were moving fast, but they were moving faster. I dropped my gaze back to the road. How long could I drive this fast without losing control?

Then the tires lost their grip and the car swerved to one side.

"What the hell are you doing?" Queenie yelled, and grabbed the wheel.

We fought for control, the car zigzagging right and left. Up ahead, the road veered sharply. We were going to hit the turn at full speed. I tapped the brakes, hoping to slow down, but Queenie kept his big foot firmly pressed down over mine.

"Stop!" I screamed. "You're going to get us killed!"

The car hit the bend. I wrenched the wheel hard and the car swiveled around. The force threw Queenie up against me. The impact of his body mashed me against the door. The Studebaker spun once, then twice, and came to a nerve-rattling halt.

Later, I would recall an eternity of silence—maybe due to a momentary deafness caused by the crash—but in reality, the whole thing couldn't have taken more than seconds. I was aware that Queenie was reaching across me, flinging open the driver's-side door.

"Get out," he whispered.

"But—"

"Get out!" He flinched as though against some inner pain. "Please! I can't hold her back much longer. Just do this for me."

"What—?" Then I saw the dark chocolate of his eyes. "Junior?"

"Go!"

In a panic, he gave me a strong shove. I fell out of the cab and landed hard, with a jolt that sent off fiery spikes of pain. Grabbing my injured side, I barely had time to scramble away. He slid behind the wheel, slammed the door, and hit the gas. The car shot forward, swerving left and right, and I had this image of Junior and Queenie battling it out behind the wheel.

I got to my feet and ran, stumbling after them, holding my side and try-ing not to slip and fall. Every step sent shards of agony through my rib cage.

The road bent in another sharp turn fifty yards ahead. The vehicle swung around it and the police car swept past me. Seconds later, I rounded the corner, just in time to see Junior headed straight for the railing. The wind whipped around my ears. The Studebaker cut through the railing like a knife through butter and flew out over the rocky incline.

For one breathtaking moment, the car hung suspended.

I could see Junior clearly. He even turned to look at me. I'd never wit-nessed a look of such utter relief. Then he withdrew, just faded away before my eyes. Relief turned to shock, then horror. It was Queenie's face now, contorted with rage as he realized what had happened. That he had lost. That Junior had succeeded in killing them both. That he had indeed "just laid down and died," but in his own way, in a place of his own choosing, and in doing so, he had left Queenie to face one last task, the ultimate task: to experience the heart-stopping, mind-numbing terror of a horrific death.

"NOOOOO!" Queenie's scream rent the air, frenzied and furious. He threw up his fists and beat the windows. Then the car tipped forward and plunged out of sight, down, down, down, to the fast-moving river below.

CHAPTER 51

T he sight of Queenie's death so hypnotized me that I didn't register the presence of the police. It must have mesmerized them too, because at first they didn't make a move against me.

Soon after, however, they took me into custody.

They knew who Queenie was, and that I had been his hostage. So theoretically, I was a victim, and there should have been no question about me going free. But there was the matter of the farmer's death: they wanted to make sure it was Queenie and not me who pulled the trigger. Since Queenie was gone, I was the only one left to face the music.

They had a doctor wrap my ribs and then let me make a phone call. I phoned Blackie. I asked him about Sam and he said there had been no change. Blackie told me he had already heard about Queenie's death and my detainment. He would be there the next day, he said. In the meantime, he would put in a call to the local authorities. He warned me, however, that since the crash happened outside of his jurisdiction, he had no official say over how long the police upstate could keep me for questioning. Though he believed they would listen to what he had to say.

They did. I don't know what he agreed to, what kind of deal he made, but it worked. I suspected that all they cared about was getting the credit for hunting down a cop-killer.

A cop-killer: that's all Queenie was to them now, just another perverse footnote in the annals of New York City's history. Given the havoc he wreaked, maybe that was all he deserved.

But his victims earned an explanation. His victims and their families, and maybe society at large, deserved to know what had created him. Queenie's murderous nature had nothing to do with his physical condition; it had nothing to do with his being a trannie; it had everything to do with the abuse he'd suffered—that Junior had suffered—as a child.

Incest, child rape, those were embarrassing, shameful secrets that no one talked about. Folks in fine homes, if they acknowledged those problems at all, claimed they were aberrations of the poor, the ignorant, the uncivilized. No doubt, Harlem's upper crust, especially, would be horrified if I wrote about the subject. We were a struggling community, trying to get white America to see us as something more than animals. An exposé on what had happened behind closed doors among one of the community's most respected members would do more harm than good. That, I knew, would be the reaction.

And maybe everyone would put it down to one family's aberration, a family that was gone now, with no one left to continue the denial or accept responsibility for the truth. I decided to try, anyway.

Those were my plans—but for the moment, they could wait.

What couldn't was Sam.

His eyes were closed when I walked into his hospital room. He still had dark half-moons under his eyes but he was less wan than before. I eased down into the chair next to him and took his hand.

"Sam?" I whispered. "Can you hear me, darling? It's over. I'm here and the whole thing's over. We can't afford to lose you. We can't lose each other." No response. I kissed him on the cheek, then brushed my fingertips over his forehead. "Sam, please. Come back to me. Please, don't leave me. Don't. I've missed you so very much." A tear slipped down one cheek and fell onto his forehead. I turned away to reach for my handkerchief and he moaned.

I shifted back, afraid to believe what I'd heard.

"Sam? Sam, darling?"

The moan came again, this time with a flutter of eyelids.

Then his eyes were open.

I thought about Hamp and about lost chances. And I thought about receiving another one, and I knew I wouldn't let this one go.

* * *

It took weeks of hospitalization and rest at home, but Sam recovered. After three weeks, he returned to the newsroom in a wheelchair. We gave him a standing ovation. Eventually, his legs healed and he could walk again on his own.

On a balmy evening in early May, I had Sam over for dinner. He and Mrs. Cardigan. She came early, and brought an apple pie. When she saw the mess I was making in the kitchen, she shooed me away, practically took over.

It was a nice dinner, quiet and happy. There was a lot of laughter too, something that house of mine hadn't heard in a long time. I resolved right then and there to do it more often, to have folks over.

Across the street, the Bernard house was locked and still. There was a big *For Sale* sign on the front door.

"No takers for the time being," Mrs. Cardigan said. "More curiosity-seekers than anything else. Every now and then, a real estate agent comes by, takes somebody in. But that's rare."

"It's going to be awhile," Sam said, "before the publicity dies down."

Mrs. Cardigan shook her head. "It's gonna take more than awhile for that."

Afterward, as I walked Mrs. Cardigan to the door, she twittered, "I'm so glad you found that young man. He's a keeper."

"Thank you. I think so too."

Her eyes twinkled. "Good night, Lanie, and thank you for having me over."

"Actually, you ended up doing most of the work."

She waved that away. "It was a pleasure."

She left and I went back to the parlor, where Sam sat sipping coffee on the sofa. I paused in the doorway, watching him. *If he's the kind of man I think he is, the kind who sees you for what you are, who you are, and still wants you, then never let him go.*

Sam glanced up and saw me. "How're you doing?"

"Fine." I sat down next to him, cuddled up under his arm.

"You're looking awfully serious."

"Just thinking, that's all. Remembering something a friend said."

"Was this friend wise?"

I thought about it, and then smiled up at him. "Yes, actually . . . in his own way." And that made me remember. "There's something I've been wanting to talk to you about." I told him about my desire to write a story on child abuse and I told him why. He hadn't heard the entire report about Junior and Queenie. I'd kept the details to myself during his recovery, but now I shared them all. He listened without saying anything until I was done.

"There'll be blowback," I concluded. "Will you back me?"

He was thoughtful, then shook his head. "It's the kind of story I once might've gone after. It's not the kind of story we handle, though."

I was so disappointed. I'd so hoped his answer would be different. "Sam—"

"Shh." He laid a fingertip on my lips. "No, we don't handle that type of story—but I guess it's about time we did."

A grin spread across my face from ear to ear. "You mean it?"

"Yes," he said. "I do."

"Oh Sam," I sighed, and snuggled up against him.